Evol
The Divine

By M.R. Forbes

Copyright 2014 M.R. Forbes
Published by Quirky Algorithms

Cover art by Mario Sanchez Nevado

All rights reserved.

CHAPTER ONE

I<small>N THE BEGINNING, THERE WAS</small> God. Nobody knows where He came from. All any of us know is that He was there. That He has always been there.

After God came the seraphim, the angels. His warriors. His army. He created them for a special purpose.

He made them to fight the Beast: a foreign creature from another place, another universe, another thread of all that is. The Beast begged for succor from Him, and in His goodness He granted it.

Until the Beast lost his mind.

Until the Beast tried to destroy all that He had made.

From the defeat of the Beast rose the greatest of the seraphim, Lucifer, and in his shadow was another, the angel Malize.

Only he wasn't an angel after all…

The universe demands balance in all things, and the goodness of God is no exception.

Lucifer turned on Him, betrayed Him, and was cast down.

To keep the balance, Hell was made.

To keep the balance, Purgatory soon followed.

From his new place in the underworld, Lucifer lusted after what He had created. Lusted to create life of his own. Lusted to destroy what He had made.

The demons were born.

The war began.

The demons came to the Earth to spread chaos and destruction. The angels descended from Heaven to fight them.

To keep the balance.

Millennia passed.

The war raged on.

Mankind evolved, blossomed, were fruitful and multiplied. The world became theirs, or so they thought. Beneath it all the war continued. Beneath it all the balance rested, a universe poised on the edge of a needle.

One good push to send it to the arms of the demons, the enslavement of man, the ravage of the Earth.

One good push to bring the faithful to their maker, all others left behind in the wake of the Rapture, no more than fodder for the things that remain.

My name is Landon Hamilton.

Once, I was nothing more than a man.

Once, I was a diuscrucis: my soul a perfect balance of human, demon, and angel descent. I was a warrior of Purgatory, a champion for mankind.

Once, I fought a god and won.

Once, I was a god myself.

That was the past, and the past is behind me.

Today, my name is Landon Hamilton. I am not a man, not a god, not an angel or a demon, not even diuscrucis, though the title remains mine.

I'm just Landon.

A grizzled veteran. An old dog with some new tricks.

The war rages on.

The balance must be kept.

The future of humanity depends on it. Depends on me.

Depends on us.

If you've found this. If you're reading this. If you can see these

words and understand them. If you want to join the fight…
  Find me.

CHAPTER TWO

THE WINTER WIND CUT THROUGH the channels between skyscrapers, pummeling against my left side, pushing my short hair into a weird non-bald combover, and snapping the unzipped front of my coat against my hip. I could feel the push of it, and hear the whistle against my ears.

I was glad I didn't feel the cold.

It was late, three in the morning. The city wasn't asleep. This city never slept. It was quiet though, most of the throng consisting of late-night partiers, people walking their dogs, that sort of thing. I maneuvered around them without paying them much attention. I was one of them, and at the same time nothing like them.

I passed the corner of a stone facade and peered down the dark alley. My stomach rumbled a complaint, a reminder that I needed to eat. I hoped the noise wouldn't give me away.

I kept walking.

It took three more blocks before they came, six in all, one from another alley, two from across the street, and three from the rooftop on my left. It was a long fall, but they could take it. They were demons.

Vampires.

"Lost, stranger?" their apparent leader asked.

He was clean-cut, in khakis and a polo shirt. I remembered

seeing him at the bar. He must have used the street over to come past and double-back. I wasn't surprised. It was typical.

Two years since I had held the power of a god in my hands.

Two years since I had rejected it.

Two years since I had been reborn, no longer a creature of the Divine.

It was strange that these were the situations that always made me reflective, that always brought me back to the memories of Charis and Clara, my wife and daughter. I couldn't help thinking about them that way, even if Charis and I had never actually been married, never even been intimate. Even if Clara had been nothing more than a construction of the the prison we had been trapped in together, a manifestation of our power. A feedback loop, in a sense. I suppose it was because the ghosts of them reminded me why I was still here. Of why I had stayed behind.

"I asked you if you were lost," the vamp repeated. He was confident, and why wouldn't he be? I was surrounded.

They didn't have their claws out, not yet. I was sure they thought they were dealing with just another mortal, a piece of meat, my age and lean frame suggesting I didn't carry the taint of the Beast's power that had poisoned half of their food supply.

Two years ago, they would have seen me as an angel, or a demon. Maybe they would have even known who I was. Those days were gone. They had died with Charis and Clara. I was different now.

Re-made.

"I know exactly where I am."

Polo looked at his cronies, slightly confused by my unexpected confidence. There was no way for them to know what I looked like, who I was.

"Bind his hands and frisk him," Polo said at last, motioning with his fingers. "If your blood is clean, you'll make a nice meal."

I put my hands behind my back, holding them together to make the binding easier.

"What are you doing?" Polo asked. His voice was a little shaky. Unsure. Most people didn't volunteer to be vamp food.

I felt a pair of rough hands take my wrists.

I had given up the Divine power. That didn't mean I was powerless.

I shifted my weight, twisting and pulling the vampire behind me, swinging him like a meat hammer and throwing him into his partner on my left. They fell into a tangled heap, even as the others hissed and bared their teeth and claws, their eyes fading to an empty black.

They came at me.

I fell into a defensive crouch, keeping my eyes trained on Polo and watching the others in the periphery. The vamp was a blur from my left, and I caught his arm in my left hand and his chest in my right. I used his own mass and inertia against him, changing his direction and burying him into the cement.

His neck broke with a wet crack.

I ducked down, reaching into my pocket and turning again, throwing my hand out towards an incoming opponent. He found himself impaled on a four foot obsidian roman spatha, covered in both demonic runes and seraphim scripture. It slid easily between his ribs and out his back, and I wrenched it free and sent it away. It left me holding a small black stone, and I clutched it while I rolled to the right, avoiding the falling vampire as he steamed frankincense and died. I came up with the blade in hand once more.

I was greeted with a single mass of teeth and claws, the remaining vampires throwing all of their energy into taking me down. Their attack was organized and ferocious. They knew what they were doing. They knew how to fight.

I had once held the soul of a centuries-old angel within my own. All of her memories, all of her knowledge had been mine. She had been an intimate part of me, a confidant and friend. Even though Josette was gone, those memories still lingered, still resonated in my mind.

They didn't stand a chance.

One took the obsidian blade in the heart, another got stabbed in the gut, and a third tried to run away. I threw the spatha, catching him in the back. He fell to the pavement and burned to ash.

I left Polo alone until then, grabbing him by the throat and throwing him against a wall. He hit it hard and slid to the ground, his claws retracting, his fearful eyes going back to their normal brown. "Diuscrucis?" he guessed, a little too late.

"I'm looking for Randolph."

"Hearst? Why?"

"He's been trying to regroup the Solen family."

They had once been the strongest vampire family in the northeast, until their patriarch, Merov, had picked a fight with his daughter and lost. The family had gone to her, and she had gone to Hell, leaving them rudderless.

Rebecca.

She was the reason the Beast had been freed. She was also part of the reason he'd been defeated. I hadn't thought about her in the two years since.

Not until recently, anyway. Not until I had discovered that Merov's former accountant was making a move to get himself installed at the front of what remained of the Solen family. He had to know that kind of work would catch my attention.

He was probably counting on it. If he had any idea who I was, or where I was, he would have just given me a call, or sent me a postcard. The Divine only saw me as a human now. It made it easy to blend in, to disappear.

"They won't accept him," Polo said. "He's a bean counter, not an alpha. You don't have to worry about that."

"Are you defending him?"

"N.... No. I know Hearst. He's a salesman. He always has an angle."

"That's why I need to talk to him. Why does his angle include me?"

"I don't know what you mean."

"Do you know where I can find him?"

Polo's eyes darted around, as if he expected him to step out of the darkness. "He likes the strip clubs. 'Inventory', he calls it. Try the Penthouse."

His expression changed. He was afraid before, but now that he had told me what I wanted to know, he was terrified. His hands moved against the cement, scrambling to push himself further away from me.

I wasn't going to kill him. There was no point.

I turned and walked away, stopping only to recover the spatha and return it to its resting place. I wasn't worried about Polo telling anyone he had seen me, or that he knew what I looked like. Soon after he left my sight and I left his, he would forget all about me.

It had been one of Malize's abilities, and I had been smart to claim it for my own when I had been reborn. The anonymity gave me time to rest, to recover, and to think, without the worry of being assaulted by demons, or harassed by angels. It let me stay hidden and secure. It made me close to impossible to find.

At the same time, it kept me closer to the people I was protecting. It let me feel more human, because I could always be myself. I knew from the Beast it was the secret to keeping the balance. He forgot who he was, what he was fighting for. I couldn't afford to let that to happen to me. I could still see the destruction his failure had caused. I could still feel the emptiness. When he lost the one he loved, he lost it all. I had lost the ones I loved, and I had survived. It wasn't always easy, and there were times when it hurt as though it had just happened, but I refused to give in. It was the responsibility I had taken, the job I had accepted. If I couldn't keep some kind of balance in myself, it wasn't just me that suffered.

I closed my eyes, an image of Charis and Clara materializing in the corners of the darkness. I had survived, because somebody had to. I had survived so that she could spread among the stars, knowing that she hadn't failed.

I looked up into the night sky, those same stars barely visible through the clouds. Maybe one day I would join her there, when mankind was strong enough to defend itself from the war between Heaven and Hell.

One day, but not today.

CHAPTER THREE

THE PENTHOUSE WAS SHORT FOR the Penthouse Executive Club. It was a higher-end so-called 'Gentleman's' club over on 11th and 45th, not far from where the Intrepid was docked. Even though I'd never been in it, I knew where it was. I knew where everything was in this town.

I watched the front from across the street, bathed in the shadows of a dark corner. I could still hear the wind in my ears, and feel it brushing my hair. Across from me, a line of limos waited at the entrance to the club, their drivers standing patiently on the passenger side, ready to accept their charges the moment they made a break from the doors. Like me, they seemed to be immune to the cold.

For some, it was because of layers of clothes beneath pressed and fitted tuxedos and wool overcoats.

For others, it was because they weren't human.

I couldn't sense Divine anymore, not in a soul-tickling expression of heat and cold, Heaven and Hell. What I could do was See them, the way even the weakest Awake human could. Looking at them, I knew them for what they were. Out of five cars and five drivers, there was one Turned, a human who had sold their soul to a demon for power, and one vampire, leaning up against the hood of a classic Rolls and looking smug.

I could guess which car belonged to Hearst.

It was three in the morning, and the club would be closing soon. There was no good reason to go inside and risk the mortals there. Instead, I watched the thin flow of pedestrians, the people coming and going from the club, and the movements of the drivers. When I caught a break in the action, I stepped out of the shadows and headed for the vamp. As I walked, the jacket and jeans I was wearing reorganized into a crisp tuxedo and overcoat, a facsimile of the chauffeur's standard dress.

"Hey, buddy," I said, walking right up to the vamp. He didn't move much, shifting his eyes left so he could see me.

"Do you need something?" He was tall and thin, and he had a soft look to him. I stared at him for a few seconds. He wasn't pure.

When the Beast had been freed from his prison, his power had begun leaking out into the world at large. This power had infiltrated mankind, seeping down into their souls, and affecting anyone with even the smallest amount of Divine ancestry, which was a much larger pool than would be expected. Some got sick and died. Some were unaffected. Some were oblivious, and at the same time became poisonous to Lucifer's creations, who needed human blood to survive.

A few, less than one percent, changed.

What they changed into depended on the ancestry, and in the vast majority of cases, that meant demons of one kind or another. After all, it was the fiends and vampires and weres who were the rapists. God discouraged His angels from consorting with mankind, and as far as I knew there was only one mortal who had inherited angelic traits.

He was in France, smitten with my sister.

"Cold night," I said.

Now he turned his head. "I'm not in the mood for small talk, *buddy*."

The last word came out like a curse.

"Me neither."

I had my arm around his shoulder before he could react, turning him so that we weren't as obvious to the other drivers. I hit him hard on the side of the head, right at the temple, supporting his weight as he lost consciousness. A real demon would never go out that easy. I half-dragged, half-carried him around to the rear of the car, holding and chatting at him like we were old friends. He hung limp in my arms, and I found the keys in his pocket and opened the trunk. I watched the other drivers to make sure they weren't paying attention, and then quickly dumped him in. I slammed the trunk shut and leaned against it for a few minutes, making sure nobody noticed the switch. When everything stayed quiet, I circled to the driver's side and positioned myself behind the wheel.

I checked myself in the mirror, adjusting the cap so it was lower over my gray eyes, creating a shadow that would disguise me for about three seconds. It was all the time I would need to make sure that Hearst hadn't brought a bodyguard.

Then I waited.

CHAPTER FOUR

I DIDN'T WAIT LONG.

THE back door of the Rolls swung open, and Randolph Hearst dropped onto the seat. I glanced over, not seeing anyone with him, while he pulled the door closed.

"What the hell am I feeding you for, eh?" he asked. "You're supposed to get the goddamned-"

"Randolph."

Hearst smiled. "Landon. I was wondering when you would get my messages."

He was old, with thin white hair and plenty of wrinkles. Every time I saw him, he reminded me of my Uncle Luther, kind and easy to underestimate. I knew Hearst liked that impression, because he wasn't the strongest specimen, and he didn't need to be. He knew how to manipulate, and he knew where to stick the knife when your back was turned. It made him a lot more dangerous than Merov ever was.

"Sending your boys out kidnapping drunks late at night… It isn't your most original move."

He laughed. "I would have stopped by, but nobody seems to know where you live. Anyway, simple is always better, and I needed to make sure you would ask questions first."

His voice was rough, with a heavy New York accent. He would

have made a great Godfather.

"Instead of just killing you?"

"Better that you don't even try."

"Pulling the Solen family back together isn't the way to do that."

"Trust me when I say that you've got bigger fish to fry."

"I take it that's the reason you wanted to talk?"

"It is." He looked out the window. "Since you seem to have incapacitated my driver, would you mind taking me home? I'm sure you already know I had Merov's old place remodeled."

"Why not?" Once I was gone, he would remember we had talked. He wouldn't remember where or when.

"You're a true gentleman."

I started the car and eased it out into the street. "So, talk."

"Have you ever heard of Matthias Zheng?"

"I can't say I have."

"He's a third generation Chinese-American. He got his doctorate in engineering at Stanford, before moving on to doing government work at a lab in New Mexico. From what my people have been able to learn, the startup was working on some kind of advanced robotics project for the military."

I laughed. "Since when do vampires care about what any government's military is doing?"

"I don't care about the military. I care about Matthias Zheng. By all accounts, the guy is a genius, maybe even as smart as me." He followed it up with a dark cackle. "He's been seen talking to the enemy."

"The angels? He's Touched?"

"Not according to my sources. Just a regular guy, same as you appear to be. Obviously, looks can be deceiving."

"I'm a special case."

"Maybe you aren't as special as you think you are. Anyway, you know Valerix?"

"The west coast archfiend? She's been quiet for a while." When a powerful demon like her was quiet, it meant they were up to no good. By telling Randolph that I'd noticed, I was suggesting I was keeping a close eye on her.

"She was the one who told me that I needed to find you, and give you the tip. If an archfiend is worried about it, there has to be something to it, no?"

"Or it could be a setup."

Hearst laughed. "How the hell are we going to set you up? We don't even know how to find you since all that bullshit with the Beast."

I turned my head to look back at him. "That only means you have to try harder. I'm not an idiot, Randolph. Getting me to come to you would be step one in any play."

He put his hands out, trying to look innocent. Like a vampire could ever look innocent. "She wanted me to tell you about Zheng, I told you about Zheng. You know me, Landon. I'm a survivor. I'm not going to start with the likes of you without some serious odds, and they just aren't there, not yet, anyway."

I couldn't argue his logic. Since he wasn't gifted with brute power, he had to be willing to be patient and highly calculating in his approach to gaining his share of the pie. I was still too much of an unknown quantity for him to take that kind of risk.

"You gave me a name and suggested he's a fan of God. You haven't told me everything you know."

"Astute, as always. Valerix said she sent a succubus over to the apartment building where he lives and set her up as a neighbor. She put the full moves on him, and he waved her off like some kind of mosquito or something. So, she thought maybe he likes boys. Nothing. He's immune to demonic power."

I glanced back at him again. It wasn't possible for someone to be immune and not be Divine.

Not unless they were like me.

"Kind of a kick in the ass, isn't it?" he asked. "There's

something going on out west, diuscrucis. The angels have been quiet for the last two years, letting you clean up the mess the Beast made and get things right again. That's two years they've had to plan, to prepare. To destroy us... or to destroy you?"

Or both.

"If you want more information, you'll have to talk to Valerix." He reached into the pocket of his suit jacket and held out a slip of paper. "Her address. She'll be expecting you to stop by at some point."

I took it. It felt like it could be a setup, but the idea that there was someone else out there with immunity to the Divine, who was working with the angels... it was a curiosity, and I was feeling very curious.

"I'm sure you know the rest of the way," I said, stopping the car in the middle of the street. We were still a good ten blocks from Merov's penthouse uptown.

"Where are you going?" Randolph asked.

"You were told to deliver a message, and you delivered it. I'm going to see what I can find out." I opened the door and stepped out. I leaned back in and looked at the vampire. "Watch yourself, Randolph. Putting the family back together... it's dangerous."

He scowled at me, clearly unhappy with his choice to either walk the rest of the way home, or have to drive himself. "You know I stay on the right side of caution."

I slammed the door closed and started walking back the way we'd come. I did know that.

It was the reason I was nervous.

CHAPTER FIVE

My current home was the corner unit of a crappy apartment in the theater district. It was a nondescript, unassuming little hole in the wall that was marked only by a small etched address in the cornerstone and a never-locked door that allowed access into the building. It was as standard as they came, and it was the truest meaning of 'hiding in plain sight'.

I made my way into the small, mailbox-lined foyer, and then through the second door into the main stairwell. It was coming up on four-thirty, and everything else around me was dark and silent. I put my hand over my stomach while it rumbled again, and then started the climb up to my tenth floor apartment. I could have taken the elevator, but it was old and cranky, and wouldn't do much to keep me from drawing the neighbors' attention.

I reached the top of the steps and rounded the bannister, finding myself looking down the familiar hallway, with its fairly new striped carpeting, and persistent smell of wet paint, even though it hadn't seen a fresh coat in at least ten years.

I paused when I noticed my door was cracked open.

Who would be at my place this time of morning? There were only three people who even knew where I lived. Dante would never go through the door, Elyse was on a run in South Africa, and Obi knew better than to just drop by.

It was another curiosity.

I resumed my walk, keeping my pace steady. The quarters were too close here for the sword to be of much use, so I found the stem of my power in the base of my soul and stretched it like elastic through my body, into my muscles, enhancing and extending my strength and speed. It was enough to give my hundred and sixty pound form the juice to keep up with the Divine.

I reached my door and put my palm to it, spending a few seconds listening before I pushed it open, the heavy creaking of the stiff hinges giving anyone inside plenty of warning that I was coming in. I stepped over the threshold and paused, taking in the air.

Perfume?

My apartment could only be described as spartan. I had a bedroom with a mattress on the floor, and living room with a sofa and desk I'd bought at Goodwill. A couple of towels and some standard toiletries rested in the bathroom, and a fridge with a freezer full of ice cream, an unused stove, and not much else defined the kitchen. To most, it would have been kind of pathetic, but I didn't need much. Clothes weren't an issue, and I didn't watch television. I kept my laptop hidden in the ceiling when I wasn't around, and the rest of the inventory was in a rented storage unit in the basement.

A purse was sitting on the corner of the sofa.

The faucet was running in the bathroom.

Whoever it was, they were female, and not very smart. The running water would have masked my entrance. I stepped quietly over to the bathroom door and pressed myself against the wall. The faucet stopped, I heard hands against the towel, and then the door began to swing open, leaving me behind it.

I saw her through the crack. Medium height, shoulder length brown hair with a modern cut. Narrow build and a chest that was out of proportion to it. She was wearing a maroon sweater and a pair of jeans.

She wasn't Divine.

When she saw the door had been pushed open, she produced a gun from under the sweater, moving with the confidence of someone who had plenty of practice with firearms.

I shoved the bathroom door closed behind her, catching her wrist as she spun and tried to aim, pinching the nerve and forcing the weapon to crack against the linoleum floor.

"I would have knocked, but I live here. Who are you?"

She had brown eyes, and a pretty face. Her face tightened at the same time she tried to punch me in the jaw. I let the strike land, and kept looking at her without reacting. She threw a kick at my knee, and I shifted just enough. It landed on my leg, hard enough to leave a bruise that would heal in a couple of seconds.

I let go of her wrist.

"It really isn't polite to attack someone in their own home," I said.

She didn't speak. She went for the gun, picking it up and putting it to my chest. I didn't try to stop her. She couldn't hurt me like that.

"Can we talk about-"

The pop of the gun made my ears ring. I felt the bullet rip into and through me, coming out of my back and planting itself in the wall. I closed my eyes and took a deep breath, feeling the energy wrapping around the wound and putting everything back in place. I'd felt pain a thousand times worse than being shot.

She dropped the gun and stepped back.

"Holy shit," she said, speaking for the first time. "You mean it's true?"

"That it isn't polite to attack someone in their own house? It's normally considered good etiquette."

She kept backing up. I picked up her sidearm and held it out to her.

"What if it wasn't true?" I asked. I had an idea what she meant. "I would be dead on the floor right now."

"This can't be real," she said. "It can't be." She blinked her eyes a few times.

"You came here for a reason." How did she find me? How did she know who or what I was? What the hell was going on?

"I... I..."

"Do you have a name?"

"Rosita. Rosita Marquez. You can call me Rose." She reached the corner of the sofa and flopped down onto it, next to her bag. "Please don't kill me."

"Why would I do that?" My stomach grumbled again. "I'm going to get some ice cream from the fridge. You want a spoon?"

Her eyes followed me into the small kitchen. When I re-made myself, I took back most of the characteristics that defined who I was before I died, traits that put me closer to being human than a soldier of Purgatory. That included hunger and thirst, and a desire to sleep even if there wasn't much of a need. It kept me grounded, helped me remember what I was doing this for, and as a side effect returned my vicious love of ice cream, now exacerbated by the fact that I could eat however much I wanted and not gain weight.

I put the gun down in the sink, found a half-gallon of mint chip in the freezer, pulled a pair of spoons from a stiff drawer, and rejoined Ms. Rosita Marquez, whoever she was, on the couch.

"Spoon?" I asked, holding it out to her. I sat next to her, far enough so we weren't touching, close enough that she could help herself to the snack.

She reached out slowly, taking it from me as if I were offering her poison. Her eyes stayed glued to mine.

"You're Landon Hamilton?"

"Yes. How do you know that name?"

Her eyes filled with tears. "I can't believe I found you."

I took a spoonful of ice cream, stuck it in my mouth, and stared at her.

She reached up and wiped her eyes with the sleeve of her sweater. "I'm sorry. You must think I'm crazy. I'm sorry for shooting you." She stuck her spoon into the ice cream, taking a small bite. "Like I said, my name is Rosita Marquez. My sister was Anita Marquez. We were twins…"

I swallowed and put up my hand. "Please, Rosita. Let's start at the middle. How do you know who I am?"

She took a deep breath and closed her eyes. Her voice was smooth and flat, projecting someone else's words from memory. *"If you've found this. If you're reading this. If you can see these words and understand them. If you want to join the fight. Find me."*

I stared at her, feeling my body go numb. Obi had helped me create the web site on the deep net nearly two years ago. It was the pot of gold at the end of a long, twisted rainbow. A test of mettle intended to bring the right kind of people into the war, the first step in my goal to bolster the ranks of my rebellion and add the fault-tolerance that the Beast had lacked.

Two years, and no one had ever found me.

Two years, and no one had ever found the site.

I'd given up on it, forgotten about it, accepted that the Awake didn't want to fight. That mankind just wasn't ready.

Until today.

CHAPTER SIX

"I can't believe you found it," I said. My hands were trembling, the ice cream rocking like a ship in a storm. "Who are you?"

"I told you, my name-"

"No, I mean... Who *are* you?"

"I was trying to tell you. This whole thing is very strange."

"You know about the Divine?"

"I know about demons." She reached into her bag and pulled out her cell. She turned it on and opened up a photo of her standing next to an identical version that could only be her sister. They even had the same breast implants. "My sister, Anita. She was killed by one, sixteen months ago."

I started to take another spoonful of ice cream before I remembered myself. Sometimes it was easy to forget what empathy was. I put it aside, close enough for her to reach if she wanted some. I put my own appetite on hold.

"I'm sorry. Tell me."

"Anita and I both went to school at MIT. We were getting our degrees in engineering. I was supposed to meet her in the library after class, when she sent me a text that she met the most gorgeous guy. She said she was leaving the library early so she could go home and change, that some guy named Jonathan was going to be picking her up at seven. They were going to have dinner together at a local restaurant. Just a date, you know?"

"I didn't think anything of it at the time. I wrote her back and told her I was happy she met someone, and that I would see her later. If we weren't going to meet to study, I thought I would go back to the lab and put some extra time in."

I didn't need a degree from MIT to know where this was going. "She never came home?"

"Not exactly. She never left home. Anita and I were renting a house together off-campus. She was smart enough not to tell him where she lived. She was smart enough to keep the date local, and public. He must have followed her, or something."

Her eyes began to fill with tears again, running down her cheeks and dripping onto the sweater as she spoke. "I got home around ten. At first, I didn't think she was there." Her face started to flush, and she looked down at the floor. "Then I heard her moaning, and I thought that maybe the date had just gone better than she expected. Except... there was something wrong about it. Its a little embarrassing, but I had heard her with other guys before, and we were twins, so I just knew...

"I ran upstairs, screaming her name. The moaning stopped. She came out of her bedroom just as I was coming up. She was dressed in her exercise clothes, and she was sweaty. She closed the door behind her. 'What's the matter with you, Rosie?' she asked me. 'I thought you were in trouble,' I said. Then she laughed. It sounded like her, but it was... I don't know... off. There was something about it. 'I'm going for a run,' she said, and she went down the stairs and left."

She shook her head and wiped at her eyes with the sweater. She was still sobbing pretty hard. "I went back downstairs to get something to eat, but I couldn't shake the feeling of wrongness. The moans I heard... it wasn't that kind of exercise, you know? I always respected my sister's privacy, and she respected mine... I got this fear in me, and I ran back up and opened her door. Anita was there, on the bed. Her face was in one piece, her eyes and mouth open like she was in the middle of the world's greatest orgasm."

She looked at me, the tears rolling from her eyes, her voice shaking, her arms covered in goosebumps.

"The rest of her... There was blood all over the sheets, enough that it was running down and dripping onto the floor. Her body was cut open from her vagina to her sternum. Whatever that thing was, it had been chewing on her lungs when I came up, and there were other parts that were already gone."

She stopped talking, turned her head, and threw up. I watched it splatter on the floor, and then silently got up and made my way into the bathroom to grab a towel so she could clean herself.

I knew my demons. The sex part sounded like an incubus. Eating the organs? A hellhound might feed on a body that way. I didn't know of anything else that would.

Then there was the fact that it took on her sister's appearance. The weres could shift from a quasi-animal form to full human, and a number of demons could cast a glamour that would make them look like someone else to mortals and less powerful Divine. They didn't get the memories of the person they glamoured, and they wouldn't be able to fool their victim's twin, not even for a second.

There was nothing that could do that. At least, nothing I had ever heard of before.

It was a day for curiosities.

I grabbed a couple of towels from the small bathroom, catching a glimpse of myself in the mirror as I did. Sometimes it was a surprise to me to see that I still looked human. Sometimes I had to look to remind myself that I was. I stared at myself, not really paying attention to my tousled hair or my lean, slightly weathered face. I focused on my eyes, bright gray eyes that were wholly unique to me in all of the universe. Eyes that belied the threads of power that coursed within my soul beneath them. They were different. They were also human.

I took a deep breath, blinked a few times, and headed back towards the living room.

She was sitting back against the couch when I returned, her eyes puffy and her nose still running. I handed her the towel, and she used it to wipe the wayward vomit from her face. I took a second towel and draped it over the mess on the floor.

"I'm sorry. It's just…"

I sat down next to her and put my arm on her shoulder. "I'm sorry about what happened to your sister. I need to know… how can you be sure it was a demon?"

She let out a dark, heavy laugh.

"Are you kidding? I didn't know what to do, what to think, so I called the police. Things got worse then, because they couldn't see what had been done to her. Her body was ripped open, and they said she had been stabbed. I told them that whoever did it had taken her appearance, and they wanted to send me in for blood work, like I was on drugs or something. Then they talked to a neighbor, who swore they saw one of us leave the house in a sports bra and yoga pants, and they arrested me as a suspect! The only reason I got out was because they put the time of death at seven thirty. I was in the lab at that time, and had the video to prove it. That little paradox still has them confused. Anyway, there's a detective assigned to the case, but as far as they're concerned it's cold as ice."

She wiped at her eyes again, her sadness slowly receding into steely anger. "I knew what I had seen, and I knew there was no reasonable way to explain it. Something had killed my sister, and her loss, the emptiness… it was tearing me apart just like she had been. I couldn't eat, couldn't sleep, couldn't think. The only thing I could think to do was try to find out what had really happened, to find whatever had done this. I went online, I did some research. I discovered SamChan, and then I started seeing things about angels and demons, crazy shit about vampires and werewolves and a war. There was this guy there, Oblitrix, always asking people if they'd witnessed anything strange like that. Part of me thought he was crazy, but after what I had seen I knew he wasn't. I knew the stuff he was talking about was really out there, and Anita was a victim of it.

"I dropped out of school, and ever since I've spent every waking hour of every day trying to find any leads I can on the thing that killed her. I also started training. I took classes in martial arts, guns, archery, anything I could think of. If I was going to find the demon, I had to be able to fight it, right? I also wrote to Oblitrix to ask him what he knew. He sent me a code."

"The code led you to me."

"Indirectly. It was a cipher, and not an easy one to break. It took months."

"It was meant to see how badly you wanted it."

"Now you know how bad." She wiped the excess tears away.

"I do. What I don't know is what you're hoping to achieve by being here."

"I wrote a program to start tracking murders that matched the description of Anita's. I got a hit or two every week going back about two years, all in the New England area. I found your site last week, with another cipher pointing to this apartment. I was nervous about coming here, afraid that what I had read was true, and at the same time hoping it was. When I picked up another hit here in Manhattan, I knew I had to come. Now I find out everything I was reading, everything you wrote is true? You took a bullet and then offered me ice cream."

She held up her cell again, so I could look at the picture of her with her sister.

"Anita was taken from me, from this world, way too soon. Other girls are being murdered. I know you can help me find the demon that's killing them."

I stared at her. After the Beast, I'd decided that the best way to help mankind was to teach them to help themselves. Now my first student was sitting right in front of me, and I could feel the anxiety and doubt creeping into my soul. Would I be doing the right thing to drag her into this? If she died or worse, and it was likely, would it be my fault? Was I ready to accept that responsibility?

"You know my fight isn't just a fight against Hell? There are demons, lots of them, but there are angels, too. They're the furthest thing from evil, and at the same time the death of humanity rests in their devotion, just as much as it does the Devil's chaos. If you want me to help you, you need to become part of that world, that fight, that war. You need to be ready to kill both sides. It isn't just about your sister. Thousands died in Mumbai because of the Beast. Thousands more have lost who they were. You made the effort to find me, now you need to decide. If I help you, my fight becomes your fight. There's no other way. If you can't accept those terms, the door is over there."

She didn't blink. She didn't sigh. She didn't waste a breath.

"I found you. I know what you're about. I'm here. You need me to sign something in blood?"

"No. No blood. It wouldn't be binding anyway."

I spent the next two hours getting Rose up to speed on the most current events. I gave her a basic rundown of what I knew about demons, and how I had never heard of one that met her description. The timing was a concern to me, because according to her the attacks started not long after the Beast was freed, which suggested we were dealing with a changeling of some kind. I didn't think any new demon types had been born from the damage. Then again, I didn't know everything.

Once that was done, I left her on the couch and went to bed.

I didn't need to sleep right now to stay strong and alert.

I needed it so I could dream.

In my dreams, I saw Charis and Clara the most often. They

would be waiting for me in a sea of grass and flowers, a picnic blanket spread out, the sun shining. It was wholly cliche, and somehow that made it more real, and more comforting. We would eat and play games. I would chase Clara through the field, picking her up and tickling her when she was caught. I would sit with Charis' head on my lap and stroke her hair, and stare down into her eyes.

It brought me peace.

Other times, I would be walking the city alone, and Josette would find her way to me. She would laugh and tease in that way she had, and goad me into sparring with her. She would point out all of the flaws in my form, her form, and then cheat by using her seraphim wings to out-maneuver me.

It brought me energy.

On the rarest of occasions, I would find myself face to face with Ulnyx, the Great Were, my first true enemy, and in the end one of my greatest allies. We would sit in a bar together and drink, and he would regale me with stories of conquest and tell me I was weak and stupid. He would push my buttons and open my eyes.

It brought me strength.

Then I would wake up, and I would be ready.

CHAPTER SEVEN

Rose was using the empty space in the apartment to do pushups when I came out of the bedroom. It wasn't the exercise that caught me off-guard, but the fact that she had stripped down to do it.

I stood in the doorway and watched her pump out fifty in rapid succession, her lean, solid muscles flexing and shifting with each rep, her naked form staying flat and perfect through the entire set. She shouted from the effort when she did the last one, pushing off with enough force to get herself up off the floor. She tucked her knees in and stood in one motion, bringing me into her field of view.

She smiled when she saw me, not the least bit embarrassed. "Hey, Landon. I hope you don't mind. I figured if we're going to be spending a lot of time together in close quarters, it would be stupid for me to be uncomfortable around you, and I didn't want to get my only pair of panties all sweaty. Besides, I'm not a shy girl by nature."

She was pretty, and I was sure the implants brought her a lot of attention from most men.

I had other things on my mind.

"Obviously." I glanced out the grimy window in the corner. The sun was up. "You don't own any other clothes?"

She laughed. "I left them at my hotel downtown. Maybe we can pick them up later? Or do you want me to stay there?"

"No. The apartment next to this one is empty. We'll get you settled over there at some point. Have you eaten?"

"I checked your fridge. You don't get a lot of visitors, do you? Ice cream and soda?"

"There's a deli downstairs. Hit the shower and get dressed, and I'll buy you breakfast."

She saluted me, teasing out a soft smile, and headed for the bathroom. She grabbed her neatly folded stack of clothes on the way.

I took a deep breath. It had been a couple of months since I had spent any amount of time around anyone, and I was getting rusty.

The water started running a minute later, followed by her mostly in-tune voice belting out some top forty hit or another. Definitely not shy. I looked up at the ceiling, extending my hand and stretching the power from it, latching it to the surface and shifting a small square of it aside.

In the past, my power had come from Purgatory, and been confined to Purgatory. When I focused my will, I was demanding change in this world, but things were really happening in that one. Those changes created a kind of ripple effect, and because Purgatory was so close, the ripples made things happen here. It was convoluted, but it had worked, though the sheer amount of power needed had kept my overall strength limited.

Now that I was working under my own power... I had only kept a small measure of it, a pin-sized sun, like an ethereal Tony Stark. I could stretch it away from me, or spread it through me, or otherwise treat it like a piece of play-doh, molding it and shaping it however I needed to do what I wanted to do. Mostly I used it to make myself stronger, or heal my wounds, that kind of thing - I was trying to fit in after all. I could also use it to push or pull, and had on a couple of occasions held the invisible energy like a makeshift lightsaber, but since it wasn't blessed or cursed, it meant having to decapitate, and that was a lot less efficient than the obsidian blade.

I shifted the energy, and my cell dropped out of the small opening and into my hand. I pushed the square back in place and looked down at the phone. When I had held the full breadth of the power, I could have done anything. Created a new universe, challenged God Himself. What I had kept was nothing more than a crumb, a pittance, and I was grateful for that.

The phone rang twice before Obi picked it up.

"Landon, man, I thought you forgot you even had a phone."

"Why didn't you tell me you gave out the code?" I asked. Obi had been my first ally after my original return from death. He'd suffered as much as anybody who had been on my side. Maybe more. Through it, despite it, he remained my closest and most dependable friend.

There was silence on the other end.

"Obi?"

"I... oh, crap, man. I didn't think they'd really find you, and I didn't want you sitting around waiting for them." He paused again. "Yeah, I gave it to someone calling themselves 'demon huntress twenty-three'. I was a little wary about that username, but she, I'm guessing she's a she, she sounded serious."

"Yeah, she's a she. She's in my shower right now. Where are you?"

"Back in Paris, man. I had a couple weeks vacation saved up, and Sarah asked me to come visit. It beats waiting around for you to decide to call me." He laughed.

"How is she?"

"You haven't talked to her lately?"

"Not in a few months. She's eighteen, I figured if she wanted to talk to me she'd call."

"Yeah, well, to be honest, between the work she's doing to bring safe haven to the Awake and the less dangerous changelings out here, and her little romance, she hasn't had much time for me either. It's all good, though. I'm enjoying doing my part to make the world a little less crazy for the ones that know about the war and want to stay out of it. It's a nice break from being on the front lines."

The Awake were the people like Rose who knew about the Divine. She was lucky because she was strong. The ones that weren't… they usually ended up homeless, jobless, and sometimes insane. It was tough to know the truth when hardly anyone else did.

"How many does she have there now?"

"Three hundred or so. More changelings than Awake. We're still trying to find a good solution for them though; they need fresh blood to survive. Cows and goats are doing it for now, but their genetics are screaming for human."

"Rebecca was investing in stem cell research way back when. Did you try to get a lead on the team that was doing it?"

"Solen family vampires? Maybe you could ask Hearst about it?"

"I will. He's going to owe me one. He tipped me to some strangeness with the seraphim and a scientist out in New Mexico."

Obi didn't respond right away, and I knew why. He was my ally, and my friend. He was also a good guy. He'd helped me fight demons, and he'd helped me against the Beast. He wouldn't help me with angels, and he didn't want to know about it either.

"Yeah, well, if you do find out, let me know," he said at last, his voice strained.

"I will. Anyway, I wanted to check in with you about the new recruit. Two years, Obi. I can't believe someone showed up."

"Me neither, man. Try not to get her killed on day one."

"I'll do my best. Tell Sarah I said 'hi', and that she should give me a call sometime."

He laughed again. "Okay, I will. Take care of yourself."

"You too."

I hung up and went over to the window, staring through the dirt to the growing volume of humanity below while I waited for Rose to finish her shower.

Today was going to be a good day.

CHAPTER EIGHT

"SO, YOU'RE TELLING ME THAT Dante Alighieri, the guy who wrote the Divine Comedy, is alive and well in Purgatory?"

We were sitting on the steps to my apartment building. Rose was downing an egg and cheese bagel while I finished the last of the quart I had carried down.

"He isn't alive, technically. His soul is in Purgatory. He's the boss there. He was the one who brought me back here, after I was killed. It's a long story."

She shook her head. "I'm still trying to wrap my pathetic human mind around-"

I put up my hand. "There's nothing pathetic about the human mind. We have our own sets of strengths that neither Heaven or Hell can match."

"Name one."

"I'll give you two. Emotional and unpredictable. The seraphim struggle because they have to follow the rules. The demons falter because they don't have any. There's a pattern in that kind of chaos."

"Okay, but I would think emotions are a weakness."

"They can be. The Beast became the Beast because of love, believe it or not. But even the strength of his destruction was born of his emotions."

"And the demons and angels don't have emotions?"

I laughed. "Of course they do, but their understanding of the world around them limits the vast majority of them. There are always the outliers, the minority. The angels who are temped by the promise of personal gain, or maybe a demon who falls in love." My mind flashed back to Izak, Mephistopheles, whose love had saved Sarah from her father. "They're good or evil. They can't be good and evil, not like you or I can. We can see the whole picture. We can feel a full range. That doesn't mean we're destined to survive, but it helps balance things out a bit. Anyway, wasn't it your love of your sister that brought you to me? Didn't the pain of her loss make you strong?"

She looked at me, and I could see the fire there. "Good point."

She didn't shed any more tears, though I could see the tightness in her face. I waited it for it to soften before I spoke again.

"So, MIT… that's a pretty serious school."

"It can get a little heavy sometimes, sure. I've always been up for a challenge."

"You said you were in engineering. What kind?"

"Biological. Genetics."

"Am I the only one who thinks that's ironic?"

She smiled and shook her head. "No. If I had known some of the origins sooner, I might have gone into a different field. In any case, I was only into my second year. I still had a lot to learn. You don't get cold, do you?"

I looked down at myself. I had stayed with the jeans and leather blazer, which were abnormally light for the forty-degree weather. "I could, if I wanted to."

"That's a nice trick."

"I could teach you, but you'd have to die first."

"I'll pass. Though I do have a question. If I'm helping you fight Heaven and Hell, what's going to happen to me when I die?"

"To be honest, I hadn't really thought about it. When you die, your soul is weighed for all the good and evil you've done in your life. The scale isn't too precise, so if you're helping me, the odds are good that you'll wind up in Purgatory with Dante. If that happens, he'll take good care of you. It won't be as awesome an eternity as Heaven is supposed to be, but I'll make sure it's cushy."

I waited for her to react. To change her mind. Losing the promise of Heaven was a powerful dissuasion.

She downed the last few bites of her bagel and got to her feet. "So, are we going to find the demon, or what?"

"We are. You said you had a lead?"

"Yeah. A girl was killed in her dorm over at Columbia University. I got her name and looked her up on Facebook. Twenty-one, attractive, smart. Like my sister. From what I read, she was stabbed to death, and her boyfriend was arrested a couple hours later."

"You don't think he did it?"

"I know he didn't do it."

"How?"

She got angry at the question. "I just do. I've been tracking this asshole, I know the signs."

"I'm not saying I don't believe you. I wanted to see how much you believe in yourself."

She cooled and nodded. "I did some research. Homicide victims get dropped off at the medical examiner's office over on First and Thirtieth. I thought if you turned out to be a real thing, we could go there first, so you could see it for yourself."

"A real thing? Former people have feelings, too."

"I'm sorry. I didn't mean it that way. I can't even imagine what it's like for you." She paused. "So, I guess you're immortal?"

"Don't worry about it. I was trying to be funny. Sometimes I end up spending too much time alone, and I start to drift away from this." I waved my hand at the world in general. "I'm mostly immortal, as in I don't age, get sick, can take a bullet or twelve.

I'm like Wolverine, or Connor MacLeod. Cut off my head, I die, except as far as I know you don't get my power. Bury me in tons of concrete, trap me ten miles underground, I don't know if I can get out of that."

"Connor MacLeod?"

"Highlander?"

"Never heard of it."

"If I were alive, I'd only be thirty-one. That isn't so much older than you that I should be getting the confused head shake at my pop culture references."

"Maybe I'm the wrong kind of geek girl? You look thirty-one to me."

I smiled and shifted my power, using it to smooth lines, tighten skin, and bring me back to my pre-demise appearance. "How about now?"

She stared at me. "You look better with a few more years on you. More trustworthy."

I used my power to go forward again. I had thought so, too, which is why I had aged myself in the first place.

"Better?"

"Definitely."

"Good. Let's go down to the morgue. I don't know if seeing the victim will help us figure out what we're dealing with, but it's a start."

CHAPTER NINE

"How are we going to get in?" Rose asked.

We were standing across the street from the Chief Medical Examiner's office. It was a plain, six-story square building located next to NYU, on the east side near the FDR drive. We'd made the walk in good time, taking the direct path across 26th. It was early enough that it was still quiet, late enough that most of the staff had already trickled in.

"Just follow my lead," I said. "What was the victims name?"

"Cheryl Paulson."

We crossed the street, my clothes shifting and readjusting into a tweed suit with leather elbow patches and a heavy raincoat as we did. When we reached the front I held the door open for Rose and ushered her through.

An older woman was sitting behind a glass-partitioned counter, looking over some paperwork.

"Excuse me," I said.

The woman looked up.

"Detective Mills. I'm on the Paulson case. Is she still here, or was she transferred out?" I didn't know if that was how a real detective would have said it. It sounded legit.

"Just give me one second." She looked over at her computer and started tapping the keys. "Paulson... Paulson... brought in two nights ago. The autopsy was already done, and the paperwork was sent over to the precinct. We're just waiting on the fax so that we can send her remains back to her family in Tulsa."

I smiled. "Well, I'm glad I made it in time. I was hoping to get a look before she was gone. This is her roommate's girlfriend, Alison. She might have some important information about the case, but she needs to see the body to verify."

The woman looked at me, and then at Rose. Then she reached over and handed me a clipboard. "You'll have to sign in. Just put your name and badge number, and I'll call the assistant to escort you."

"Thank you, Miss..."

"Wells."

"Miss Wells."

I smiled at her again, and took the clipboard. I scribbled John Mills as poorly as I could on the blank sign-in page, and added Obi's former badge number at the end. I handed it back to Miss Wells and waited while she picked up the phone and dialed an internal line. She worked the computer at the same time, glancing back to the clipboard and then to the screen.

"Hi, this is Erica. Can you come up to the front and escort a Detective Mills back into the morgue to view the Paulson cadaver? Yes. Yes. Okay. Thank you, Michael." She hung up. "He'll be with you shortly."

Rose and I retreated away from the desk to wait.

"Roommate's girlfriend?" she asked. "How do you know she had a roommate?"

"I don't. I doubt they do either."

"You're lucky they didn't ask to see your badge."

I reached into my pocket and pulled out a small leather case with a gold badge pinned to it, also sporting Obi's number. "You mean this?" It was really a simple square of plastic, the kind used in 3d printers. Like my clothes, I could mold it and alter it to be whatever I needed. It was more than passable for a quick flip.

"You're like a regular David Copperfield."

"I have better tricks than that hack."

The door next to the glass partition opened. I was expecting a white-coat. Instead, I got a security guard. His gun was drawn, aimed squarely at my chest.

"Don't move," he said.

"What is this?" I asked.

"I don't know who you are, but impersonating an officer, especially a deceased officer, is a serious crime," Miss Wells said from behind her desk.

She had run Obi's badge while we waited. Damn.

"I can explain."

The guard kept the firearm steady. "Just stand there."

The front doors opened, and two police officers walked in.

"Turn around, spread your arms and legs," one of them said. "Both of you."

Rose glanced over at me, a hint of fear in her eyes.

I started turning, and Rose did the same. I was powered to fight demons and angels. I could kill all three of them without too much effort.

That didn't mean I was going to.

"Show me what you can do," I whispered to Rose, at the same time I leaned forward and put my hands up against the wall. I needed to see her toughness, to know she could take care of herself. The Turned, the Touched - they were humans, stronger and faster than most, but still mortal. If she couldn't handle a cop...

Her eyes registered surprise at the statement. She responded with a short nod. The officers came up behind us, cuffs in hand, and I felt a foot push against my ankle, spreading me a little wider.

"You have the right to remain silent-"

Rose's elbow snapped back, catching her target in the shoulder with enough force and surprise to knock him off-balance. Before he could recover, she turned and wrapped her arm around his neck, lifting her legs from the ground and using her weight to pull him over. My guy saw what was happening and grabbed me tight, shoving me hard into the wall and pinning my arms behind my back.

My head was turned to watch Rose, and I saw she had the officer's gun in her hand by the time they hit the ground together. She put it up against the side of his head, dropping the safety with practiced expertise. "Drop it," she ordered the guard.

He stood still, his weapon aimed at her. She was beneath the policeman, his body blocking any kind of shot at her. My first impression of her move had been raw force, not much form. Seeing that every part of it had been intentional, that she had planned to wind up below him in possession of his sidearm - I was impressed.

I pushed the energy out, wrapping it around the guard's weapon and ripping it away, snapping it against the officer holding my arms, breaking his grip and turning. I put my hand around his neck and held him lightly.

"We just came to see the body," I said. I stared into his eyes, waiting to see any kind of spark that might signal he understood that little bit 'extra' that set the Awake apart from the Sleeping.

There was nothing.

"Get off me," Rose said. "One wrong move and I'll kill you."

I watched the officer get to his feet, Rose springing up behind him. She kept the gun trained on him, and then guided him over to the guard.

"Cuff yourselves," I said, letting my officer go. "My partner and I are going to go and identify the corpse, and then we're going to leave. You aren't going to remember any of this."

It wasn't completely true. They would remember putting the cuffs on. They just wouldn't know why. It would be awkward for them to explain later, but it was better than having to kill them. Rose had done well with the situation. I had been sloppy. The people here weren't the enemy, and I should have done better to avoid the confrontation in the first place.

Once the cuffs were on I locked the front door and went back to the desk. Miss Wells was still sitting there, frozen in fear and shock.

"Erica, if you wouldn't mind directing us back to the morgue yourself?"

She pursed her lips and stared at me. I leaned in closer, taking a deeper look into her soul.

"What have you seen?" I asked.

"I don't know what-"

"Yes, you do. Tell me what you've seen. Angels? Vampires? Things that everyone tells you aren't real, but you know they are?"

She kept staring at me.

"The girl, Cheryl Paulson. She was killed by a demon. You know they exist. You know they're real."

"I... I... no. It can't be. It's just my anxiety."

She said it. She didn't believe it.

"I'm not going to hurt you, Erica. We're hunting it. We need to see the body, to understand."

She pushed her chair back and walked to the door on shaky legs.

"Go down the first hallway, all the way to the back, turn left and go down the stairs. Its the second door on your right." Her eyes stayed locked on me. "You aren't one of them."

"No."

She nodded and then pointed at the policemen, sitting quietly with their wrists cuffed together. "What about them?"

"They're going to forget. You are, too."

"Everything?" Her eyes lit up in hopefulness.

"Not everything. I'm sorry."

"My brother. He was... taken... when I was seven. We were

playing outside. I can see them. I can feel them. I've been to therapy, I've taken pills. It isn't enough. I thought I was crazy. I never told anyone."

"You aren't crazy."

She laughed. "I think it would be better if I was."

"I know the feeling." I turned back to Rose. "Come on."

CHAPTER TEN

WE WENT DOWN TO THE morgue, walking with enough purpose that none of the others we crossed paths with questioned two new faces. I had never been to a morgue before, and I was surprised to find that it was one of the things television got mostly right. The room was cold and sterile, a wall of corpse storage, a desk with a computer. The chair behind it was out and turned, its occupant currently absent.

Cheryl Paulson's body was already out on a gurney, wrapped and ready for travel. I unzipped the body bag, whispering an apology as I did. I hated to have to disturb her.

What I saw was disturbing.

The body was in one piece. What was left of it, anyway. As Rose had claimed with her sister, the face was in a frozen look of ecstasy, locked with eyes rolling back, mouth open and smiling. Her neck, arms, legs, and upper body were all good, untouched. Her lower abdomen... that was a different story. It was as if a massive hand had reached in and ripped away her organs.

"I knew it," Rose said. She came up next to me and looked down at the corpse, her face hard. "My sister's wounds were more ragged, and less of the internals were missing, but it's the same demon."

I kept staring at the body, focusing on the wounds. "What kind of demon?" I asked, more to myself. I gathered my power and cast it out, letting it drift away from me, to settle on the flesh of the victim. When it had finished dropping I examined it, tracing the rise and fall of the mold it had made, running my attention along every edge, every fold, every missing piece.

"The ovaries are gone. So is the uterus. The lungs. Whatever did this..." I could feel the outline of the damage with my power. Not teeth or claws like I expected. "A blade of some kind. A razor, or a knife. I don't think it was cursed." It was hard to know for sure on a human. I pulled the energy back and shook my head. "The good thing about demons is they have a general profile. Vampire bites, werewolf claws, easy to identify. This - I don't know any kind of demon that does this."

Every part of it was getting stranger and stranger. Was Rose wrong?

"There is, Landon. I saw it. Whoever it was, they looked just like my sister. They attacked her, mutilated her, ate parts of her... and became her." The tears threatened, but she didn't break.

I looked down at Cheryl Paulson. Demon, human, whichever it was, she was too young to die this way. "You could have been in shock. They could have knocked you out. There are other things that explain what you thought you saw."

Were there?

"Bullshit. If you get knocked out you don't remember anything, and I wouldn't have been in shock before I knew she was in trouble. There's something out there. If you don't know what it is, then you don't know what it is. That doesn't make it any less real."

I took a deep breath. She believed, and nothing was going to alter that belief. "Okay. Let's assume it is a demon. Let's say it's a new kind, or that it somehow got out of Hell. I'd venture to guess that it looks just like Miss Paulson here, and there are thirty million people in this city. How the hell are we going to find it?"

"You destroyed a god, and you can't find a demon?"

"Like I said, demons have profiles. They prefer certain environments. I don't know anything about this." Dante might, and if he made an appearance I would ask him.

"What about the boyfriend? We could go and question him."

I shook my head. "I don't know what we'd get from him that you don't already know."

"Probably nothing, but we can't just leave him there. They think he killed her."

"How are we supposed to change that? Go down there and tell them we think it was a demon?"

"I was in his shoes. You don't know what it's like, to have someone accuse you of doing something so horrible."

"You're right, I don't. There's nothing we can do." I put my hand on her shoulders and looked her in the eye. "You came to me for help, and to be part of this war. You need to understand, it's just us. Against the angels, against the demons, and unfortunately sometimes against the people we're trying to protect. What that means is that a lot of times we have to do things that we don't want to. Things that suck, like leaving an innocent person accused of murder. It's part of the balance."

She stared back at me for a few seconds, took a deep breath, and nodded. She didn't have to like it, only accept it, and she had.

"Most of the victims were picked up at colleges. We could start there?"

I zipped the bag back up, and started for the door. "How many schools are there in the northeast?"

She sighed. "Let's go back to my hotel so I can get my stuff. All the work I've been doing is on my laptop, including a map of every place the asshole has already been. Maybe we can narrow it down?"

We didn't have much else to go on. "Where are you staying?"

"Milford Plaza."

"The lullaby of all Broadway?"

"What?"

"Try Youtube."

We went back out the way we came in. The policemen were gone by then, and Erica looked confused when we exited, tilting her head and narrowing her eyes. She didn't say anything, or try to stop us.

"Walk, or cab?" I asked.

"These attacks happen every few days. We need every minute we can get if we're going to catch up before anyone else has to die."

"So, cab then?"

We walked to the corner, and she flagged a taxi like a true New Yorker.

"Hold on," I said as the car stopped against the curb. "The Divine love taxis." I opened the passenger door and peered in at the driver. "Good morning."

He looked back at me. "Good morning, sir." He was Sikh, with a thick beard and a turban. "Where are you headed today?"

I stared at him for a few seconds. He was clean. Mortal. I got in, with Rose trailing right behind me. "Milford Plaza."

"Yes, sir."

We were there ten minutes later. Rose's room was on the third floor, a small space in a random part of the hotel. It was obvious she had dropped her suitcase on the bed and gone right to my place, because nothing else had been touched.

She unlocked and unzipped it, retrieving a laptop and flipping it open. A minute later she picked it up and turned the screen towards me.

"Here's the map, with all the pins."

They were spread across the New England area. Boston, Maryland, and of course New York.

"Here's a map with pins added to all the nearby colleges."

There were red, demon pins surrounding the city, and a single new pin at Columbia University, where Cheryl Paulson had been enrolled. A sea of green pins rested around it.

"There are a lot of potential targets left on that map. Manhattan has more than fifty schools by itself."

"I know. Even if we split up, the odds of picking the right place still suck."

"We need a better approach than that. Demons are chaotic, but even chaos has a pattern to it. Are the locations all you have?"

"You mean a history?" She sat on the edge of the bed, patting the spot next to her. I joined her there, and watched her flip screens. "I've been keeping a database of the attacks. Names, dates, locations - all correlated with any related info I could find: news articles, Facebook posts, tweets, whatever. I wrote some data analysis tools to go with it. I can step through it, if that's what you're thinking." She scrolled the data, too fast for my eyes to follow.

"That's exactly what I was thinking."

"Not a problem. Ready?" She hit a few keys. A loading bar popped up for a second, followed by the map again. Pins started dropping, fast at first, then slowing as the dates progressed. "You can see, there's not much of a pattern to it. At the same time, our demon doesn't typically travel too far between hits. I have a feeling they might be on foot most of the time, and maybe hitchhiking the rest. The distances seem to bear that out."

I watched the pins fall. Each one was a dead college girl whose body had been mutilated. I hadn't known anything about this. The disturbance was too small to affect the balance, and I didn't have Obi or Dante to feed me this sort of information anymore.

I didn't normally feel guilty for this kind of thing. Then again, the consequences didn't normally show up at my door.

I turned towards Rose, getting her attention. "I'm sorry for your sister. I should have seen this, known this was happening. I should have stopped it sooner."

She shook her head. "Look, I don't know that much about you, other than the fact that you claim to have already saved the world once or twice. What I do know... you gave back the god power, right? That means you can't possibly know everything. You're doing something about it now, that's what matters."

Absolution? Not complete, but her words helped. "Can you play that back again?"

"Sure."

She hit a couple of keys, and the history repeated.

I watched it three more times, a fuzzy idea in my mind clarifying with each reset.

"Can you make this thing connect the pins with a red line or something?"

"Of course." She closed out of the map, opening up the code that powered the whole thing. She went through it in a hurry, adding lines here and there.

Ten minutes later, it was done.

"The lines will be straight. I can add curves if you need it, but the algorithm is a little more complex."

"This should be more than enough."

"What are you looking for, anyway?"

"The points... It sounds crazy, but the pattern reminds me of demonic runes. Like our target is drawing them in their path."

"Are you serious?" She looked back at the screen, and her chest heaved in rhythm to a rising heartbeat.

"Let's see."

She started the animation. I watched while the pins dropped, the lines appearing, connecting each as the murder occurred. As the series progressed, one thing was clear.

"It is a demonic rune. A few of them. Imperfect, maybe because of the straight lines, or maybe because our target likes a specific profile."

"What is it for?"

"I'm not sure. Runes are hard to translate when they're incomplete. It usually takes the entire thing to describe the meaning. It's intentional, an encryption of sorts."

She stared at it, tracing the lines with her finger. "Does it help us?"

"It might. Look at the last line. The shape." I reached forward and tapped my finger against her screen. "This should be the next point. Which school is it?"

She zoomed in until we could read the labels for the streets, and for the college.

Juilliard.

"I never liked drama students," I said.

Rose smiled as she closed the laptop and stood, slipping it back in her bag. "You're sure this is the place?"

"As sure as I can be."

She took a deep, nervous breath in. Her exhale was anxious. "Okay, we have a location. Now what do we do about the fact that we don't know what our target looks like?"

"You're Awake. You can See demons. So can I." I paused, considering. What if it didn't register as Divine? What if I was flat out wrong about it being a demon? We might only have one shot to catch it. "Just to be sure, we'll bring it to us." My eyes traveled from her brown hair, to her ample chest. "We already know you're its type."

She crossed her arms over her breasts. "You want me to be bait?"

"Isn't that what you've been waiting for? A chance to catch up to the demon that killed your sister?"

"Yeah, but we were twins. It knows what I look like. Don't you think it will remember?"

"Appearances are easy to change. A haircut, some dye, makeup and new clothes. Perfume, in case it has a strong sense of smell."

She stood and stared at me. I could read the conflict on her face.

The desire for revenge, the fear of having the opportunity to get it.

"All this time... I spent over a year chasing it, and you figured it out in less than a day."

"You figured it out. You tracked it, collected the data. Without that, we have nothing."

"I would never have recognized a demonic rune." She shook her head, her body trembling. "We're talking about a demon. I knew it was real, and you're here, and real. I'm still having trouble believing it. I've wanted to catch this asshole for so long. I suppose it's as impervious to bullets as you are?"

"I'm afraid so."

She laughed. There was no humor in it, only nerves. "I can't fight a demon. Not on my own. Even if I had found it, even if I knew it for what it was. I would have shot it, and it would have killed me."

"You can fight it, just not with guns. All your research on demons, and you never learned about blessed and cursed blades?"

"Not directly. There was one guy online who claimed that King Arthur used Excalibur to kill demons."

"It was also known as the Redeemer. It did more than kill them. In any case, they're weapons, made by angels and demons and covered in runes and scripture. Other than cutting off the head, you can't kill a Divine without one. Don't worry, I have a collection." I motioned to her stuff. "Is that all you have?"

"Yeah. Kind of pathetic, right? I have to go to a laundromat twice a week."

"Have you looked in my closet? I don't have any clothes."

Her head tilted, and she smiled mischievously. "You mean you're actually naked right now?"

"Not quite." I grabbed the edge of the jacket. "This is going to sound really geeky, but the best way I can think to describe it is that I use my god-energy to manipulate the atomic structures, and change the molecules into whatever I want or need."

My explanation of how it worked was simple, because my own understanding was simple. I knew what was happening, though I didn't have all the details. In my mind, I only thought about the energy, and what I wanted to do with it. The reaction was literally magic.

"That is geeky. So, you could make your leather jacket into steel or something, if you wanted to?"

I looked down at the jacket, then at her, then back at the jacket.

"I never even thought of that."

CHAPTER ELEVEN

We spent the rest of the day taking cabs around the city, collecting the things we would need for our inception into Juilliard. We went to Macy's to find some tight faux leather leggings and a body hugging sweater, hit up the Lance Lappin Salon to have Rose's hair cut and colored, and spent an hour wandering the aisles of Whole Foods, picking up some food fit for someone who still needed to worry about calories.

It was strange to move through the day in such a 'normal' fashion, and I felt myself responding to the simplicity of it as the day wore on. It was as though everything around me took on a new dimension, a rhythm and clarity that I thought I recognized, like an old song. I knew I had been too isolated and out of touch. I hadn't realized how much.

We brought our haul back to the apartments, and I opened the unit next to mine for her to call home. It was similar to my own, and furnished with seventies throwbacks that had been left by the prior resident. I thought the decor was tacky, but Rose loved it. Seeing the reaction made me happy in a way I hadn't experienced in years.

I almost felt human again.

"I'm having trouble getting used to this," Rose said, running her hands through her hair. The brown was now a multi-toned blonde with hints of strawberry, cut into fashionable pieces that fell lightly over her scalp.

It was morning. I was sitting on the couch in Rose's apartment, waiting for her to finish getting ready. Based on the timing of the prior attacks, we were expecting that the demon would be looking for his next victim today, and we had done our best to ensure that she would be the one it chose.

"It looks great," I replied. "It really suits your face."

She turned away from the mirror and smiled. "Thanks. What do you think of the outfit?" She spun around, showing off the clothes.

She really was an appealing woman. "I just hope you don't attract *too much* attention." I reached behind my back. "I have something for you."

"You bought me a present?"

"Sort of. I didn't buy it." I brought my hand out, holding up the blessed knife I'd recovered from my storage unit in the basement. It was long enough to kill a demon with, small enough to stick into the heel of the ankle boots she was wearing.

"How romantic." She laughed and took the knife, examining the scripture etched into the metal. "It's beautiful." She ran her finger along the edge, pulling back as it sliced easily through her flesh and drew blood. "Sharp, too." She sucked the blood from her finger. "What would happen if I stabbed you with it?"

"It would hurt. Give it a try though, you gave me an idea yesterday and I wanted to test it out."

"Are you sure?"

I nodded. "You can't do any permanent damage."

She took the knife and flipped it in her hand, putting the blade up against her wrist. She rushed forward and slashed across my chest.

I pushed the energy out along my shirt, changing it to something denser and more resilient, something more like spider-silk than steel. The knife started skidding off, and then sank through, cutting into my side.

"Oh, shit. Landon, I'm sorry."

I looked down at the wound, pushing the energy to it. It was harder to recover from Divine weapons than it was to bullets, which is why I had wanted to put the shield idea to the test.

"It's okay," I said. "I didn't make it strong enough." Both the wound and the clothes mended while she watched. "I didn't want to do something heavy, because it will pull the rest of the cloth down and move it off the impact point. I can't do the whole thing, or I won't be able to move."

"Maybe it wasn't the best idea."

"It has potential. I'll have to think about it some more."

She knelt down and tucked the blade into her boot. "Thanks again for the knife."

We left the apartments, deciding to walk the sixteen or so blocks north to Lincoln Center. The sun was out, and the weather temperate for the time of year. If it hadn't been for the map, the pins, the runes, and the demon, I would have enjoyed the chance to get to know Rose a little better.

Instead, I was more nervous than I had been since my rebirth. I didn't like not knowing what we were walking into, or who or what we would find. It had been a long time since I had felt so clueless, so unprepared and vulnerable.

"There's the school," Rose said.

We had reached the intersection at Broadway and 65th, leaving the sharp corner of the school pointing at us like the tip of a dagger, though it bore a closer resemblance to the bow of a ship, or the mouth of a whale. I watched the people near the building with a close eye, searching for that internal sense that they were not what they seemed, and at the same time wondering which of the girls I saw entering the school today might not be coming back tomorrow if we failed in our plan.

"Nothing out of the ordinary," I said. "Which isn't much of a surprise."

"No. Let's find out where the library is."

We crossed the street and made our way towards the entrance to the school: a row of glass doors leading to a reception area and a set of stairs. I repeated my aging trick as we did, reversing myself back to my pre-death appearance.

"I still like you better older," Rose said.

"This is a little less suspicious. Are you ready for this?"

"I'm nervous, scared, angry. Yeah, I'm ready."

We didn't stop at the help desk, instead heading straight up the stairs together, laughing and making small-talk and doing our best to look like we belonged. There were a few other students around us, and I eyed each one carefully, making sure they were pure mortal. I knew Rose was doing the same.

It took a bit of wandering, a few missteps, and a couple of reversals, but we managed to locate the library without attracting the wrong kind of attention, and without spotting any demons.

We split up as soon as we got inside.

Most libraries had a similar setup, and despite housing one of the most complete collections of music related resources in the world, Juilliard's wasn't much different. An open space on the ground floor with tables for studying, bookshelves ringing the walls and aligned in columns, and two more floors of material rising above it. Rose kept to the ground floor, heading straight to a table to put her props down and act studious, while I hit the stairs and climbed to a vantage point that allowed me to scan anyone who entered.

After that, there was nothing to do but hope we'd picked the right place, and wait.

CHAPTER TWELVE

WE WERE THERE FOR FOUR hours.

Then five.

Then six.

Rose spent the entire time at her table, laptop open, a stack of books aligned around her. I spent as much time as I could near the steps where I could see the door, moving just enough to not look like a stalker. I wandered back and forth with a book in my hands, open to a random page, my eyes peering over the edge to the position below.

Seven o'clock came. The library was closing in a couple of hours, there were only a half-dozen people left milling around, and we still had nothing.

I had been wrong. That was the only way to explain it. Maybe the rune was a coincidence, or maybe I had picked the wrong school. In a city as dense as New York, the minor differences between the straight lines versus the actual sweeping curves of the shape could have brought us to the wrong place.

Didn't Fordham have a campus nearby?

Or maybe the demon had already come and gone, picking its victim and setting a date. Maybe it had gone against its penchant for libraries, choosing the stage or the orchestra.

I headed for the stairs, ready to collect Rose and try to figure out what to do next. If the demon kept up his killing pace, someone was going to die tonight, and it was my fault. Not that people didn't die every day. Not that demons didn't kill a fair number of them. It didn't usually bother me, except... Rose had come to me for help, and when she did, she came to me on behalf of every girl that either had been killed, or might be killed. She had jumped through my hoops, she had cut through my red tape. She had worked out the tough ciphers that Obi created, and believed strongly enough to come to my apartment to see if I was for real. No one had ever done that before, and the idea of that made it all the more meaningful.

It also made it personal.

I was halfway down when I noticed someone had approached her; a tall, skinny guy with shoulder length black hair in tight jeans and a leather jacket. Where the hell had he come from?

I went back up the stairs, going straight along the railing, trying to get to a spot where I could see his face, his eyes. Rose was talking to him, and she looked calm and comfortable, not what I would expect if she were face to face with her sister's killer.

I circled around behind her, finally getting a look at him. He had a narrow face, angled features, and dark eyes. I stared at him, expecting the alarms to go off.

Nothing.

He reached into his pocket and handed Rose a business card. He brushed a piece of his hair away from his face. He glanced up, his eyes passing over me for just an instant.

Then he left.

The place was almost empty, so I vaulted the railing, letting myself drop to the floor, pushing off with my power at the last second in order to land easy. I came up behind Rose.

"What do you think?" she asked me, holding the card up behind her head. It was glossy and colorful. I took it from her and scanned it. "He's a musician. His name is Peter."

The card was an advertisement for a club his band would be playing at in two hours. "Entropy?"

"Short and sweet, I like it. He gave a card to everyone in here."

"I didn't see him come in."

"He was here for a few hours, studying at the table over there." It was below the overhang. "You must have been sleeping or something when he came in. Anyway, he didn't register on my demon warning system, and if he already has a band and a gig, I doubt he's new to the school. I don't think he's our asshole."

She was right. There was nothing suspicious about him.

"Do you like rock music?" I asked.

CHAPTER THIRTEEN

Entropy was playing at a club a few blocks away, a place called the Underground, probably because the entire thing was located in the sub-basement of a residential apartment building, a place that supposedly had once been anything from an upscale brothel, to an opium den, to a Mafia hangout.

Now it was a stage, a pit, and a bar. There were lots of multi-colored spotlights, lots of grafitti-coated bare cement and pipes, and lots of people.

They were dressed in an assortment of short skirts, blue jeans, and leather, and crowded into the place at least a few hundred strong, leaving little enough room to maneuver through the flesh, and little enough fresh air to breathe. They were mostly college age, though I could spot a few that were a bit too old to be there, and even more that were definitely too young. There had been a bouncer at the door up the steps, but apparently he wasn't very picky about checking ID, or actually preventing anyone from entering.

"Anita would have loved this place," Rose said. We were near the center of the space, halfway between the bar at the rear and the stage at the front. A DJ was spinning tracks from a cage hanging over our heads, and bodies pounded and shifted around us.

"What about you?"

"Back then, yeah. Life has made enjoying stuff like this a challenge."

"I'd love to say it gets easier-"

"But you don't want to lie to me. I know. I get it."

A girl came out at me from the left. She had tripped or something, and was on her way to taking a painful fall. I lunged forward and caught her, one hand resting on her shoulder, the other on her ass.

"Are you okay?"

She looked at me. A vampire.

"Landon, what the-" Rose had noticed. She could See the girl I'd caught well enough to know she wasn't human.

"Landon?" The vamp was scared. She squirmed in my arms, trying to get free. "Let me go. Please."

"I'm not here for you," I said. I lifted her upright. A young guy came out of the crowd and took her arm.

"What the hell are you doing, touching my girl?"

"David-" She tried to intervene. I'd inadvertently walked right into her mark.

"Just trying to keep her from smashing her head on the floor," I said. "No harm done." I put up my hands.

"Yeah, right. No harm done? Your hand on her ass is no harm done?"

"David-" she said again, still trying.

David's hands curled into fists.

I took one quick step towards him, hitting him hard below the temple. He had no time to react. He dropped to the floor, the rest of the crowd making room for him.

"Sorry, you'll have to settle for frozen," I said to the vampire.

She looked down at David, and then back at me. Then she took off.

"Of all the stupid luck," I said, turning to Rose.

"She was a vampire," she said.

"Yes."

She took a deep breath, trying to calm herself. "I've never been that close before. What was she doing with him?"

"Vampires can't survive without human blood. Since she came to party with him, I'm guessing she was planning to keep him around as a source. She'd take him home, have sex with him, have a little drink, rinse, and repeat until his body couldn't take it anymore. Otherwise, she might have brought him somewhere and drained him out, drinking enough to be satisfied, and collecting the rest to either save for later, or put onto the exchange."

"The exchange?"

"Vampires have a global marketplace where they buy and sell blood, valued by the source."

"Seriously?"

"Yes. I shut it down temporarily a few years ago. It started up again while I was gone, and it hasn't been worth the effort to go after it again."

"They kill people for their blood, and that's not worth the effort?"

"You know the war on drugs?"

"Yeah."

"How well has that gone?"

She stared at me for a few seconds, and then accepted it.

We turned towards the stage, even as five guys appeared on it, walking out from the left. A drummer, a bassist, a guitarist, a girl in a tight cocktail dress, and Peter.

The DJ faded out the music, and the rest of the eyes turned to the stage.

"Hey bitches!" The girl shouted into the mic. "DJ Spinz is hot, but I know you all came to hear some real, live, kick-ass rock music!"

The crowd erupted in cheers and whistles.

"Hell yeah!" she agreed. "We've got some killer music for you tonight. Here's Entropy!"

More cheers, clapping, whistles as the girl retreated from the stage and Peter took up the mic. The band started playing behind him, and they blasted into the first song of their set.

"We need to get up front," I said. "You try to get his attention, while I get behind the stage."

"Okay."

We moved forward, making slow progress through the pits that had formed all around the floor, trying to keep outside of them and avoid the distraction. The music blasted around us, and to be honest, it wasn't bad. Peter had a great singing voice, and his riffs were tight.

How could this guy be our killer? It seemed ridiculous, impossible, and it probably was.

I'd gotten screwed by impossible too many times to risk it.

We had nothing else. If we were wrong, we would have been wrong even if we hadn't followed him. If we were right? There was only upside.

It took me four songs to get to the stage. There was a bouncer there, keeping a bunch of screaming females from passing through. It only took a thought for my clothes to morph into a replica of his 'security' t-shirt and jeans, a badge around my neck.

"Hey," I said to him. "They asked me to head into the back."

He was a lot bigger than me, and he tipped his head down and nodded, stepping aside with the end of the rope barrier. I slipped in behind him, thankful to have some room to move again.

I climbed up to the corner of the stage and put my eyes on each of the band members, just in case. They didn't register as anything other than mortal, and so I turned my attention to the crowd, searching for Rose. I found her getting closer to the front, her hands over her head, waving towards Peter.

Perfect. I left the stage, following it around to the dressing rooms in the corner. I knocked on the door before pushing it open and going in. Instrument cases were laying open on the floor, half-empty water bottles resting on simple tables on either side of an old couch. I took a look around, hoping to sense something Divine.

There was nothing.

I retreated from the room, and went to the next one. It was little more than a closet, with a chair and a mirror amidst the cleaning supplies and toilet paper. There was a tiny bathroom in the back corner behind a narrow door, a toilet and sink that looked like it had never been cleaned.

Again, nothing.

Entropy played their set straight through, two hours without a break. By the end, they were coated in sweat, and Peter had removed his shirt to reveal a slim, toned torso. I was standing at the corner of the stage when a sweater landed on it and he picked it up to wipe his forehead.

It was Rose's.

I found her behind the bouncer, her frilly silk bra drawing his eyes. She was giving all of her attention to Peter, hooting and cheering and jumping up and down, making sure her breasts made themselves known. It must have been working, because as soon as Entropy was off the stage, Peter went over to the bouncer and had him let her through. She took his hand, and I retreated to the closet ahead of them.

She was going all-in on figuring out who or what he was. Would she regret it when she discovered he wasn't the demon we were looking for?

Something told me she wouldn't.

CHAPTER FOURTEEN

"Did you like it?" Peter asked.

I peered out from a crack in the bathroom door, watching him. He held the door for Rose, who kept her eyes locked on him while she walked in.

"You're amazing," she said.

"I think this is yours?" He laughed and held up her sweater. It was damp with his sweat.

"This can be yours, too," she replied.

He closed the door, and she pushed herself into him, bringing her lips to his. He was warm to the affection, and he returned it with enthusiasm.

"You're wild," he said, between kisses.

"I know." She turned him around and pushed him down into the chair. Then she straddled his lap. "Do you like it?"

I wasn't sure if I should keep watching or not. I wasn't interested in being witness to what was about to happen.

"I love it."

More kissing. I backed away from the door when Rose took off her bra. How had I ended up in this situation?

"I can be wild, too," Peter said. "More wild than you've ever had, I bet. You want to see?"

She moaned her consent.

I sat down on the can and closed my eyes. I would have closed my ears if I could.

I heard his lips on her skin. Her soft purring of enjoyment.

Stuck on a toilet. If Obi could see me now.

I didn't catch it right away, and I don't think I would have if I hadn't been sitting there. It was a smell. A light, sweet, strange smell, that traveled from the closet to the closest air duct, which happened to be in the tiny bathroom. It was a smell I sort of recognized, the slightly sulfurous edge making a connection in my mind.

I opened my eyes, jumped to my feet, pulled the black stone from my pocket, threw open the door, and stepped out into the room.

Rose's head was back, her mouth open in ecstasy, her neck long and exposed. Peter removed his lips from it and turned towards me. I could See him now, his hot aura unmistakable.

How the hell had he been hiding it?

He stared at me, standing up with Rose wrapped around him. She was still moaning, still moving in his arms even though he'd stopped. He turned and put her on the chair, extracting himself from her.

I summoned the spatha, pulling it into this world. The black blade appeared in my hand, pointed squarely at the demon. "You've been a bad boy," I said. I noticed his lips were moist, too moist. A dark mucus was resting on the edges. Poison.

It had left Rose in some kind of strange high. She squirmed in the chair, oblivious to me.

"What do you know about it?"

"I know what you are, and I know what you've been doing."

He looked at the blade. He looked at my face. Then he ran, taking three quick steps and getting out the door before I had a chance to move.

"Shit." I took two steps and paused at Rose's side. I remembered the wounds on Cheryl Paulson's body. The poison was to incapacitate, not to kill. "I'll be right back."

I gave chase.

The spatha vanished and I pocketed the stone, even as I flew out the door and turned my head just in time to see him round the corner. I raced along the hallway, past the main dressing room, towards an illuminated 'exit' sign mounted on the wall. Ahead of me, I heard an old door squeal open.

I pushed the energy into my muscles, increasing their strength and upping my speed. I went horizontal to bounce off the wall with my legs, pushing off and rolling to my feet, launching towards a metal door ahead. I reached out and yanked it open before I got there, hitting the steps without slowing, taking them up three at a time.

They fed to a second door, and that door led out into the alley behind the apartments. I came out and skidded to a stop, my head going left and right, then up in search of the demon. I had gone as fast as I was able.

Somehow, he had gone faster.

The alley was deserted. Bags of garbage rested against the wall next to an overflowing dumpster. A trickle of water dribbled from a pipe near my feet. I could just barely hear the thumping of the club through the cement.

A cough near the mouth of the alley drew my attention. I walked towards it, keeping the stone in my hand, ready to summon the sword. As I approached, I saw a homeless man on the ground, his back against the wall. He was almost invisible under all of the threadbare clothes he was wearing.

I stepped right up to him. His head shifted, and he stared up at me. He was old, his skin wrinkled and veined, his fingers narrow and bony.

"Spare some change?" he asked with a nearly toothless smile.

I summoned the spatha, and shoved it up against his throat.

"Huh? What are you doing?" He tried to push himself further back against the wall. I caught the smell of his urine rising below us. "Please, don't hurt me."

"Did you see a man with long hair come down here?" I asked. I knew the demon could change shape, but the vagrant was clearly terrified.

"I... He went that way," he raised his hand and pointed down the street. "Please don't hurt me. I didn't do-"

I didn't hear the rest of what he said, because something hit me.

I didn't see it, didn't hear it, didn't sense it. I felt a heavy blow to my ribs, and then I was airborne, twisting and coming to ground back down the alley, sliding through the grime. I tried to breathe in, finding it labored. My ribs were broken by the strike, my arm by the fall. I pushed the energy into the wounds, pulling myself back together at the same time I got to my feet and looked down the alley.

There was nothing there.

"What the hell?"

I felt the rush of air from an incoming mass, and then was back in the air, my body slamming into the wall of the apartments hard enough to crack the cement. I threw some of the energy into healing my spine, the rest into throwing myself away from the impact point. I landed in a roll, facing back towards it.

The attack had taken my first breath.

What I saw stole the second.

He looked like a medieval knight, six feet tall, in matte steel armor with a simple helm covering his head. He was covered in scripture, angelic scripture, dense and tight, etched into the armor and glowing a soft blue in the darkness of the alley. His fist was planted in the wall where my head should have been; a wide, flat blade slung below it, stabbed directly into what would have been my neck.

An angel? It couldn't be. Angels weren't allowed to strike first.

It was against the rules. It made them fall.

The knight's head turned. His face was visored, the eyes hidden by black shadows. He started towards me, feet almost silent against the ground. A second blade extended from beneath his other arm.

I got to my feet. The first hit had forced the spatha from my grip, and I backed away, trying to get a second to find it on the ground.

The knight was fast, ridiculously fast in that heavy armor. He took a dozen steps towards me and then leaped, jumping high in the air in an arc that would bring him down on me. When he reached the top of his leap, his arm pointed out and his wrist turned over, revealing a set of six small bolts mounted to the forearm. A small spark, and one of them shot towards me.

I swung the power out like a cape, using it to knock the missile aside, and letting the momentum push me. I slid back a few feet, the knight hitting the ground right in front of me.

"Who are you?" I asked, still trying to see through the visor.

It answered with its blades, coming at me again in a flurry of attacks. I sidestepped the first blade, and managed to back just far enough away to avoid the second. It launched another bolt as its arm swept past. The missile dug deep into my flesh, puncturing a lung and leaving me breathless again. I stumbled away, my new fall to the pavement helping me avoid getting stabbed.

It wouldn't miss me again.

I gathered the energy around me and pushed it out, driving it all into the knight. It slammed against it like a tidal wave, throwing my opponent away, sending it into the wall across from us. I fought to breathe, pulling the energy back and redirecting it into healing.

The knight started coming again, unaffected.

"Wait," I said. "Damn it, wait."

He didn't listen. He didn't slow. I threw the power against him again, and again he was thrown. It was a delaying tactic, and I couldn't do it indefinitely.

I finished healing, the bolt falling out of my stomach and

clattering on the pavement. I reached out with my power, lifting it and firing it at the knight like a bullet. It rocketed into the chest plate, the force sending it through. A blessed weapon couldn't kill an angel, but it would still hurt going in.

I waited for a scream that never came. He still didn't slow, raising his arm to make the killing blow as he arrived.

"Landon."

The homeless man was on his feet, the spatha in his hand, hilt out. There was no time to wonder who the man was, or how he knew my name. I latched onto the sword with my power, pulling it to me. I was just fast enough to catch the knight's blade on it, and I poured energy into my muscles to keep steady against the force of the blow. The angel had lost the element of surprise, and now it was a fair fight.

I turned the blade and used the momentum to spin to his side, swinging the side with the demonic runes on the edge, hitting it up against the armor. The scripture there flared brighter, pushing me back. I spun the other way, caught the incoming blade, and threw out the energy to shove the other one aside. I kicked out with enhanced strength, knocking the knight back. It fired a third bolt at the same time it tumbled to the ground, the missile catching me in the shoulder.

I cursed in pain and switched sword hands, not taking the time to heal just yet. The arm was coming up to fire again, and I shoved it aside and then came down hard on the elbow, the spatha leading with the scripture edge. The blade sunk into the metal, and then straight through, severing the hand.

Again, I expected a scream of pain.

Again, he didn't make a sound.

The second blade came around and caught me in the thigh, slashing across and creating a deep wound. I did cry out, even as the bolt it fired from the same hand caught me below the arm. The damage made me drop the blade again, and I fell away, bringing the power back to heal.

The knight started getting up.

The vagrant appeared in front of me. He lifted the hilt of the spatha with his foot, bringing it up into his hand in a smooth motion. He hopped onto the knight's chest, kicked the arm away and drove the blade down into the angel's head.

It fell back, but it wasn't over. The homeless man repositioned himself at the knight's side and pulled the blade from his head, raising it and bringing it down in a strong chop.

The helm rolled away.

That should have been the end of it. Instead, the body started moving again. My savior hit it with the sword, leaving deep marks in the metal, even as it regained its feet, ignoring the attacks. As it did, I could see that there was no blood, and in fact no flesh at all.

Hearst's message resonated.

The angels were consorting with a leading robotic engineer.

The body raised its arms to the sky, holding them together like it was praying. I heard the whisper, and I tracked the trio of angels that swooped in. Two took it by the arms and lifted it away like a broken toy, while the third landed between it and us, sword out, ready to defend. He didn't speak. He didn't even look at us directly.

Then they were gone.

I pushed myself to a sitting position, feeling the burn of the energy healing my body. The vagrant approached me, the obsidian sword in his hand. My mind was racing to catch up, to make sense of the entire sequence of events.

"Who are you?" I asked.

One moment, I was looking at a homeless man.

The next, long-haired Peter.

The next, Cheryl Paulson.

Finally, I was gazing up at a man I recognized.

A man I hated.

CHAPTER FIFTEEN

"It can't be," I said. He was still holding the blade. I waited for him to plant it in me.

His smirk twisted every part of my soul.

"Surprise."

Gervais. The archfiend responsible for more of my pain and loss than any other demon. He had imprisoned and raped his own sister, the angel Josette, to produce Sarah, to create a creature outlawed by both Heaven and Hell, a true diuscrucis, a true balance of demon, angel, and human. A creature that could wield untold power. Enough power to rule the world.

Or destroy it.

Gervais, who had sided with the Beast, taking the smallest thread of his power and becoming an undead… thing. A thing with no soul, evil or otherwise. A thing that had plotted to capture the rest of the Beast's power. A thing that had been destroyed when the Beast's power had become mine.

Or so I had thought.

I bounced to my feet, tensing to attack, ready to rip the smirking demon apart.

"Landon, wait." He flipped the sword in his hand, and held it out to me, hilt first. "I don't want to fight you."

I laughed, filled with anger and hate. "Are you kidding me? I don't give a shit what you want."

He pushed a lock of curly black hair away from his angled face. "You should, diuscrucis." He kicked the helm of the knight towards me. "This is bad for both of us."

I glared at him, seething, the head laying at my feet. I could see the wires and actuators in my peripheral vision, along with the etched scripture along the surface of the metal.

"I know. I know. You are angry with me. I don't blame you. I hurt Sarah. I tried to destroy the world, and yes, given this new chance I would like to do so again. I know about the balance, Landon. That thing at your feet, that is a threat to the balance, not me. Look at me. I'm a pathetic little piss-ant now compared to that. Compared to you."

My hands clenched, my heart pounded, my breath was shallow.

"I saved your life. I helped you fight it. You didn't know the hobo was me. I could have escaped."

I took one more deep breath, pictured pummeling him in my mind, and then let it go. Damn him, because he was right.

"That is better, no?"

I took the spatha from him and sent it away. "How are you even here? Sarah killed you."

He shrugged. "Not quite. When I sided with the Beast, he destroyed my body, and he ravaged my soul. He wrapped it up in his power, both to make me stronger, and to compel me to do his bidding. I was a slave, you see. Something he didn't mention when he offered me the opportunity to be second to a god.

"Then you put him away, and I was free. I knew I could capture his power, and have it all for mine. I would have succeeded, but I underestimated my sweet daughter. Oh, you should have been there, Landon. To see her make the change. To see the power of her. Power that should have been mine. Power we were supposed to share. You and Josette. You made her… good."

He spat the word like it was poison.

"When you destroyed the Beast and took his power, you didn't destroy my soul," he said. "It went back to Hell. Back to Lucifer. He tortured me for being a traitor. An eternity of torture in an instant of time here. When he had enough, he decided to send me back again, as a new kind of creature that he has been developing."

I liked the part about the torture. The part about a new kind of demon? Not so much. "A creature that can hide their demonic aura, and change shape?" Talk about evolution.

"Yes, that and more. I don't just change shape. I become the person. All of their memories, all of their knowledge. Everything. I can become any of them, so no one would ever know the difference."

His body changed. Back to Peter, to Cheryl, to the vagrant, cycling through dozens of forms.

"Enough," I shouted. It was Rose standing in front of me. No, not Rose. Anita.

He went back to being himself. "Except the design is imperfect. He said as much. I am the beta test. The first field trial. It isn't enough to drink the blood of mortals. To stay hidden, to be able to change, I need the true flesh of life." He shook his head sadly. "I have done horrible things and enjoyed them. Even I find that part distasteful."

"Lucifer has millions of souls he could have used for his experiment. Why you?"

"You think this is a boon?" He laughed. "It is part of my torture. Send me back to the world where I was once top of the food chain, as a creature so flawed that there would be no chance that I wouldn't draw your attention, or the attention of the seraphim. A creature so weak that I cannot win in a fight. That's right, diuscrucis. I ran from you, because I cannot defeat you." He pointed at the head. "I helped you, because I know there are no demons that can defeat them. How can I rise up again, if the balance is broken before I am dominant once more?"

This whole thing was getting shittier by the minute. He expected me to, what? Let him help me? "If you can't defeat me, then give me one good reason why I shouldn't just kill you right now. You've made it clear you intend to work your way back to where you were. I'm sure the runes you were drawing with the bodies has something to do with that."

He held out his hands. "I am what I am, diuscrucis. Neither you or I can change that. So, why try to be dishonest with you about my motivations? Yes, my path of feeding does have an ulterior motive, one that I was hoping to complete before I was discovered. One good reason that you shouldn't kill me? Because I am not the only demon who knows of it. I am not the only demon who might like to copy it. You need me, to keep it from happening."

"Keep what from happening?"

"It is a ritual. A summoning ritual."

"What does it summon?"

"Of course, I'm not going to tell you. Not today. I need... assurances."

"You're bargaining with me? I could kill you right now."

"Which is why I wish to bargain. I have something you want-"

"You claim to have something I want. You could be full of shit."

He laughed. "I am not, as you say, full of shit. Not with this. Why would I waste two years for something that had no value? For you? Please. I care only enough about you to hope to kill you myself."

Whatever it was, he wouldn't be summoning it unless he was going to have control over it. He wouldn't be summoning it unless it was enough to bring him back to power. If he was as weak as he claimed to be, which wasn't definite but seemed likely, it wasn't something I could just dismiss.

"So, I have something you want," he repeated. "And you have something we all want. Wherever that creature came from, it is obvious to me that you are the only one that can stop it."

"You destroyed it, not me. And, it almost killed me."

"Yes, it would have, if not for me." He gave me a smug smile. "In your defense, you were caught off-guard. You still weakened it. Otherwise, I would never have been able to get close. Even the largest fire demon will fall to one of those bolts. How they have gotten the full blessing on them is a terrifying wonder. No, there is no demon here that can stand up to something like this. Which if I am not wrong, and I rarely am, is the point."

"They were beta testing it, weren't they?" I said. "To see how it would do against me."

He nodded. "It seems likely."

"How did they know where to find me? I'm as hidden as you are without line of sight."

"Perhaps they have been following me? Or perhaps they knew where to follow you?"

Rose.

Could it be? Was she working with them?

"What do you say, diuscrucis? I will help you against the angels, and once they are stopped I will cease my activity in the summoning, tell you its purpose, and give you the names of the other demons here who know how to perform it. In exchange, you will allow me to live, you will not stop me from feeding as I must, and you will help me fight the angels until this business is done."

Gervais was smart. He was cunning. He couldn't be trusted. No demon could be trusted. I had a choice. I could still kill him now, and take my chances with the summoning. His new power did have its value though, and I had a feeling I could put it to good use. Keeping the balance meant putting personal shit aside. It meant shifting tides and strange alliances. The… thing whose head was at my feet almost killed me, and it was a prototype. It was the greatest threat I had seen since the Beast. Gervais was right about being a piss-ant. At least right now.

"I want a solid binding. The kind that will cripple you if you try to go against the bargain." Demons made deals by shaking bloody hands. It created an internal contract that could be broken more or less easily depending on the strength of the deal, and the strength of the other party. That strength was determined by volume. "Oh, and I want you to stay the hell away from Sarah. If I even think you're trying to get near her-"

"Yes, yes. Fine. I will leave her be. I'm not eager to find myself impaled on her wingtips again." He produced a small, cursed knife from somewhere on him, the same one that had cut open his victims. "Take what you want. I'll find another way eventually. I always do." He ran the blade along his wrist, so that it ran down into his palm.

"Both hands," I said.

He did the other without comment. I stepped forward, took the knife, and made the slightest cut in my own flesh. Just enough blood on my side to seal the deal. Then I clasped his hands.

We exchanged the terms of the deal. As we did, I could feel the weight of the binding growing on my soul. I could tell from the way Gervais' face paled that he felt his end much more heavily.

Would he regret the decision?

Or would I?

CHAPTER SIXTEEN

"Whatever you did, you need to undo it," I said.

Gervais and I were back in the Underground, standing in front of Rose. She was still contorted, her mouth open, eyes rolled back in her head.

"I cannot undo it. It is a toxin that overstimulates the pleasure center of the brain. It will wear off in an hour or two. Do not worry for her, diuscrucis. She cannot help but enjoy it."

"What about the way she threw herself at you? Was that her, or you?"

He smiled. "Pheromones. I passed them to her in the library. Normally, I make a date, I get them to bring me home, then I disable them with the toxin and do what I must. This was more convenient today, and the positioning was better than the dormitory."

"Convenient?"

"Yes. A question for you: how did you know I would choose her?"

"You've been predictable. Besides, you already took her twin sister. We had a feeling you'd go for someone similar."

He started laughing. "I killed her sister, and now you are going to what? Introduce us?" His cackling grated on me.

"Shut up." The craziness of it hadn't eluded me, I just didn't have much of a choice. If she was going to be with me she had to learn the rules, as lousy as they could be sometimes. If she couldn't… at least I'd know that now, before I invested more time with her.

Then there was the fact that she might be a plant.

Of course he didn't shut up. He kept laughing until the humor of it ran out. "What of this?" he asked, holding out the knight's head.

"I have a lead on that. A message from Valerix to come see her."

His eyes lit up. "Valerix? Really? You haven't done that saucy minx in yet? Now that will be an adventure."

"Can you go do something useful, like call a cab? We need to get her out of here."

"Of course, of course. Your wish is my command." He put the head on the floor and morphed into Peter. "I'll tell the guys I wore her out." He laughed again, and vanished from the room.

As soon as he was gone, I took a deep breath and tried to release some of the tension from my body. Dealing with the Beast was easier than this.

I found Rose's sweater on the floor. It was still disgusting with Gervais' sweat, so I slipped it over my arm and pushed the energy into it, watching it break apart and reorganize in the blink of an eye. Then I gently titled Rose's head so I could slip it back on her and cover her naked upper torso. She didn't react at all to my manipulation. It didn't seem she could react to anything. I could only imagine what it would be like to be trapped in a paralyzing orgasm. At what point did the inescapable aspect of the pleasure turn it into hellish pain?

Gervais returned a minute later, still looking like Peter, the drummer trailing behind.

"Oh shit, man," he said, seeing Rose sitting there. "What the heck did you do to her?" He looked up at me. "And who are you?"

"I'm her brother," I said.

He wasn't sure how to react, so he laughed. "Dude, are you

serious? This is so screwed up."

"Just help us get her to the cab," Gervais said. "She's tripping pretty hard."

"Yeah, yeah, no problem, Pete. I'll take her legs. Man, she has a nice-"

"Do you mind?" I asked.

"Oh, yeah. Sorry, man." He took her legs, while Gervais took her arms. I picked up the head and guided them through the hallway, opening the doors ahead of them.

"That's a sweet rig," the drummer said as we walked, pointing at the head. "Must crank some massive sound."

I didn't know what he thought it was. "You bet your ass."

We waited a couple of minutes for the cab, keeping Rose propped up so she only looked drunk.

"I'm gonna make sure she gets home okay," Gervais said to the drummer after she was loaded in. "I'll see you guys tomorrow for class."

"Okay, Pete. Peace." He backed away from the car.

"Hey, is she okay?" the driver asked.

"She's fine. She just needs to get home to sleep it off," I said.

He looked concerned, but didn't argue. I gave him the address, and we were back at the apartment inside of ten minutes. Rose had loosened up a little by then, her head slumping forward and her limbs twitching.

"Now I know where you live," Gervais said, helping me get her out of the car. "Not even bourgeoisie. More like a sewer rat."

I looked back at him, holding my tongue against the surfacing anger.

I was going to have to move again when this was over.

CHAPTER SEVENTEEN

For the second time in as many days, there was someone waiting in my apartment.

He was sitting on my sofa, his feet up, his cane laid across his lap, the big ruby at the end sparkling despite an absence of direct light. He was wearing a suit, white with large blue pinstripes, and a matching bow tie. His hair was slicked back, his beard neatly trimmed.

"Signore!" Dante said, as I angled in through the door, holding Rose's top half.

Her silence had turned to mumbles, and her eyes had closed.

"Get out of the way," I replied, leaving the Lord of Purgatory to scramble. He planted his cane on the floor and vaulted over it, his athleticism betraying his aged appearance.

"Is that any way to greet me, when-"

He fell silent, his mouth hanging open.

Gervais had turned the corner.

"Ah, the poet," he said, on seeing Dante. "Still carousing with the rabble?"

We laid Rose down on the couch.

"I'll go and get the other package." Gervais glanced at Dante. "Maybe you'll be gone by the time I get back?" He walked out, closing the door behind him.

"Signore, a word."

I leaned down over Rose's face, brushing the hair away from it. "Rose?"

She mumbled and settled back.

"Signore." He tapped me on the shoulder with his cane.

I turned and got back to my feet. "Dante. You picked a strange time to make an appearance."

"My apologies. As you know, it has become increasingly difficult for me to track the movements of Heaven and Hell since I lost Mr. Ross. Alichino is proving to be less than an ideal replacement. Anyway, that is of little matter. How and what is that demon doing here?"

"You didn't always have your Collector. How did you manage then?"

"Things were simpler when everything had to be spoken in person, or sent by messenger. Technology… she has made my work all the more complex. You didn't answer my question. The archfiend… I believed him destroyed."

Rose groaned again. "Landon?"

I knelt down. "I'm here."

"Signore!" Dante cracked the cane across my back. "I asked you a question."

I closed my eyes, pushed out the pain, took a deep breath, and turned around again. "Mind your temper, Dante. I'm not in the mood."

He smiled weakly. "Yes. Again, my apologies. I am a bit… distraught, over your choice of accomplice."

"Landon." Her voice was groggy and dry.

Her hand reached up and grabbed mine.

"It's okay, Rose. We're back at the apartment."

"Did you kill him?"

"Signore."

"Rose, just give me one minute. Close your eyes and try to relax.

You're safe."

"Who's there?"

"Signore, beyond your new... ally, I have news of great urgency to discuss with you."

"Dante, I haven't seen you in over a year. You finally decide to drop by, and you can't give me two minutes?"

"A year is nothing to you."

"That's not the point."

"Did you say Dante?" Rose said.

Gervais came back into the room, holding the severed head.

Dante saw the head, Rose saw Gervais. He wasn't broadcasting his aura, so I don't know how she knew who he was, but she did.

"Landon?" She started trying to get up, her body fighting her mind.

"Landon?" Dante was staring at the head, growing angry at who was holding it.

"Rose, wait. It's okay. He isn't going to hurt you. Dante, just give me a damn minute."

"This is bullshit," Rose said. She'd managed to get her hand to the knife I'd given her. She fell off the couch trying to get at Gervais.

"Was it as good for you as it could have been for me?" Gervais asked.

I threw out my energy, slamming it into him and driving him to the ground. "You shut the hell up."

He started laughing.

I helped Rose off the floor. She twisted and yanked herself away from me, spinning and slashing with the knife.

"You asshole. I trusted you. You're supposed to help me."

"I am helping you."

She was unsteady on her feet. "Are you kidding me?"

"Children, enough." Dante raised his hand, and Rose fell back to the couch, out cold.

I jabbed my finger at Dante. "If you can't help me with the important stuff, don't help me with this."

He already looked old, and somehow his face aged another fifty years.

"No, I suppose I can't help you, signore. I came to warn you about the angels. It appears my warning was too late."

His sad-old-dog look calmed my own temper. "You're too late to tell me that they're building robots. Do you have anything else?"

"They've recruited a mortal."

"Matthias Zheng."

He seemed surprised I knew the name. "Yes. Who told you?"

"Valerix, via Randolph Hearst. This is a problem for demons, too." I pointed at Gervais, who was sitting up on the floor. "Even this one."

"Especially this one," he said. "It should please you that I'm not what I used to be, poet. Not by any shot at all."

"Yes, I can see that. Alichino told me a new demon had been sent through a rift. If I had known it was you, that your soul had survived, I would have paid more attention to the news."

"I don't want to work with him either," I said. "The fact is he has some skills that may be useful, and he knows as much about fighting angels as anyone. This is kind of new ground for me." Ground I had been dreading having to traverse. As long as it remained a matter of busting up some machines, it wouldn't be a problem.

Gervais finished getting back to his feet. "You can be useful, too, my Lord." The last two words were sarcastic, mocking. "Someone needs to examine this. To see if it has any weaknesses. To determine what it is made of."

"I don't take orders from you," Dante said.

"Of course you don't, you old fool. You're probably so ignorant that you'd rather not do what I suggest just so you can not listen to me."

I could tell Dante was fuming. He remained silent while I took the head from Gervais and handed it to him. "Can you bring this back with you?"

He shook his head. "No, signore. I will have to bring Alichino back to examine it. I can carry it to his old workshop in Brazil and drop him there." He glared at Gervais. "Only because you are asking, and because it is the logical next step. Agents of Heaven that can attack without provocation, that are armored against demonic claws and teeth... This is an escalation that cannot be allowed to occur."

"It's more than that," I said. "This thing shot bolts at me. They've miniaturized the scripture or something. The entire blessing fits on a small projectile."

"It is worse than I realized. Let us not waste any more time on old wounds. The balance is of the utmost priority."

He vanished.

"Always a pleasure," Gervais called out. "Old windbag."

"How did you and Josette turn out so different?" I said it softly, not expecting the comment to be heard or answered.

"It is simple, diuscrucis. She always believed that no matter what occurred in the mortal life, God would lift her into His Kingdom of light, beauty, and eternal happiness. I always believed that if you want something, you need to take it. That is the only way you are guaranteed a chance to achieve the kingdom you desire." He chuckled softly. "You know what that Kingdom did to her, don't you? You know how it used her, just as much as I used her. I never pretended to be something I wasn't. I never kept a hidden agenda. Not from her.

"Can you say the same for Heaven?"

CHAPTER EIGHTEEN

I KICKED GERVAIS OUT OF my apartment so I could deal with Rose. His parting words lingered in the back of my mind, his laughter tracking behind it the entire time. Regardless of what the demon thought, Josette had never regretted her decision to return to Earth as an angel. She had always trusted in God's path, and she walked it with humility wherever it took her.

Even her death, her final death, was dignified.

Gervais didn't know the difference. He would always grasp for material power, and never understand the true strength of spirit. It's what made him such an asshole.

"Rose."

I was leaning over her, ready to hold her still if she woke as angry as she had been when Dante knocked her out.

Her eyes fluttered and opened. "Landon." A tear pooled in her eye. "I don't understand."

"I was attacked in the alley. By the seraphim, the angels. By a construction of mortal engineering and Divine power. I would have died, if he hadn't helped me."

"What?"

"They can't sense me, Rose. They don't know who or where I am unless I'm in direct line of sight. I was in a dark alley, between two buildings. How did they know I was there?"

She was looking up at me from the couch. Her breath hung. "Are you suggesting I betrayed you?"

"I'm asking."

"No. I didn't tell anyone. I'm not working with them."

I watched her eyes. I didn't have my Divine truth-telling mojo anymore, but it was a crutch that was too easy to be fooled by, and a power I didn't need. I was smarter. More experienced. I could read the signs better.

She was telling the truth.

"I believe you. How are you feeling?"

"I... I'm not sure. He did something to me. It felt good, really good, but in a bad, bad way. I'm trying to deal with it, trying to work it out. I don't feel violated, or dirty. Just... confused. A little dizzy, like a bad hangover. All of this is happening so fast." She squeezed her eyes closed, and the tears flowed from behind the lids. "I don't know if I can do this. I wanted to find you. I wanted to be part of this. You let him live. You brought him back here with you. He's killed how many girls? Anita... She was innocent. She never hurt anybody. He..."

She trailed off. Opened her eyes. Looked up at me, the fire and anger replacing the pain. Her voice was quiet venom.

"How could you?"

I was calm. I had expected this, and worse. "I told you. I was attacked. He saved my life."

"One life saved, and how many taken? He doesn't deserve to live."

"No, he doesn't. It isn't that simple. The balance... it's never that simple."

The anger cooled a little. She shifted her head, as though getting a different angle would let her see deeper into me. "There's something you're not telling me."

I was impressed that she saw it.

"I know him. His name is Gervais."

We talked for a long time. I told her everything. How he captured and raped his own sister so that she would give birth to a true crossbreed, a mortal whose potential dwarfed that of any angel or demon. How he sided with the Beast to get to her. How he killed my friends. I told her everything I could think of. It took hours. Not because I had planned to. Not because I thought she needed to know it all. She had enough to try to make sense of already, and I was only adding to it.

Except I found that once I started talking, I couldn't stop. I found that there was no god-power that could salve the pain of what I had endured. Of what I held inside.

She listened. Despite her own pain, she listened. She didn't speak, she didn't move. She sat and absorbed the words without question or judgement.

By the time I was done, my own face was wet with tears. I had spent time alone to recover after defeating the Beast, and I had cried for Charis and Clara, for my friends, and for the thousands of others who had died at his hand.

Two years.

It was the first time I had cried for myself.

When it was over, when my emotions were spent, we sat together in comfortable silence. At some point, she reached out and took my hand in hers, and I focused on that connection, that simple human affection. That basic, primal comfort.

"I understand," she said a while later.

"Understand?"

"Why you didn't kill him. I don't like it, but I understand."

"It's going to get worse. What the angels are doing... You can still change your mind about helping me. I didn't hold up my end."

There was no hesitation.

"I'm not changing my mind. The things that are out there... I get that the angels want to help, and think they're helping, and I like the idea of getting rid of demons. To trade the many for the few?

Anita wasn't a believer. Neither was I, before all of this. I don't think that made us bad people, and at the same time we would have been left for food when the Rapture happened. Now that I *do* believe in God… I'm not convinced He's got the right idea." She smiled and squeezed my hand. "Besides, you need someone to watch your back. To make sure this Gervais doesn't stick something in it."

I laughed at that. "Do I need to watch his? To make sure you don't stick something in it?"

"No. Not as long as you need him. Since Anita died, everything that has happened, it's made me stronger than I ever thought I could be. Strong enough to deal with the demon who killed her. I never imagined I would say that."

"I felt the same way after I died."

She laughed and leaned in, kissing me softly on the cheek.

"I'm going to go back to my room, have something to eat, and try to get used to all of this. Goodnight, Landon."

"Goodnight, Rose. Thank you for understanding."

She got up and walked out.

CHAPTER NINETEEN

I HAD A TRICK UP my sleeve that allowed me to cover large distances faster than conventional air travel. I knew it would be necessary, a counter to the angels' globe-hopping airspeed, or the demons' use of transport rifts. In simple terms, I could use my power to destroy a pocket of space-time in front of me and recreate it behind me, essentially folding space. The trouble was that I could only use it for myself, and it generally left me disoriented and tired when I came out the other side. It was the stretch at the very edge of my limits.

As a result, we lost most of the next day catching a flight from JFK to LAX. As promised, Rose was neutral around Gervais. Not happy, not warm. She didn't speak a word to him, but she didn't try to stab him either. The demon returned her ignorance with ambivalence, staying fairly quiet himself and only making an occasional rude comment.

The flight was tense and awkward. I wound up in the center seat, with Rose on the aisle and Gervais against the window, to keep the demon from having easy access to the attendants. He must have fed after he left the apartment, because he was looking healthier and stronger. More like himself.

I hated it.

We landed six hours later, a car already waiting at the airport to take us to Valerix's home near the coast. It was late evening, warm, and dry.

"I can't remember the last time I was in California," Gervais said. "Eighteen forty-nine, perhaps? That was a fun vacation."

We were in a stretch limo, on our way to pay the archfiend a visit.

The demon turned to me. "Did you know Valerix was already establishing her territory back then? Ah, she was a spit-fire. You'll never meet another demon who is better with a sword." He paused, took a swig from the champagne bottle he'd found, and smiled. "Except for me, of course."

"Of course."

"We dueled. Not with swords, with pistols. Did you know that? We couldn't do any permanent damage. We had a fresh crop of virgins. So young. So delicious. And a bet."

Rose was sitting against the window, keeping her eyes locked on the scenery. I saw her face tighten as she tried to ignore him.

"I need a name for myself," he said. "You have the vampires, the werewolves, the nightstalkers. You have your devils and your succubi. I'm the only one of my kind right now, so I should get to decide what I am called, should I not?"

He took another pull from the bottle.

"Can you shut up?" I asked.

He put his hand on my shoulder. "Oh, come now, Landon." He laughed and looked past me. "Or do you want to, again?"

Her head whipped around, and the blessed knife I had given her was in her hand almost before I could grab her wrist.

"Rrraawwrrrrr." He stuck his tongue out at her, and then ran it around his mouth.

"Just ignore him," I said.

She relaxed, put the knife away, and returned her gaze to the window.

"It's all in good fun." He laughed again, and finished the

champagne. He held the bottle out and looked down at the label. "That was disgusting."

I was wondering how much I really needed him when the limo turned onto a long, narrow driveway.

We were there.

He drove us up to a large, wrought iron gate, where a man in a dark suit waited. Not a man, a were. He approached the driver's side as we came to a stop.

"Don't ruin my surprise," Gervais said. He changed form, back to Peter. "I'm just another of your new recruits."

"The Mistress wasn't expecting nobody," the were said. Like most weres, his voice was deep and rough.

"I have a Mr. Hamilton here to see her," the driver replied. "He said she's expecting him."

"I don't know that name." A wire was running to his ear. He leaned into it. "This is Jackson. I got a Mr. Hamilton here to see you." He listened for a few seconds, then leaned down, sticking his head into the driver's side window. He looked back at me. I could see his nostrils flare as he caught my scent, and recognized that I was different. "You ain't alone."

"My associates," I said. "Anything Valerix has to say to me, she can say in front of them."

He pulled his head out. "Yeah, it's him, I guess. Smells funny. He's got two others in the car with him. Nah, they're human." He paused. "Yeah, okay." He raised his hand and motioned in a circle. The gate started to open.

The driver eased through. The other side started with a large, open field and ended with a circular driveway with a huge, twisted fountain in the center, a brutal, carved depiction of chaos and violence. It was a good reference for what I thought Hell probably looked like.

Behind the fountain was a large, white, columned mansion, with a huge colonnade and lots of dark tinted windows. There were a dozen small steps leading up to a huge door, which was nicked and dented with thousands of runes.

Protection from angels.

The car stopped and the driver got out, circling around and opening the door for us. Gervais exited first, his balance a little unsteady, and he leaned against the car to keep himself upright. I followed, and took Rose's hand to help her out of the car.

"Thank you," she said softly.

I answered with a smile, and turned back to the doorway.

I could see her there, on the other side of the threshold. She was half-bathed in shadow; a fiery-haired, green-eyed beauty of a woman. Her skin was porcelain, her clasped hands ending in long, nimble fingers. She was wearing a short red leather skirt and a silk blouse, with gem-encrusted sandals on her feet that twinkled in the moonlight.

Two more weres came down to greet us.

She stayed behind the doors.

She was afraid.

"She's only gotten hotter," Gervais whispered.

"What did you say?" one of the weres asked.

"It sure is hot out here." He started giggling. Had he known the booze would go to his head? I couldn't believe this was the same demon who had nearly stolen away the Beast's power.

"Mistress Valerix welcomes you," the other were said, stopping in front of me and moving into a sweeping bow. "Please, accept her invitation as an honored guest in her home."

"I accept," I said, staying upright. "I expect my companions will be afforded the same honor?"

The were huffed. "Of course."

"Peter, Rose, let's go."

I started walking, leaving them behind me. It was the proper decorum for meeting with an archfiend. If it had just been Rose, I wouldn't have bothered.

I heard a grunt behind me.

"Damn it," Rose cursed.

I turned around. Gervais had started to fall, and she had caught him. She held him like a dirty diaper, trying to keep him upright and touch him as little as possible.

I caught her eyes in mine.

"Go," she said. "I've got him."

She set her jaw and put his arm over her shoulders, helping him walk. I could only imagine how hard it was for her.

CHAPTER TWENTY

"Diuscrucis." Valerix held out her hand, palm down so I could kiss it. Now that I was closer, I could see her eyes were cat's eyes, bright and predatory, tapering at the edges in an interesting and physically appealing way. She was an archfiend, which meant she had once been human, a human so evil that Lucifer allowed her to leave Hell to regain our world as her almost immortal playground.

I could see one of the ways she had risen to power.

"Valerix."

She looked past me. "Is your companion well?"

"Peter? He'll be fine."

She laughed. "Peter. A very… godly name."

"I'm not on a side. You know that."

"Yes, of course. The Great Equalizer. Since you're here, I assume you got my message."

"And then some."

"Do tell."

"Once we're all inside. I'm guessing you have those wards on the door, and won't come away from them, for a reason."

"I've put myself at great risk for you, diuscrucis."

Rose reached the doorway, still helping Gervais along.

"Good evening, Miss…"

"Rose. Just Rose." She looked back at the demon, and I could tell she was trying to quell her fear. She would be able to feel Valerix's aura, an aura that was likely much stronger than anything she had already encountered, even in passing.

Valerix's eyes ran the length of her body, an act that was anything but innocent. "Rose. By any other name, would you be as sweet?"

"I'm Peter," Gervais said, blurting it out. He shifted in Rose's arms. "I think I'm going to be sick." His face paled, and his stomach made a horrible gurgling noise.

Valerix looked horrified. "Take the sheep up to one of the guest rooms," she said to one of the weres. "Do not hurt him."

"Sheep?" Rose said.

"Baaaaa!" Gervais laughed. "Baaaa!"

"Come on." The were grabbed him roughly and pulled him away from Rose. She looked thankful to be rid of him. "I'll bring him upstairs."

"Landon, if you will." Valerix turned, walking ahead of us. The second were pulled the doors closed, and then lifted a heavy slab of iron across to reinforce it.

"Sheep?" Rose whispered to me, coming to walk at my side.

"You're human. She only sees you as food, or a toy. For now."

We kept walking, following Valerix down a marbled hallway and into a large sitting room. It was modern, with square, white leather furniture and huge, minimalist canvases lining the walls.

"Your companion," she said. "He is-"

"A little rough around the edges."

"Why did you bring them here? What do you hope to gain by consorting with mortals? They will only get in your way. Make you soft."

"That's a demonic perspective if I've ever heard one. Have you forgotten what your own human spirit was like?"

"I remember my desire to hear how other spirits beg and scream."

"Watch your tongue, Valerix," I said, taking an aggressive step towards her. "You invited us in. Have some respect."

She pursed her lips, bristling at being challenged in her own home. I don't know how much she feared me, but she feared the bigger picture enough to back down. "My apologies, Rose. I don't spend much time around sh… mortals, these days. I have forgotten my platitudes."

"Apology accepted," Rose said.

The answer made her bristle more. Her face flushed, and her eyes burned. "Please, sit. Make yourselves comfortable. Would you like some tea?"

"We can skip the polite hostess part." I took a seat on a cream colored sofa. Rose chose a white, gothic looking chair, declaring her independence from me. It was a smart choice. "You have information."

Valerix sat on the love seat opposite the couch. Her leather skirt rode up as she dropped, an intentional maneuver to try to entice me, or maybe Rose, with a sneak peek.

I knew how to play the game. My eyes stayed on her face.

She smirked. "Hearst told you about Matthias Zheng?"

"Yes. I've already seen the fruits of his labor."

Her eyebrows lifted. "What?"

"The machine. The angels threw it at me last night."

"And you survived?" Was she disappointed, or excited?

"Human spirit."

"I've seen the fruits of their labor, too. They dropped that thing into a vampire nest. Over a hundred vampires against one. You can guess who won."

"That's why you warded your door?"

"The entire house, underneath the wallpaper. I spent six days without interruption inscribing it myself, wondering every minute if they would show up with their weapon before I was done."

"Why would they target you?"

"They know I contacted you. That I tried to warn you. I also may have… detained, one of their Touched. He was a boastful sh… man. Certain that the 'Fists of God' would destroy our kind once and for all. I enjoyed bl…" She caught herself and glanced at Rose, and then returned her attention to me. "Oh, and you."

Fists of God? It was a cool name. I wasn't too happy about the plural.

"They're tough, but not indestructible. We decapitated one. I've got someone studying the scripture as we speak."

"Templars?"

"No. Since the Beast was destroyed, the few that were left have faded into the background. A scientist. Speaking of which, Randolph mentioned that Zheng is immune to Divine power."

"It is an oddity, isn't it? I sent my most powerful sex demons to meet him. Their power did nothing. I sent them back with a glamour I placed myself, changing their appearance completely. He saw right through it. He has no Divine aura, so I know he's mortal. Even stranger - he acted like he didn't know they were demons."

I was silent while I considered it. Gervais could disguise his aura. Was it possible Zheng was a demon, or had been replaced by a demon?

A well-placed rift would make for fast travel. Was it possible Gervais was Zheng? I couldn't rule it out.

I got to my feet. "If you could excuse me for a minute. I need to check on Peter."

Valerix stood, confused. "We weren't done with our conversation."

"We can pick it up in a minute. Can you have your dog lead me to where you stashed him?"

She didn't look happy. "Zel, will you please escort the diuscrucis upstairs."

"What's going on?" Rose asked, also rising from her chair.

"I just want to check on Peter. I trust Valerix will be a gracious host while I'm gone." I eyed the archfiend. Her eyes flared red.

"Of course. Please, Rose. Sit. Do you like designer handbags?"

Rose didn't look happy either. "No. I like knives."

Valerix smiled and ran her tongue against her lips. "Well then, I have something to show you, I think you're going to love."

"This way," the were, Zel, said, motioning me towards the door.

I started following. We made it halfway to the door when something outside caused the whole building to shake. A moment later, Zel reached up to his earpiece.

"Mistress, there are angels outside."

Valerix hissed. "Why now?"

"Maybe they know I'm here?" I said.

"How would they? You only arrived a few minutes ago."

It couldn't have been Rose, she was with me the entire time. Gervais on the other hand…

The mansion shook again. I heard a faint scream from outside.

"Zel, send out the alarm. We need to be ready in case the wards don't hold. Do they have any Fists with them?"

The were growled and shook his head. "I don't know, Mistress. I'm not getting any reports from the outer security."

Valerix hissed again and hurried out of the room.

"Are you ready for this?" I asked Rose on our way out behind her.

"No." She drew a cursed knife. "I don't want to kill the good guys."

"You should never *want* to kill anything. Just remember, if they win, all of this is gone, and only the few will be going someplace better."

"I know."

We trailed the archfiend out into the hallway, the building shaking every few seconds. If Gervais was behind this, if he was double-crossing me for the angels, he wouldn't be doing it for much longer.

We reached the foyer, coming into sight of the warded door.

The other were, the one who had brought Gervais up to his room, was standing next to it.

He had just pulled it open.

CHAPTER TWENTY-ONE

"Elyx!" Valerix shouted. The were looked towards her, hopping aside as a gout of hellfire launched from her fingers towards him. He turned and galloped towards the stairs, bounding up them at full speed, vanishing from sight in a matter of seconds. "You'll spend eternity in Hell for this, you flea ridden mongrel!"

"Get down!" I grabbed the archfiend with my hands, at the same time I threw my power into Rose and pulled both of them to the ground.

The seal of the wards broken, the door flew open and six of the bolts whizzed through the air above us. I heard them buzz past and slam into the wall.

The Fist came in behind the volley, extending the wrist-mounted blades and charging like a bull. I pushed the energy into my muscles and rolled to where Rose was laying face-down. I got her aside even as the machine and another blast of hellfire converged on the spot. The blue runes on the Fist's surface grew brighter while the fire poured into it, absorbing the heat and energy. The blade retracted from its right hand, which adjusted to face Valerix and angled back so the palm was out.

A blue beam of light launched from it, striking Valerix full in the chest. She had two seconds to scream, and then she vanished in a pile of ash.

"Oh my god," Rose said, her voice cracking with fear.

I pulled the stone from my pocket and summoned the obsidian blade, throwing myself forward at the Fist's back, bringing the blade up to make a hard stroke on its vulnerable neck.

Its hand swung around, cuffing me in the shoulder, catching my momentum and redirecting me. I braced myself and slammed hard into one of the warded windows and then through, hitting the pavement and rolling to a stop against the base of the fountain. I healed myself as quickly as I could and got back on my feet. I could hear the Fist moving, and it stormed out the front door in pursuit.

At least it had ignored Rose.

"Landon."

A voice from behind me. A voice I knew. I turned around.

"Adam?"

He was standing on the other side of the fountain, flanked by three angels on each side. His handsome face was sharp and serious, his long, golden hair falling in waves across broad, muscular shoulders. My eyes trailed down them to the white toga the angels preferred, to the reddish gold clasp that identified him as the Inquisitor Prime, to his right arm.

Gervais' undead demons had broken the arm during the fight to destroy the Beast. It was a unique wound, not wholly demonic, a wound that I knew would never heal. A wound he had overcome.

"Why?" I asked him, staring at the arm. It was metal, like the Fist now standing still behind me, and also covered in glowing scripture. It had been fused to his skin just above the elbow, the mechanic actuators visible beneath his forearm. He extended the fingers and closed them back into a fist, showing off the prosthetic.

"Why? Landon… I'm sorry, my friend. I have nothing but respect for you, but what did you expect? Your existence is a problem for us. It's even more of a problem now, because we've developed a tool to finally rid the world of demons."

"That thing is going to lead to the downfall of man."

"Not all men. The believers will be brought home. You know that."

"How many is that? How many are left behind? Three billion? Four?"

"It is His infallible wish."

"Did He tell you that?"

"We are His children. We know His will."

"So He's okay with you circumventing the rules of engagement?"

"He allowed us to have the idea, and He provided the means."

"You're reaching."

"I haven't fallen yet. What does that tell you? This isn't something I want to do. It's something I have to do."

"Again, why? Why you? Shouldn't you be out capturing lost artifacts?"

He laughed. "I wish I were. After the Blades were destroyed, the archangels gave me a new task. 'Discover a way to defeat the diuscrucis.' Those were the exact words. I did, though you've been a hard man to find."

"It helps to have a demon on your side."

"It is uncommon, but there are a few who are willing to trade their services for the promise of forgiveness."

Gervais? After everything, would Heaven bargain his soul?

"Anyway, my friend, I came to give you a chance to save yourself. To save your soul. God forgives all who repent."

It was my turn to laugh. "You want me to repent? To screw over the rest of mankind? Are you serious?" He was. I knew he was. "Forget it. You already got one of your toys back with its head ripped off. It's fine by me if you want to keep adding to my collection."

He looked at me. I didn't see any conflict, though I did see regret. He was being honest when he said he didn't want to.

We both knew that wasn't enough.

I spun around, throwing my hands out, directing the energy. The Fist's bolts came in fast, in a wide enough spread to hit me no matter which way I turned.

Thankfully, I didn't need to turn.

I focused on the power, splitting it into six distinct streams, using them as funnels to capture the bolts, dropping to the ground and spinning on my knees, redirecting them around me and through the cascading mist of the fountain.

Into the angels.

One bolt for each of Adam's companions. They slammed into them, disappearing in an explosion of blood and the heavy crack of bone. All six of the angels fell back, reaching for the metal that was buried in them. It was blessed, it couldn't kill them. It did keep them otherwise occupied. More importantly, it showed Adam I wasn't about to give any quarter.

He didn't move. He didn't react. His artificial limb flexed, fingers tapping a strange cadence. The Fist was coming hard.

I gathered myself and leaped away from it, backwards over the fountain, twisting in mid-air, summoning the obsidian blade. I cleared the grotesque centerpiece and angled downwards towards Adam, leading with the sword.

He had a sword of his own, and it appeared in his hand just in time for him to backstep and parry my attack. I landed and pressed in, flooding my muscles with the power, slamming my sword against his. He was good, very good. He wasn't as good as Josette had made me.

"What do you hope to gain by this?" he asked, backpedaling with each new stroke, his face twisted in concentration.

"I was hoping I could convince you to surrender."

His wings unfurled behind him and he bounced backwards, using them to carry him further and faster. I sprung after, covering the distance in one strong leap.

"I can't, Landon. This is His will. Break the diuscrucis, break the balance, win the war."

"You saw what happened in Mumbai. When you win... the entire world will be like that."

He turned and lashed out with a wing, getting more desperate as I continued pressing, the black spatha whistling through the air in combinations of cuts and jabs. I took the hit off my shoulder, planting myself to keep from being thrown aside. He managed to slow my attack long enough to get a couple of breaths.

"All of His children have the opportunity to ask Him for forgiveness and pledge themselves, up until the very moment of the Rapture. The ones who don't..." His face tightened. "They will get what they have asked for. A world without Him."

I let him block me again. This time, I reached out with my power, pulling the ground behind him, raising enough earth that he stumbled on his next backstep and lost his balance.

His wings spread and twisted. He shot into the sky, just barely escaping my reach. The blessed end of the blade caught his abdomen, cutting through the toga and leaving a thin line of blood that trailed him upwards.

I noticed that the fingers on the metal hand were still moving.

I ducked just in time to avoid the Fist's heavy blade, turned and smacked against it with the spatha. As before, the scripture flared, making the blow of the razor sharp artifact more like a stick against a stone. I knew from the first fight that the joints were vulnerable, so I changed my tactics even as I rolled away from it.

It followed after, twin blades making alternating stabs, torso turning independent of its legs to follow me more quickly. Its form was shit, its approach pure brute force. I could duck and weave for a while to keep it away. Eventually, I would get weary.

I doubted that it would.

I pushed out with my power, shoving the arm out and bringing the cursed side of the blade down towards the joint. It was smarter this time, and it shifted just enough to move the joint out of line, leaving the stroke to bounce off the scripture. It followed up the bold attack with a solid kick to the ribs that sent me tumbling, and left them shattered under my skin.

"You can still repent," Adam said, from his position fifty feet over my head. "He'll forgive you."

Angels. They were all about forgiveness, love, charity. When it suited them. Otherwise, they were more than willing to throw you aside.

I could hardly breathe, but I didn't bother healing myself. The Fist was coming for me.

If Divine weapons were ineffective, maybe I needed a different approach.

I took a deep breath, steadying myself on my knees in front of the onrushing machine. I reached out with the energy, casting it like a massive net.

Then I pulled.

The twisted artwork of the marble fountain cracked as it was yanked from its base and sent hurtling in my direction. I followed the path and clenched my muscles, as though that could somehow give me more leverage with the energy to better direct the heavy stone missile. Maybe it did. Maybe it didn't. The end result was the same.

It slammed into the Fist, not four feet from where I was kneeling. Both objects met in an echoing collision. Both objects went airborne for a few seconds. Then the sculpture came down on the machine, twisting and crushing it beneath the weight.

It didn't get back up.

I flopped onto my back, bringing my sword up to defend myself from Adam. He wasn't coming after me. He floated above me, looking down and shaking his head. A moment later, the other six angels joined him.

They all left together. As they did, I could swear I saw him smile.

CHAPTER TWENTY-TWO

I FOUND ROSE WAITING FOR me inside the mansion. She was sitting on the floor, her back pressed against the wall, her blessed knife laying on the ground between her legs.

It was bloody.

"What happened? Are you okay?"

She nodded. "I'm fine. Happy to see that all that training paid off, even against werewolves." She pointed towards a pile of dust a dozen feet away. "After that thing chased you outside, Valerix's servant thought it might be fun to try to rape me. It didn't turn out the way he planned." She smiled. "I saw the fight. The best part, anyway. I'm impressed. What was with the cyborg angel?"

I couldn't hold back my smile, and I felt a bit of heat rising to my cheeks. "Thanks." I held out my hand and helped her to her feet. "His name is Adam. He's the Inquisitor Prime, which in simple terms means he runs Heavenly Special Ops. We were allies against the Beast."

"He's pretty handsome."

"Yeah, he is."

"So are you, in your own way."

More heat. "What's that supposed to mean?"

She laughed. The adrenaline had left her a little giddy. "I don't know… he's a male Thor kind of handsome. You're more like a

James Bond, or Captain America."

I shook my head. "You didn't just call me Captain America."

"Or James Bond. Somewhere in there. It works for you."

"Thanks, I guess. Have you seen Gervais?"

"Not since the were took him away. Do you think he's in trouble?"

We started for the stairs. "I know he's in trouble. I'm going to wring his damn neck."

Neither of us knew the layout of the place, so it took us some time to wander through all the hallways and check each room for the demon. It wasn't enough to just peek inside, we had to look in the closets, under the beds; anywhere he might have decided to hide after I crushed the Fist. I could picture him watching the confrontation with Adam from one of the windows, the quiet of the room interrupted from time to time by his annoying french giggle. He'd played me for a fool.

The last door we hit wasn't a single room. It was Valerix's suite. It fed into a massive bedroom with a four-posted double-king bed as its centerpiece, draped in red velvet and silk with various different leather straps and chains positioned along the sides of the posts. Thick fur rugs lined the floor around it, and four candled chandeliers hung above. To the left of it was an open bathroom, decorated in black marble and leather. To the right, an office.

Gervais was sitting behind the desk, his feet up on the mahogany, a big smile on his face.

"Ah, there you are, Landon."

Just the sight of him made my temper flare. I threw out the energy, slamming it into him and launching him backwards. He lost his balance on the chair, and wound up laying on the floor.

I rushed into the room, vaulting the desk and landing on top of him, my hands around his throat.

"Ouch," he said, looking up at me. He didn't seem very concerned about his predicament. "You're angry with me for not helping you against the machine?"

"You sold me out to the angels, you son of a bitch."

He started laughing.

"What the hell is so funny?"

He laughed harder.

I squeezed harder.

He tapped on my forearms, and pointed to the desk. There was a laptop there. The screen was on.

I let go of him.

He coughed twice and got up, rubbing at his neck. "For one, you should know me better than to think I would ever join forces with those buffoons. For another, you're welcome."

A photo of Matthias Zheng was on the screen, along with the beginnings of a full profile. "You didn't let them in?"

"Of course not. I feigned my drunkenness so I could get into Valerix's office. It was her were that ratted you out. The idiot came up here after he opened the door. He wanted the very thing that you're looking at right now."

"Why?"

"I imagine to keep anyone else from seeing it. It seems that our minx did quite a bit of digging and spying on Mr. Zheng. She was trying to both figure out the reason for his Divine immunity, and determine where the angels had taken him."

"And?"

"And the information is incomplete. She never did learn the secret to his immunity, and she lost his trail a week ago."

I skimmed through the data on the screen. Matthias Zheng, born Xin Zheng. The only son of Bo and Celia Zheng, an accountant and a housewife from San Diego. Finished high school at age twelve, graduated with a doctorate in engineering and robotics at sixteen. Not married, no kids, apparently no friends either.

A real nerd.

According to the file, Valerix had tracked him to a safe house in

San Francisco. Then the fiend that was following him disappeared.

I turned my attention from the computer to Gervais, who had climbed back into the chair. It was possible that he was still playing me. That he had opened the door in the form of the were, and then come back up here to play innocent. It was also possible that he was telling the truth. The data on the screen couldn't have been manufactured in the last ten minutes.

"You left me out there to fight that thing on my own."

"You had Rose to help you."

"No offense to her, but she's not exactly ready to take on a Fist of God. You, on the other hand-"

"I would have been splattered against the dirt. I caught the... Fist, is it?... in the alley off-guard. I disposed of the were for you, and I got into Valerix's computer to get this information. It isn't as though I've just been sitting here twiddling my thumbs."

"I could have been killed, and we could have just asked her for this stuff. You should have been downstairs with us."

"Don't be stupid. She may have been afraid, but she was still a demon. There would have been some kind of bargain involved. This way was more efficient, and it all worked out for the best. Maybe when we're done, I'll come back and claim this territory."

"You don't have the strength to claim the west coast. And if you try, I'll kill you myself."

Gervais grinned. "I will keep that under consideration."

"What's our next move?" Rose asked, interrupting us.

I turned the screen so she could see it. "You know how technology is. You start with a prototype, a proof of concept. Then you iterate. You make improvements, you fix weaknesses. He's the one supplying the technology. We need to find him before he has a chance to make these Fists any stronger than they already are." I picked up the laptop and handed it to her. "Your other job is to see what else you can learn from the data Valerix collected, if you don't mind."

"Not at all."

"If you don't mind," Gervais parroted behind me, raising his voice in pitch. "Not at all." He got up off the chair and walked out ahead of us. "We have what we need. Can we go?"

I glared at Gervais' back as he left the room. I needed to keep a closer eye on the demon.

"Let's get out of here before Adam decides he wants a rematch," Rose said.

I couldn't have agreed more.

CHAPTER TWENTY-THREE

We needed to get from L.A. to San Francisco. A plane would have been an obvious choice, but a plane meant going airborne, and airborne meant angels. While we weren't giving off any kind of Divine aura, and Adam would have forgotten about our confrontation by now, I was still feeling skittish about the risk. I could survive a fall, even from thirty-thousand feet. Gervais probably could, too. Not that I cared. Rose on the other hand…

So we drove. We were fortunate that Valerix had a nice collection in a large garage in the back of the property, a cavernous expanse of black Escalades and Camaros for her small Turned army and her vampire and were henchmen, most of whom had fled the scene at the sight of the Fist. We found one of them hiding behind the door of the locked room where they kept the keys. She tried to knife me on my way in, and was rewarded with a blow to the head that would leave her at rest for a few more hours.

Growing up in the city, I'd never cared much for driving. Rose's eyes lit up when I offered her the keys, and she hopped in on the driver's side without hesitation, quickly adjusting the mirrors and seat.

"I've always wanted to drive one of these things," she said.

She pulled us out of the garage and onto a narrow road that led around to the front of the mansion to the main driveway. When we reached it, I noticed that the broken bit of the fountain was still laying on the grass. The Fist was gone from beneath it.

"How do you think they managed that?" Gervais asked.

I didn't know he had actually seen any of the fight.

"Some kind of self-destruct?" Rose said.

I reached out with my power, pushing hard and shoving the marble away. The ground beneath it was black, as though the Fist had burned up. There was no sign of any dust to mark its disintegration.

"Probably. I can imagine they don't want anyone getting their hands on it."

"We have the head," Gervais said. "And they carried the rest of it away."

"That one wasn't too badly damaged. Maybe they thought they could fix it up. If the destruction mechanism is in the body, severing the head would keep it intact."

Gervais kept his eyes on the spot, examining it. "Burned to nothing? No ash? No dust?"

"What are you suggesting?"

"I don't know. A thought, only."

"Care to share?"

He looked at me and smiled. "No."

"Maybe I should rephrase that. Tell me."

"You can't Command me, diuscrucis."

"No, but I can kill you."

He leaned back on the plush leather seat. "Stop the car."

Rose hit the brakes. Gervais jumped out and walked over to the dark circle in the ground. He knelt down and wiped his finger along it, and then lifted it up for me to examine.

"Sulfer?"

"Someone took it."

"Who?"

"What do I look like? A demon powerful enough to sneak in

here and send it through a Hell rift in the thirty minutes we were in the house."

"Don't you need runes for a Hell rift?"

He nodded and walked around the scorch marks. He stopped on the other side and pawed at the dirt. "Here. They scratched it out when it was done."

"What's a Hell rift?" Rose asked.

"A portal," Gervais replied. "A transport mechanism. You can guess where it goes."

Her face paled.

"How do you think we get here?" he said.

"If the rift is here, why didn't the statue go through?" Rose said.

"It isn't Divine. It would need to have been held or touched by a demon to make the trip," I said. I turned to Gervais. "So, they brought the body back to Hell. They're going to try to reverse engineer it. They're going to try to make their own."

"They won't be able to fully reproduce it. You crushed most of it," Gervais said.

"Future plots aside, it means someone was either following us, or following Adam." I eyed the demon again. "It seems there have been a lot of strange coincidences since I picked you up."

"It is what it is. That isn't my fault, though I can't deny the circumstantial evidence. Leave me here, if you want. Kill me. I still have information. Information you won't get."

I walked across the center of the abandoned rift. "Which could be just another misdirection so that I'll bring you along. I figured you had some value, and it was better to keep an eye on you. Now... I'm not so sure."

I summoned the spatha, the black blade appearing only inches from Gervais' neck.

"Wait," he said. He put his hand on the side of the sword and pushed the tip off his throat. "I'll give you a name. A token of faith."

"No. You could give me any name. You know we don't have time to go chasing some random fiend right now."

"What do you want from me, diuscrucis? I'm trying to help you in this."

"You don't help anyone without getting something in return. Is that it?" I pointed back at the rift. "Or maybe you just wanted to get Valerix out of the way? What's your game, Gervais?"

"Just kill him and be done with it," Rose said. "Whatever small way he can help can't compare to having to put up with his smell."

"Thank you," Gervais said, glaring at her. "Of course there's a game. You know as well as anyone that there always is. It took some time for the dust to settle once you defeated the Beast, and now the pieces are all starting to shift and move again. Heaven has made the first maneuver. Should it surprise you that Hell has an interest, the same way that I have an interest? They can't count on you coming out on top. I, on the other hand, have cast my lot with you. I didn't call Adam here. I have nothing to do with whoever took what was left of the Fist."

He was a consummate liar. A perfect manipulator.

"Your words don't mean anything."

"I have one that will."

"Do you?"

"Abaddon."

I felt my body turn cold. "What about him?"

"The summoning is to bring Abaddon back from Hell. Lucifer won't let him out, and the rifts aren't strong enough to carry him."

"Who's Abaddon?" Rose asked.

"Why the hell would you summon Abaddon?" I said, ignoring her.

"The summoner has control over him, the most powerful demon ever made. I'm weak in this form, relegated to parlor tricks." He changed his form twice for effect. "With Abaddon, I could regain my former glory, and more."

I stood and stared at him, feeling my heart thumping against my chest. I had made a promise to Abaddon.

A promise to destroy him.

The binding of the deal had been lost in my transformation. It didn't mean I had forgotten. I'm sure the demon hadn't either.

"Who is Abaddon?" Rose asked again.

"A demon. *The* demon. Lucifer modeled him after the Beast. We've crossed paths a couple of times. If anyone brought Abaddon back to this world, they would instantly become the greatest threat to everything here, Divine or not." I shifted my eyes back to Gervais. "Why would you give that up so easily?"

"You think it was an easy choice to make? I can't rise to glory if I'm dead, if we're all dead. I told you, I'll find another way. As long as you can keep the others from completing the summoning."

"You need to tell me who they are."

He smiled. "I know."

Right. He would tell me when we defeated the Fists. If we defeated the Fists. The situation had circled back around. At least now I knew what he was after. At least now I knew how important the names he was withholding might actually be.

Assuming he wasn't full of shit.

CHAPTER TWENTY-FOUR

WE DROVE UP THE COAST. It was four hundred miles from Los Angeles to San Francisco, and we made good time. Rose had a heavy foot and an aggressive style, honking, cursing, and flashing her lights at anyone who dared cross her path in the wrong way.

Her road rage kept the ride from being too quiet or tense.

I spent the journey halfway inside my head, trying to work through the overload of information I'd been given in the last twenty-four hours. Abaddon worried me, but it was a problem I could deal with later. Gervais was two years into the summoning and hadn't been too close, so I had to believe I would get at least a couple of weeks to finish working through this mess before I had to start cleaning up the next one.

That left me with Matthias Zheng.

I didn't know what to make of him. Smart, yes. A good guy? He must have believed it, to be helping the angels. Was he the kind of guy you could talk to? To persuade? I hoped so.

The only other option was to kill him.

I wondered if that was even a good idea. The now destroyed Canaan Blades had been forged in Heaven. What was to say Matthias' soul wouldn't just rise up, or that he wouldn't decide to join the seraphim as their new high-tech armorer? He could keep making the Fists, could keep improving the tech. Right now, I could fight them - well, one at a time, anyway. What if he had an eternity to perfect the work?

I was still stuck on that line of thought as we drove past the airport and made our way into the city of San Francisco itself. It was funny, because for all the Divine power I had witnessed, for the little bit of energy I had saved for myself - we still needed to rely on GPS to get us close to the safe house address.

We stopped the car almost a mile away. According to the nav, the safe house was near Islais Creek, and the satellite view we pulled up showed it to be a pretty ragged industrial area. Lots of concrete and big, square buildings. Lots of pickups and older model cars. Even here, the homes and apartments were proving their proximity, most of them small and suggesting lower income inhabitants. If the SUV had been mine, I might have even worried about it.

I was tempted to ask Rose and Gervais to stay behind, and not for any other reason than because I didn't trust the demon, and thought it would be safer for Rose. I wanted to protect her, when I knew that I couldn't. If mankind was going to learn to fend for itself, it started with her.

So we left the Escalade parked in front of a small green house with a busted fence, and walked down cracked sidewalks towards the creek. I kind of wished we had a pickup to ride in on, because walking was almost as conspicuous as the SUV. At least losing the roof had made it easier to watch the skies.

We walked in silence, with Rose at my side and Gervais trailing behind, his eyes sweeping back and forth, scanning rooftops, the sky, and our backs as we moved. If we were fortunate, the angels didn't know that we knew where they had stashed Matthias. The wrinkle was that Valerix had lost her informant over a week ago. Was the engineer still holed up inside? There was only going to be one way to find out.

The address turned out to be a large, aluminum sided building in the middle of the industrial area. It was nothing special compared to its surrounds, ringed by a chain link fence with a semi trailer resting on the west side. The place had no windows, and the only other visible doors were two roll-ups near the trailer. I expected maybe there would be some security cameras mounted to the exterior, or near the corners of the fencing. There was none of that either.

The entire place was deserted. The businesses around the building were closed - it looked like for good. We hadn't Seen any Divine on our way in, and there was nothing about any of it that suggested anyone was home.

Which made it the perfect place to hide.

The lack of people was the biggest clue. The Divine had a special power over the mortal, their very presence causing a subliminal, subconscious response that tended to cause humans to shy away from areas where they gathered, especially in areas of recent or upcoming conflict. It was almost like an unknown, unrecognizable sixth sense.

Was that why the surrounding businesses were shuttered? Or was there a simpler explanation? Heaven and Hell both had their share of supporters with deep pockets. Buying out the area around the building wouldn't have been out of the question.

"I have a bad feeling about this," Rose said.

We were up the street from the building, crouched at the corner of one of the other buildings, staying in the shadows.

"A specific feeling, or just general unease?" I asked. The Awake could See the Divine. They also had a better handle on that innate sixth sense. What she was feeling might have been caused by a buildup of Divine power.

"I don't know. A little bit of both."

Gervais sighed from behind her. "Can you be a little more specific?"

"I'm nervous. I also feel like something is… I don't know… off."

"He's probably still inside," I said.

Gervais nodded. "I agree. Or seraphim at the least. I didn't sense any demons while we were coming in, but that doesn't mean they aren't out here, watching from a distance." He pointed back the way we'd come. "High powered binoculars or a scope could keep an eye on this place from further back."

"What should we do?" Rose asked.

"We need to go for it," I said. "If there are demons out here they aren't working for Valerix, or they would have been reporting in. We need to get in and grab Matthias before they can stop us or take him themselves."

"They might not even know what they're watching," Gervais said. "If they came upon Valerix's minions and decided there could be something valuable inside, they may have killed them to claim the prize. Of course they'll scout it first, if they know the seraphim are involved."

"Seriously?" Rose said. "How do you demons ever threaten the balance when you can't even cooperate among yourselves?"

Gervais smiled at her, a condescending smile. "Landon can tell you how close I came."

"The squabbling is the only reason the angels are able to keep the balance, considering they are far fewer in number," I said, not giving the archfiend credit for anything.

Gervais spat on the ground. "Pah. The other archfiends are pathetic and small-minded. That is why they don't succeed."

I returned my attention to the building. We needed to be fast, to break our way in before who or whatever was inside had a chance to react. If there were demons watching the building, forcing them to enter would give us a better chance to pick them off before they could amass.

The question was: how were we going to get there fast enough? Gervais had been plenty quick back at the Underground, and I could force more power into my muscles to speed myself up. What

about Rose? It wasn't enough for me to handle everything.
I turned back towards her to discuss it.
She was gone.

CHAPTER TWENTY-FIVE

"Where did she go?" I asked.

Gervais shrugged. "Who?"

He just *had* to be an asshole. "You know who."

"Your bitch went that way," he said, pointing across the street. I saw her vanish behind a tall, square cement building.

I wondered what she was doing. A few seconds later, I heard a rumble, the release of heavy brakes, and the roar of an engine.

"Not exactly subtle," Gervais said.

Not exactly. A cement truck appeared from behind the building, making a tight right turn in front of us and chugging down the street. It bounced and rolled as Rose changed gears, pegging the accelerator and getting it moving as fast as it could.

"Not the worst idea either." It was brute force instead of stealth. Maybe it would attract the occupant's attention. Maybe they would see her coming. They wouldn't be able to stop a cement truck.

I pushed the power into my limbs and started running, getting up to the back of the truck and hopping on. Gervais did the same, moving with a speed and agility that no mortal could match. I didn't feel anything when the machine slammed into the fence, ripping it down without slowing. I leaned out from the edge, watching the building approach at breakneck speed. I ducked back behind it as it slammed into the wall, and kept going.

There was a clatter and ringing as the truck pierced the building, passing through anything that was in its way. Aluminum siding fell around me, and fibers coated me in a layer of dust. Then there was a jolt, a whine and crushing of metal, and we came to an abrupt halt that sent waves of pain up my neck. I pushed myself to heal and jumped off the back, rushing to the driver's side.

"Rose?"

The door flew open and she hopped out, her knife in hand. "He's here. Come on." She ran ahead of me, vaulting the mangled mess of steel she had crashed the truck into. I turned and leaped, following her over it.

Whatever the building had once been, it had been gutted and converted to something somewhere between a lab and a penthouse. The space was huge and open, a long corridor lit by sharp LEDs that hung from plain wires looped around the ceiling cross-beams. At the near end was the lab, a workstation with massive monitors hanging in front of it, a large, flat table with scrolls laid out and weighted so they wouldn't roll up again, and a bunch of equipment and machinery that I didn't recognize, and would have no idea what to do with.

The far end was a living space. A bed, a couch, a large-screen television. A kitchen, and an enclosed area that must have been the bathroom. There was a man there, standing in front of the couch looking at us, the video game controller still in his hands. I could hear the music of whatever he was playing blasting through the speakers.

There were no angels here. There was no one here, except for him. Matthias Zheng. I recognized him from the profile.

Was it really going to be this easy?

The controller fell from his hand. He watched us coming, showing no signs of distress or panic, no indication that he was worried about us at all. He reached down onto the couch, removing an object that looked like a baseball.

We were still twenty feet away. I had sprinted ahead of Rose, and was closing on him in a hurry. I could see Gervais gaining out of the corner of my eye. He had his own weapon in hand, ready to use it on the man. I really wanted to reach Matthias first, to make sure we captured him, and got to talk to him.

I gathered the energy and pushed, using it to propel me off the ground towards him in a dive that probably made it look like I was flying. The baseball fell from his hand and rolled onto the floor.

I reached out, lunging with my arms, my hands grabbing his shoulders, my momentum pulling us both to the ground. We rolled a couple of times and he fell away from me, coming to a stop on the carpet a few feet away. I ignored the pain and shoved myself to my feet, scrambling to reach him before Gervais could, watching helplessly as the demon leaped onto him, knife raised.

"Gervais, no," I shouted. I gathered the energy and threw it at him, knocking him away.

Too late.

The knife rested in the engineer's chest.

Only he didn't scream.

He didn't make any sound at all.

He hadn't made a sound when I tackled him either.

The three of us converged on him almost at the same time. There was no blood pooling up from the entry point. Instead, there was a clear, slick fluid.

"Synthetic oil," Rose said. "He's a fake."

A fake? They had known we were coming long enough to arrange the doppelgänger. No. How could they? We had only known we were coming five hours ago.

"Landon," Gervais said softly. "We have company."

I turned and watched as the demons streamed in around the truck. Mostly vampires and weres, along with a contingent of armed devils, summoned from Hell by the fallen angel at their head. There had to be fifty or more. Too many to fight.

"Don't move," the fallen angel said. He was easy to identify by the demonic runes painted across the part of his arms that were visible, and the dark wings that folded out behind him. He wanted us to see them, and to know what he was.

"Who are you?" Gervais asked.

The runes on the angel's arms glowed, and Gervais fell to his knees, clutching at his throat. The other demons continued moving, filling in around us, blocking us in.

"You don't question me." His voice was calm, confident. His eyes scanned us. "What are the Nicht Creidem doing here, I wonder? What prize have my brothers been stashing, that have attracted such acute interest?"

He thought because we had no Divine aura that we were Nicht Creidem - a cabal of mortals who had been bred and inbred to a partial immunity to Divine power, who trained from birth to fight the Divine, and who spent their resources hunting down the Divine artifacts that existed in the world, hoping they would give them an edge in seeing their ultimate goal achieved.

Destruction of all the Divine, regardless of consequence, regardless of whether or not it meant the end of man as well. They were another player, and while we had similar goals, I understood that the Divine were a necessary evil, that they were an equal part of the balance, and that without them, without that balance, mankind would simply destroy itself instead.

Not that we didn't seem to be on the brink sometimes, anyway.

"This," I said, kicking the fake Matthias Zheng. "There were other demons who were watching this place. Did you kill them?"

"I said, you don't question me." The angel's eyes burned, and he moved his hand. I heard Gervais take a heaving breath, and stared back at the fallen while he tried to choke me. I pushed my power against his, keeping my own airway clear.

I was about to take a step towards him, to challenge him, when Rose nudged me with her elbow.

"Landon, look," she said, motioning past the angel.

The object that fake Matthias had dropped was still resting on the floor. There was seraphim scripture carved into it, and it was glowing.

I was wrong. It wasn't a baseball.

"Praise be to God in the Highest," the doppelgänger said in a synthesized voice.

I clenched my stomach, taking my power and wrenching it in. The not-baseball vanished in a burst of white light, followed by the red and blue of intense heat.

I pushed the power out, a hemisphere of energy that expanded enough to cover Rose and Gervais, that caught the fallen angel in its protection as well. The blast tore through the assembled demon army, the heat destroying those that were susceptible to it, the cold blue of the Heavenly flame killing the rest.

It continued outward while I crouched and gritted my teeth, pushing my own power back against it, keeping the explosion from reaching us. I could feel the sweat on my forehead, the strain in my muscles. Everything vanished, leaving us submerged in a sea of red and blue flame.

It was replaced a few seconds later by the force of the building collapsing around us. I closed my eyes, concentrating on keeping us safe, using every bit of my strength to do it. Metal beams and aluminum siding came to a rest against my invisible shield, covering us and leaving us in darkness. I felt Rose take my hand in hers. I heard the slap of flesh against flesh, and the fallen angel grunted.

Ten more seconds, and it was done. I made one last push, throwing the debris away and freeing us from the burial. I opened my eyes. We were under open skies, the building around us reduced to ash and twisted metal, the roof gone, the entire west side, gone.

A bomb designed to kill demons. They had known they were

being watched.
　　They had been prepared.

CHAPTER TWENTY-SIX

Rose put her hand under my shoulder and helped me to my feet. I stumbled a little bit, disoriented by the massive use of the power. I could feel it churning in my soul. It couldn't be diminished, only disturbed, and the disturbance left me weak.

"Are you okay?" she asked.

"I will be. I need food, rest."

Gervais was standing over the fallen angel, having knocked him to the ground during the explosion.

The dark seraph looked up at us, his nose bloodied. "What was that?"

"You don't ask questions," Gervais said. "You're outnumbered now." He kicked him in the gut again for good measure.

"Let him up," I said. The demon looked at me and backed off.

The fallen angel got to his feet. "What kind of artifact holds such power, to protect us from this?" He motioned at the destruction around us.

"None of your business," I said. It didn't matter who he thought we were. Not now. "Do you know why we're here?"

"Why do the Nicht Creidem turn up anywhere? To capture something of power, I'm sure." He looked around again. "I don't think you're going to find it here."

"Is that why you were here? Is that why you were watching?"

"Something valuable, yes. Valerix's spies took a strong interest in this building. We saw the angels come and go from here. We knew they had something she wanted."

"You don't know what?"

"What does it matter? We were preparing to take it. Then you showed up and we were forced to act. Lucky for me that I had already created the rift to carry in the soldiers." He shook his head, looking over at the mess again. "I wasn't prepared for this."

"It was a bomb," I said. "A bomb made to kill demons." Maybe the Nicht Creidem, too. Why else have a physical explosion to go with the holy flame? "They were waiting for you. They knew you were watching."

"No. They couldn't have. We never came close. I dispatched Valerix's spy myself. No one saw."

Someone saw. Unless this whole place had been a honeypot from the beginning. Angels had their own way of being sneaky.

"Who are you working for, if not the archfiend?" Gervais asked.

"I'm not some sniveling vampire. I don't work for anyone. Coming across that horny bitch's lackey, that was pure luck."

"Bad luck," Rose said.

The fallen angel glared at her. "You saved my life. What do you plan to do with me?"

"I didn't save your life on purpose. That part was good luck for you. I don't really care what you do. The treasure you wanted, the treasure we came for, isn't here." He didn't need to know we were looking for a person, something I doubted he would find any value in at all.

"You're letting him go?" Gervais asked.

"Why not?" I snapped. I was already pissed enough at him for stabbing Matthias before we knew he wasn't the real deal, and his questioning wasn't helping.

"Information. He'll find someone to sell this story to. Someone who will bring it back somewhere that it may get intercepted, or traded on to the seraphim."

"So what? This was a trick and a trap rolled into one. What does it matter if Adam finds out we were here?" The angel wouldn't even remember what I looked like, though I was sure he would derive the truth from whatever tale reached him.

"Fool. It isn't just Adam you need to worry about. If word starts to spread that the Nicht Creidem are searching for an artifact powerful enough to go headlong into an angel safe house for, you can be sure it will make things much more complicated."

"If you let me go, I won't say a word about this," the angel said.

Gervais stepped in and grabbed him by the throat. "You lie."

"No. Look at me. I've lost my army. I'm starting over."

"All the more reason for you to sell whatever you can." Gervais turned to me. "You know I can be useful, diuscrucis. As you said yourself, I know demons better than anyone."

"Diuscrucis? What?" The fallen angel took a step back and fell to his knees. "I can help you."

"You turned your back on your God, and you think you can be trusted?" Rose said. "I hate to say this, but I agree with Gervais."

I looked at her, surprised.

"It's not just about one demon," she said, using my own words against me.

Of course, she was right.

"Do what you need to do," I said to Gervais. "I'm going back to the car. I need to sit for a while."

I turned my back on the two demons and started walking away. I was weak and tired, and my stomach was making itself known. Rose kept her arm around me, lending me a little bit of support as I moved.

The fallen angel didn't scream or beg or cry out. I heard the soft sound of Gervais' knife sinking into his flesh and got a whiff of the frankincense that followed.

I didn't look back.

CHAPTER TWENTY-SEVEN

THE FIRE TRUCKS SCREAMED PAST even as we piled back into the Escalade, with Rose behind the wheel and Gervais in the back. I didn't say anything to the demon, not yet. I didn't say anything to Rose either. I wanted something to eat. I wanted to close my eyes. I was lightheaded, unbalanced, the power feeling like a stormy ocean in my soul.

"Rose, can you find us a hotel or a motel or something? Deflecting explosions isn't good for my health. I'll need a few hours to recharge."

She leaned over and tapped some buttons on the navigation system. "Looks like the Happy Bay Inn is the closest."

"I'm not picky."

She put the truck in gear. Five minutes later I was alone in the car with Gervais, while Rose went inside to get us a room. The place wasn't much to look at, and was probably lacking in any kind of comfort beyond four walls, a ceiling, and a bed. It was more than good enough for me.

I had one more thing to do before I could rest. It was the reason I'd asked Rose to do the check-in.

"What the hell were you thinking?" I said, shifting in my seat so I could see Gervais. The demon was laying across the rear bench, picking his nose.

He flicked his prize away. "What do you mean?"

"With Zheng."

He shrugged. "He's dangerous. I was thinking I would end the danger."

"I wanted to talk to him."

"What for?"

"What for? For one, I'd love to see if he knows why he's immune to Divine power. For another, I'd like to try to talk him down from helping Heaven."

The demon sat up, putting his face too close to mine. He smiled. "Convince him to help you instead? All the more reason to kill him."

"I don't want to convince him to help anyone. I just want him to stop. What if he dies and continues his work? He'll be upstairs. He'll have access to anything he needs."

"He's mortal. That will happen sooner or later, regardless of your best intentions."

"If we can talk to him now, he might refuse to help out once he passes."

He laughed in my face. Right in my face. "Are you serious? He made a bomb that kills demons. No, not just demons. It obliterated that entire warehouse. It was meant to kill whoever or whatever came after him. A man like that is not one to abandon his ideals because some wanna-be godling has a chat with him." He sat back. "Better to kill him first, and then deal with the consequences."

"No. Maybe I wouldn't be able to convince him not to help the angels. We would have at least gotten him to talk. To tell us about the Fists. There's no saying Alichino is going to find anything helpful in that head."

"Are you suggesting torture? Hmm... you do still surprise me sometimes."

I took a deep breath. "If it came down to it, yeah, I guess I am suggesting torture. This has already gone beyond just the Fists.

I've never seen anything like that bomb before. Heavenly flame? That's a new one to me. Give Zheng another month, and he'll have the Divine nuke that the Nicht Creidem have always wanted."

"Except it will only vaporize demons," Gervais said. "Heavenly flame... I've heard of the seraphim's cold fire, though I believed only the archangels could wield it." He rubbed his chin with his hand, silent for a moment. "It is troubling."

"Yeah. Anyway, the angels have to be building these things somewhere, right? Somewhere here, in this realm. Zheng can tell us where. If we can shut it down then it doesn't matter if he tells them how to make things, because they'll still never get made."

"An interesting theory. I can admit that I may have been a bit premature in my decision to end his life. I suppose it's fortunate for both of us that we attacked a replica."

"We got lucky in that, at least. Let's get one thing clear here, Gervais. This is my work, my team, my rules. I lead, you follow. It isn't a democracy."

"Are you certain? I seem to recall you being outvoted on the matter of the fallen angel not ten minutes ago."

"No. You made a suggestion, and I saw the value in your logic." I was trying not to let him get under my skin. I was failing.

"Whatever you want to call it to feel like you're in control. I don't see you having a tantrum at your little plaything for her cowgirl antics."

"How I handle Rose isn't your concern."

"Of course." He leaned over and pushed open his door. "I'm going to go for a walk. Don't worry, I'll stay disguised." He morphed into Anita, just to piss me off even more. "I can imagine how you'd like to handle Rose." He fondled his breasts suggestively, blew me a kiss, and then hopped out and started walking away, morphing into Peter as he did.

I watched him go for a couple of seconds, and then turned my attention back to the hotel. Rose pushed her way out of the lobby and came over to the car, holding a set of keys in her hand.

"Where's Gervais?" she asked, sliding into the driver's seat.

"He went for a walk."

"To walk, or to eat?"

"I don't know. I don't want to know."

She started the truck and drove us to a spot a little further down. "That's our room there," she said, pointing to the door in front of us. "Are you okay?"

"I will be. I don't usually get like this unless I time walk. That bomb packed a punch."

"Time walk? Is that what it sounds like?"

"Maybe. It's like teleportation."

"Another cool trick. I might be willing to die for that one."

I smiled at the joke, opened the door and slid out of the Escalade. "Can you grab Valerix's laptop?"

"Okay. Thanks for saving my life, by the way."

"You're welcome."

She got the computer, and we went into the hotel room. It was predictably shabby, with dirty walls, a rust colored carpet, and a thin, queen-sized mattress on a squeaky frame. The bathroom was done up in polka-dot wallpaper and matching shower curtain, a pattern that made my head hurt even more.

I sat down on the edge of the bed. "Rose, can we talk for a minute?"

She put the computer down on the dresser, next to the old tube television. "This is about the dump truck, isn't it?"

"Yes and no. It's more about the fact that you didn't wait for us to make a plan, or even give me a warning."

She took a deep breath, walking over and dropping down onto the bed next to me, putting her face close to mine. It was much more enjoyable than having Gervais six inches away.

"I understand if you're upset. The thing is - I want to help you. I really, really do. It's just... I don't know if you've been paying attention the last twenty four hours, but I'm outmatched. Seriously outmatched. Your power is amazing, and even Gervais is stronger and faster than I can ever be. That fallen angel? The Fists? Hell, even the bomb. Without you, I would be dead three or four times over. In less than twenty four hours."

I was surprised, because she hadn't seemed like the type to have doubts. "You handled yourself with Valerix's were."

"I did. That was *one* were. How often am I going to get odds like that? Don't get me wrong, I'm not trying to complain, and I don't regret meeting you." She paused, taking my hand in hers. "I can't rely on being stronger, or faster, or tougher than what I'm fighting. The vast majority of the time, I doubt I will be. That means I need to rely on my human strengths, on being emotional and unpredictable."

I was the one who had said it. At least she was listening. "There's nothing wrong with that."

"I want to believe that. If it hadn't been for the bomb, we would still be in a world of trouble. I gave the demons an easy way in."

I couldn't argue the truth of it. "You've been doing this for one day. You'll learn. I wanted to talk to you about it, because I want to help reign in some of your impulsiveness before you get yourself killed."

She smiled. "I feel like I could get killed just sitting next to you."

"I can't make any guarantees."

"I know. Isn't that the point? I'm part of this now. It's scary as hell, and also one of the most exciting, liberating things I've ever done. I'm human. I know I'm going to make mistakes. I know I can't hang with you demi-gods, but I'm trying to prove that I'm worth having around."

"You don't have to do anything to prove you-"

She kissed me.

She didn't just kiss me. She put her arm across my chest, pushed me back down on the bed, leaned over me, and pressed her lips to mine. It was aggressive and impulsive, emotional and unpredictable.

I didn't kiss her back. It wasn't that I didn't think she was attractive, or that there wasn't a part of me that was tempted. I was still a virgin. I was sure Rose wasn't. Maybe it was old-fashioned. Maybe it was stupid. I didn't want my first time to go down like this, and I didn't want to complicate our relationship before we even had a chance to be friends. Right now, I needed an ally a lot more than I needed sex.

She pulled away.

"That's a new one," she said, looking down at me in disbelief. I could imagine she wasn't accustomed to rejection.

"Rose…" I took a deep breath and huffed it out. I could feel my heart pounding, my body reacting even if my mind was unwilling. "You don't have to try so hard. You don't have to prove anything to me, or do… this, for me to feel like you're worth having around."

Her eyes narrowed and rolled, and she pushed herself away from me, pissed. "Is that what you think this is? I don't know what kind of girls you've had around before, but I have a little more self-worth then to just throw myself at you because I feel like it's the only thing I can help you with. Maybe I just thought, you know, you're here, I'm here, maybe it would help us both unwind a little bit, have a little fun and forget about this Divine stuff for a while. It's fine if you don't want to. It's fine for you to say no thanks. You don't have to be an asshole about it."

She hopped off the bed, leaving me laying there and feeling like an idiot. All the power in the universe hadn't made me any better at this sort of thing.

"Rose, I'm sorry. I didn't mean to insult you."

She smiled, the anger fading from her face. "Just forget it. You needed rest and food, right? I'll go and get you some ice cream. Do you have a preference?"

"Cookie dough," I said, returning her smile.

"Good choice." She walked over to the door. "I'll try to be a little less impulsive. I'm not making any promises."

She slipped away, leaving me tongue tied and tired.

CHAPTER TWENTY-EIGHT

I SLEPT FOR THREE HOURS, feeling a lot better when I woke up. Gervais was still out, but Rose was there, sitting on the bed next to me, Valerix's laptop open.

"Shit. The ice cream," I said, sitting up.

Rose turned her head and laughed. "Don't worry about it. There's a freezer behind that door." She pointed at the dresser.

"Thanks for picking it up," I said, sliding off the bed and going over to get it.

"How come you don't just use your special sauce to grab it?" she asked.

"I wouldn't feel very human if I used the power to let myself be lazy."

"Are you sure you wouldn't feel more human?"

I opened the freezer and grabbed the ice cream. There were two spoons laying on top of the lid.

"I got some teriyaki before, but I left room for dessert."

I brought it back over to the bed and plopped down next to her. "About before-" I started to say.

"Forget it, Landon. No harm done on my end. I shouldn't have been so horny. The adrenaline, you saving my life. It hit me right here." She smiled at me, motioning between her legs. "It was my fault for pushing you, especially when I knew you were tired."

"I don't want things to get complex," I said.

"If that's what it is to you, I understand, and I respect that. To me, it's just good fun. No emotional attachment needed, and no expectations after."

I just wasn't built that way. I handed her a spoon and popped the lid. We both dug in.

"So, what have you found?" I asked, after savoring a nice chunk of dough.

She turned the screen so I could see it better. "The profile is incomplete. To be honest, it's pretty lousy. Yeah, they got the history from the time our guy was adopted, but I mean, they totally missed his special assignment to Los Alamos."

"The National Lab? I didn't know they did robotics?"

"They don't. Not publicly, anyway." She hit a few keys. "Your friend Obi helped me do some digging while you were sleeping."

"Obi?" I was confused. "You talked to him?"

"Oh yeah, I borrowed your phone." I noticed it on the bed between us. "Oblitrix, Obi... I made the connection. I didn't realize it was short for Obi-wan though."

"Okay. So what did you and Obi find?"

"Zheng was working for a startup in New Mexico, RoGen. It's a mashup of robotics and genetics. Basically, they were working on technology to make robots that had biological components. Self-healing skin, living muscle, that kind of thing. Like a modern day Frankenstein."

"Why would they do that?"

"Cost. Growing parts is a lot cheaper than importing rare earth minerals from China."

"Interesting."

"Yeah. Anyway, Matthias spent six months over at Los Alamos. We couldn't figure out what he was working on, but I bet its related to his work for RoGen."

"And the Fists of God?"

"Most likely."

"How do you know he was spending time there?"

"Obi was the one who figured that part out. He noticed that RoGen wasn't too far from the lab, so he decided to check their gate records. He matched up the plate on Zheng's car with daily entrance and exits, six days a week for six months."

Good old Obi. I owed him a quad latte with extra caramel the next time I saw him. "When did he start carousing with angels?"

"I don't know. What I do know is that he quit RoGen a week after he stopped checking in at Los Alamos."

I grabbed another spoonful of ice cream and shoved it into my mouth. Rose did the same, and we were silent while we ate.

"We need to find Matthias Zheng," I said. "The safe house was a trap, and we have no other leads. My gut says we should make the trip to New Mexico and try to find out what exactly he was working on. If it has anything at all to do with the Fists, we might be able to get some kind of information that can help us find him, and fight them."

She pursed her lips and nodded. "It sounds like a reasonable plan to me."

"You did great work. You and Obi, both. Human ingenuity."

She blushed. "It was more Obi than me. That guy is too smart for words. Hey, I wonder how Dante is doing with that head you gave him?"

I had almost forgotten. I picked up the phone from the bed and searched the contact list. Somehow, between the time Dante had visited and now, he had added Alichino's phone number. I put it on speaker and made the call.

"Yeah, what do you want?" The harlequin demon's voice was a thin rasp on the other end of the line. I could picture him in my mind, his spindly black and white body, his toothy snout, the lycra bicycle shorts he favored to keep himself modest.

"What's so funny?" Rose whispered.

"I'll tell you later. Alichino, it's me, Landon."

"Oh, it's you, Landon. Great. Just the guy I wanted to hear from. I bet you're calling about the head, right? Not to say 'hey', not to see how I'm doing. We haven't talked in two years, and now you only call because you need something."

"You've been in Purgatory. I can't reach you there."

"Yeah, like that's an excuse. Whatever, meat sack."

Rose started laughing.

"Who's that?" the demon asked. "She sounds sexy."

"My name is Rose. I'm helping Landon."

"You a succubus?"

"No."

"Are you sure?"

"Yes. I'm human."

"Humph. Well, nobody's perfect."

"Alichino, what can you tell me about the head?" I asked.

There were a few beats of silence. We heard clattering through the phone, like the demon had spilled a bucket of screws on the floor. It was followed by a loud bang.

"Sorry about that," he said. "I was looking for my webcam. You got a computer with a camera there?"

"Yes," Rose said.

"Good. My Skype name is Alliequin. A-L-L-I-E-Q-U-I-N. I'll be waiting."

He hung up.

"Who is he?" Rose asked while she hit the net and downloaded the software.

"A demon. He got kicked out of Hell for letting some guy named Bonturo trick him. He's been trying to get back in ever since. I promised to help him get there at one point, and since discovered that once Lucifer kicks you out, the only way to go back is with his permission. He's kind of pissed about it, which is why he's a little abrasive."

"I don't think he's abrasive. I think he's cute."

She finished installing Skype, and logged in with her 'DemonHuntress023' name. She added 'Alliequin' and made the connection. The demon's face popped up on the screen, just like I had imagined it.

"You are sexy," he said on seeing Rose. He glanced over at me. "Here, let me show you."

He shifted the camera so that it was pointing at a desk cluttered with wires and books, and a computer monitor sitting in the corner. The head sat in the center, with what looked like jumper cables running from the ends of a pair of exposed wires to somewhere off-camera.

"Okay, so this thing, it is absolutely swimming in scripture. I mean, it makes the Sistine Chapel look like it was painted by a two year old. And this is just the head. You get me?"

"I get you."

"Yeah, two things about that. One, there's no hand in the world that can make these kinds of marks at this size with any kind of consistency, except maybe the hand of God Himself, and I doubt he's finger painting on armor these days. Two, the scripture isn't just on the outside. It's on the inside, too. On the circuits."

"Did you say on the circuits?" Rose asked.

"Yeah. The lettering is almost microscopic. It's printed right onto the circuit. That means whatever is making it, it has to be industrial."

"So you think there's a machine that's pressing it?" I said.

"A few different kinds of machines. One for the circuits, one for the metal. I saved the best for last though. The wiring is made from living tissue."

It wasn't that surprising, considering what Rose had just told me. "We figured that part out already. Have you been able to work out the meaning of the scripture?"

"You see those books? I got some of it. This thing is protected against pretty much any kind of demonic attack you can imagine. Teeth, claws, blades, even hellfire. It's also reinforced against ballistics. Bullets, arrows, regular swords, and all that. That's the outer scripture. I'm still working on the inside. It's slow going, because I have to look at all of it under a microscope."

"You did a lot of work in only a little time," I said. "Any weaknesses?"

The demon snickered. "Other than cutting off the head? You could probably drop a rock on it or something to get it to stop moving."

"Already did that. Do you have any idea what's powering it?" Something that big and heavy had to have a pretty massive battery. It was likely in the torso, but maybe the wiring would give some indication.

"No clue. Like I said, the wires are all organic, so whatever it is, I think it's pretty unique."

"Okay. Last question. Does it have a brain?"

"If you consider a couple of memory chips to be like a brain, then sure."

"So, no. Rose, do you have any other questions?"

"Yes, I'll go out with you," Alichino said. His snout split in a sharp grin and his tongue flicked out between his teeth.

She shook her head. "No. You've been very helpful, Alichino. Maybe we can go out when this is over."

He nodded enthusiastically. "I hope you aren't lying to me, too."

His eyes shifted to me, pushing the guilt.

Then he disconnected.

"What do you think?" Rose asked.

"I think we need to stick to the plan. Head to New Mexico and see what we can find out. It's obvious they've built some kind of machinery to create the Fists. Maybe it's hiding in Los Alamos? I-"

My stomach clenched and released, and I lost my breath. I closed my eyes for a second and put my head in my hands.

"Landon, are you okay?"

I opened my eyes and straightened up. The sharp change in the balance had caught me by surprise.

"We need to pick up the pace. It's started."

CHAPTER TWENTY-NINE

We were on a plane to New Mexico a few hours later. Gervais had reappeared from his extended 'walk' not long after we disconnected from Alichino, and I filled him in on what we were planning to do without mentioning what the demon had told us. Discounting his usual insults and jibes, he was more than willing to follow my lead, and seemed almost relieved that I had some kind of plan.

It was mid-morning by the time we touched down, the flight going a little smoother than the first now that everyone had gotten to know each other a little better. That wasn't to say Rose was growing any warmer towards her sister's killer, but she was getting more accustomed to his presence, and had managed to fully accept him as a necessary evil.

I didn't get any more shocks in the interim, the balance staying steady beyond the initial hit. Whatever had happened, whoever the angels had sent the Fists after, the needle moved. Not near enough to be a problem. Just enough that I would notice.

Was Adam sending me a message?

Los Alamos was a stark departure from the crowds and hustle of New York. Sparse and spread out, with lots of low lying brush and brown grass, and surrounded by brown hills. It had it's own specific beauty to it. A beauty that I didn't think I was able to appreciate. After making the drive from the airport to the town outside of the National Laboratory, I missed the concrete and glass, the crowds and the congestion. At least it would be easy to spot Divine.

"It sure is beautiful out here," Rose said. We had rented a mid-sized Hyundai or something at the airport, and she was driving.

"It reminds me of Hell," Gervais said.

"I wouldn't be surprised," I replied.

"Oh, come on. This is peaceful. Elemental. Don't you ever get tired of the noise? The people?"

"If I did, I could think of a lot nicer places to escape than a desert," I said.

"You should visit France sometime, Rosie. Picnic along the Rhine, a nice bottle of merlot or maybe a sauvignon. Just you and your thoughts."

"The idea of you alone with your thoughts is terrifying," I said, looking back at the demon.

"That isn't the point I was trying to make. There is nothing beautiful about this barren landscape."

Rose turned the wheel, bringing us off 502 and into the heart of the so-called city.

"So, now what?" she asked. "We're here."

"Do we have an address for RoGen?" I said.

"It should be in an office building a mile or so down Central."

"Let's head over there first."

She kept us on the small avenue, driving us past a shopping center, some houses, a few apartment buildings, and some other office buildings. The whole thing seemed kind of random, like the developers here just put stuff wherever, no real zoning needed.

A few minutes later, we pulled into the small lot of a three story office building. It was newer construction, with reflective, tinted windows and white concrete. There were about a dozen cars parked outside, suggesting the building wasn't heavily occupied.

"Rose, would you mind waiting in the car?" I said once she pulled into a spot. "It's going to look strange for three of us to go up, and we need someone on the outside keeping lookout."

I was hoping she wouldn't think I was punishing her because of the incident in San Francisco. If she did, she didn't show it.

"No problem. What should I do if any Divine show up? How am I going to warn you?"

"Blast the horn. I'll hear it."

She nodded, reached down, and pulled the blessed and cursed knives from her calves, putting them on her lap. "Do you think this is a trap, too?"

"I can't rule it out. I would have preferred to go right to the Lab, but we need to come up with a way in first. I don't want a repeat of the CMO's office if we can help it."

"Are you coming?" Gervais asked. He was already out of the car, his form morphed into an older man in a business suit. A fresh kill?

I got out, adjusting my own clothing to match the demon's.

"So, what are we pretending to be?" he asked.

"Feds," I replied. "Working missing persons."

"Fun."

We made our way into the building. The lobby was clean and bright, filled with the scent of the fresh flowers that lined the reception desk. There was no indication that anyone ever worked behind it.

"Elevator's over there," I said. There was an office directory between the two sets of doors. It only had eight names on it. RoGen was listed by itself on the third floor.

We got in and rode up in silence.

The elevator stopped. The doors opened. I had no expectations.

I was still taken by surprise.

There was nothing. No desks, no cubes, and no people. There wasn't even a sign hanging anywhere with the company name on it. Just a large, blank room, with a soft blue carpet and windows ringing the perimeter.

"Another trick?" Gervais said. "I didn't think the flying monkeys had it in them."

I looked around the room.

"No, I don't think it was a trick." The light was streaming in through the windows, showing that the carpeting was still slightly compressed in some places. "Something heavy was sitting in that corner. There was a desk over there. Someone used to be in this office, and they only left recently."

"Bah. It doesn't matter, diuscrucis. Everything is gone. We should be, too. Focus on what we can find, not what is missing. If RoGen was here, they dismantled it."

It couldn't be a coincidence that the company had vanished. Was the whole thing a front to the work Matthias Zheng had been doing? Either way, Gervais was right. There was no point for us to delay here, especially since checking the RoGen office had been a target of opportunity, not the main reason we'd made the trip. Part of me was hoping the angels were somehow watching us in secret, and that they knew we had stopped by. Maybe they would think we'd reached the end of the trail and smashed hard into their wall.

Maybe this time, we could catch them by surprise.

"We need to find a way into the Lab that won't attract too much attention," I said.

Gervais morphed back into his true form. "Leave that to me."

The maliciousness of his smile gave me chills.

CHAPTER THIRTY

OF COURSE, YOU COULD ONLY get so close to the Lab without proper credentials. The entire site had a secure perimeter to prevent against potential terrorist threats, and was managed through three guarded vehicle entrances. That meant that in order to get onto the site, we would need a badge. To locate and gain access to whatever facility Zheng had been stationed in would take a bit more than that.

It was the reason I was sitting in the Fabulous 50s Diner with Rose.

It was the reason we had spent the last three hours waiting there.

It was the reason Gervais wasn't with us.

I didn't tell Rose what the demon was up to. I didn't need to. It was obvious that there was only one way we were going to get into the Lab, and it wasn't a pretty one. She was handling it. Not well. Well enough. I'd brought him along because I thought he would be useful. This was his big chance.

"He left two hours ago," Rose said. "What the hell is taking him so long?"

She'd been edgy since he had excused himself from our table and made his move, leaving the diner and returning a few seconds later, morphed into a really, really handsome muscle type. We'd watched him approach a very plain looking woman in a linen suit who was wearing a LANL badge. We had overheard her talking to the waitress about how she had to work overtime today, and had just taken a break for some of their delicious pie.

His charm and pheromones had gone to work, and they had left together not long after. The demon had winked at Rose on the way by, causing her to bring her napkin up to her face and start choking, trying to hold down the vomit. I was sure he had gotten a great kick out of that.

"Knowing him, he's trying to make you squirm," I said. Her foot was tapping a fast rhythm on the floor, and while I'd ordered and eaten four pieces of cherry pie in the last two hours, her first was still untouched. "It's working."

She tried to calm her foot. It was still for about five seconds, and then started smacking against the table again, shaking up the silverware.

"Another?" our waitress, Cathy, said, stopping by to check on us for the four hundredth time. She was a grandma type, plump and grey and full of spunk. She picked up my empty plate.

"Why not?" I said. "Maybe a different flavor this time. Do you have pecan?"

"Sure do, sweetie." She glanced over at Rose's pie. "You might as well eat hers, too. Can I get you something else, dear?"

Rose looked up at her and shook her head. "No. Thanks. I'm fine."

Cathy's eyes caught mine for just a second, and she turned away. "One piece of pecan pie, and I'll grab you a warm up on your coffee." She headed off.

The door to the diner opened, and the woman in the linen suit walked in.

"He's here," I said.

Rose closed her eyes and inhaled, clenching her lips. Trying not to get sick again.

Gervais sat down next to me. Across from Rose.

"How do I look?" he asked. He stared at her and smiled, then morphed back to himself.

"Enough," I said. I shifted and found Cathy. "Excuse me. I'm sorry, can you cancel the pie? Just the check, please."

She smiled and nodded, and a minute later we had the check.

"How do you pay for anything?" Gervais asked me. "You don't have any rich sympathizers to support you."

I pulled the same bit of plastic that had been Obi's badge and put it with the bill, changing it as my hand went from my pocket to the table. I had spent some time in prison once for identity theft. After Dante had brought me back, I had sworn I wouldn't get back into that business.

It was one promise I hadn't been able to keep. My expenses were light, and I tried to do it as little as possible, but sometimes I needed some quick liquidity. I figured it was a fair price for humanity to pay. In any case, Elyse payed the rent on the apartment, using the millions she had inherited after she killed her father. Money the rest of her Nicht Creidem family was still trying to get back from their former leader's deserter of a daughter.

"You aren't the only one with tricks," I said, handing everything over to Cathy. "Do you have what we need?"

"I have what I need. Ah, yes. I also have the badge, and the brain. Her name is Sarah, if you can believe that. Sarah Mitchell. She's in procurement."

"Procurement?" Rose asked.

"She places the materials orders for the scientists."

Cathy came back with the card. I signed us out, leaving her a nice tip. "Any materials we would be especially interested in?"

He tapped his skull. "Not in here, but I can get us into her computer. She has decent access to the rest of the network. I trust our Rose can do the work from there?"

"What's the matter, are computers too advanced for you?" Rose asked.

"No. I just like to have the underlings handle the menial tasks."
"Can we just go?" I said.

CHAPTER THIRTY-ONE

THE BADGE GOT US PAST the armed guards and through the vehicle access point, though there was a minute of tension while Sarah/Gervais explained why he had two guests with him. It was the moment at which his unique abilities proved themselves, because without his victim's memories and intimate knowledge of process and procedure at the Lab, we would have never gotten in.

"Did you doubt me?" he said. "I never doubted myself."

We were riding in Sarah's car, a late model Ford with an 'I love science' bumper sticker on the back fender. I had changed into a standard black suit for the occasion and we had picked up similar business formal attire for Rose before we drove over. She looked pretty good dressed down. She looked even better in the white blouse and skirt, with her hair pinned up and wearing a pair of low magnification reading glasses.

"I'm sure you must have doubted yourself when Sarah killed you," I said.

"Not really."

He pulled into a large parking lot and stopped near the center, in a numbered space that matched the sticker on Sarah Mitchell's car. We got out and followed him to what I assumed was an administration building - a very normal looking concrete and glass structure. He swiped the badge at the door and pulled it open.

"Ladies first," he said, waving Rose through. She glared at him as she passed.

We took the elevator up to the third floor. The place was deserted save for a janitor who was vacuuming the carpets in the hall. Gervais gave her a warm hello and led us down a corridor to an office near the middle of the space. It was small and windowless, with a simple desk and workstation, a file cabinet, and a few photos hanging on the walls. One was of Sarah, with a man I could only assume was her husband and their two children. It was a hard one to look at, but I forced myself to do it.

There were always victims. There were always casualties. The day I felt nothing about them was the day I became the Beast.

Rose must have noticed, because she took my hand and squeezed it. I knew it wasn't easy for her either, so I returned the favor.

"Aww, how cute," Gervais said. "Rose, if you would." He motioned to the desk chair. She went over and sat behind the workstation.

"Username and password?" she said, turning on the monitor.

"Sarah period mitchell, all lowercase. 'Love my kids', lowercase, all one word." The demon stood behind her, looking over her shoulder. I stayed on the other side of the desk, giving her space to work.

"It didn't work," Rose said.

Gervais smiled. "No? Try, 'I'm dead because of you'. Again, lowercase, all one word."

We both shot him a dirty look.

"What's the damn password, you asshole?" Rose snapped.

"M-X-Y-Z-T-P-L-K-1-9-4-4. All lowercase."

She typed it in. "Now what?"

"Go down to the menu and click on 'eProcure'," the demon said. "Do a search for Zheng."

"Nothing," she replied a few seconds later.

"Hmm. Sarah didn't know what department Zheng was working in."

Rose typed something in. "Here's a list of orders for robotics," she said. Gervais leaned in, putting his face close to hers. She tried to angle herself further away from it.

"Standard parts, I think. Try searching on orders from RoGen."

"Nothing."

Gervais growled impatiently. "This might take all night."

"We don't have all night," I said. "Is there a way to get a list of departments?"

Rose looked at Gervais, who walked her through the steps.

"Anything promising?" I asked.

"Everything has a department number and a title," Rose said. "Mechanical engineering, biology, those are fine. This one," she pointed at the screen. "Classified. This one, too. There are three listed that way."

She clicked a few times, scanned the screen, clicked a few more times.

"Do you know the password to get into the screens for these departments?" she asked Gervais.

He shook his head. "No. She didn't have access. Find another way."

"Just like that? Just find another way?" she snapped. "No password, no entry. We can try to brute force it, but that *will* take all night."

I turned to Gervais. "You don't have anything else that can help?"

He tapped his index finger on his chin and closed his eyes. Then he smiled again. "Personnel records. Maybe we can find out who has the highest security clearance."

"Great. Then what?"

"Then I don't know. You have power. Can't you use it to get a password from their computer?"

"Just like that?" I asked. "I know it looks like magic, but it has limitations."

Rose twisted so I could see her past the monitor. "Wait. You can affect things on an atomic level, right? Do you think you'd be able to tell which keys had been hit the most frequently on a keyboard?"

I thought about it. "I might. How will that help?"

"It might not. These workstations are set to lock down after sixty seconds of inactivity. That means any time the person went to a meeting, got up to use the bathroom, got distracted by a phone call - they'd need to put their password in again."

"So the most worn keys are probably used in the password?"

"Yeah. It will still take a little time to get in because we have to try the combinations, but not as much as using the whole range of alphanumerics."

"Not as dumb as you look," Gervais said. "It may be the best approach."

"Okay. Check the personnel records."

She leaned back and starting typing and scrolling again.

"I got an org chart. Top floor, corner office. Nathan Rogers. Director of Special Operations."

"That sounds promising," I said. "What's his birthday?"

"June sixteenth, 1969."

We abandoned Sarah Mitchell's office, heading back down the hall to the elevator. Gervais swiped the badge, and we moved up to the tenth floor.

It was indistinguishable from the third floor, at least from the hallway. The same neutral carpeting, the same off-white walls. We walked all the way down to Nathan Roger's office. The door was locked. Opening it was trivial.

"It's good to be the king," Gervais said, leading us in.

The office was massive, surrounded by full length windows that provided a great view out to the rest of the complex. A leather couch sat close to the door, while a private conference table and whiteboard rested on a slightly raised floor near the window, opposite a dark wood desk. Like Sarah, Nathan kept photos of his family on prominent display. A large one of his wife on one side of the desk, and another of his labrador on the other side.

I sat down behind the workstation, closing my eyes and casting the energy out. As with Cheryl Paulson, I let it sink onto the keyboard while I focused on it, running my mind over it and picking it apart molecule by molecule.

I couldn't see the wear on the keys. Instead, I had an innate sense of it, a subatomic topography. The 'e' key was the most warn, and had the greatest buildup of oils on it. The 's' key, the 'g', the 'q', the 'u', the '1', the '7', the '9'. I rattled them off to Rose, who wrote them down on the board.

"I think that's it," I said, opening my eyes. I looked over at the letters and numbers.

"Clearly a man of great intelligence," Gervais said. "He very obviously used at least part of his birthday in the password."

Rose nodded. "And only four letters are especially warn. I'm not so sure about 'e' though. That's the most popular letter in the English language."

"How do we know if a letter is used more than once in the password?" Gervais said.

"We don't," I replied. "We just have to try them. Let's start simple, and work our way up."

Rose took over at the computer, while I worked with Gervais to start outputting combinations of letters and dates. The number of possibilities was still quite large, though the demon seemed be able to create and track them with no amount of effort.

It took an hour to come to 'squeegee61669'. In the end, it was the 'q' and 'u' that helped us narrow it down. We made the assumption they went together, and if they were together that the password was an actual word, and not a random combination. I was amazed by Gervais' knowledge of the english language. It was as though he had a dictionary in his head.

"Check 'eProcure' first," I said, once Rose was in. I wandered over to the doorway at the same time, making sure we were still alone. We were.

"Landon, I think I have something," she said a few minutes later.

"What is it?"

"The 'classified' titles are gone. One of them is called Project Fog."

"As in, Fist of God?"

She smiled. "I think so. I'm inside the shipping system. There are dozens of deliveries here. Looks like part numbers and abbreviated descriptions. I can't make out most of them, but it seems one is for a laser engraving machine."

"A machine like that wouldn't be able to make scripture small enough," I said.

"An early effort," Gervais said.

"Anyway, that's not the most interesting part. There are a ton of imports. There's one export, out to Shenzhen, China. Get this, the listed contents are two workstations, a 3d printer, and a 'project prototype'." She did the air quotes for effect.

"Does it say who it was delivered to?"

"Hang on." Her eyes followed her scroll. "Here it is. Some place called THI."

I felt my heart bang against my chest. "Taylor Heavy Industries."

"You know it?"

"The founder, Rachel Taylor, was a friend of mine. She was Touched. THI is a subsidiary of Taylor Enterprises, a publicly traded company whose shareholders indirectly include the Vatican, among other wealthy Christian entities."

"Oh. Do you think she knows anything about this?"

I shook my head, feeling an old wound threatening to reopen. "I doubt it. She's dead."

Her lips formed a thin line across her mouth. "I'm sorry."

"Me, too."

"At least we got something out of this trip," Gervais said.

"Let's see if we can get more. Rose, can you find out where Project Fog was being developed? I have a hard time believing that the United States government was funding angelic research, which means that there are probably other engineers here who worked on parts of it besides Zheng, and who didn't know who or what it was they were actually doing the work for. They may have left evidence on their workstations. Blueprints, research notes, that kind of thing."

"Sure. Just one second, I can see which building the incoming orders were delivered to." She starting tapping the keys for a second, and then stopped. Her head turned towards the window on her right. "Landon. Oh, shit. We've got company."

CHAPTER THIRTY-TWO

I THREW MY POWER OUT towards the window, even as the trio of angels swooped in and through it, sending shattered glass pouring into the room. I clenched my jaw, using the energy to catch it, to keep it from exploding onto Rose.

She pushed the chair backwards, rolling away from the desk, and at the same time ripping open the top of her blouse and tearing her cursed dagger away from its hiding place beneath her breasts.

The glass fell to the ground in a neat line.

The angels straightened up.

"You must be the diuscrucis," one of them said, looking down at the glass. He stepped forward. "My name is Abraham."

"Abraham, there are only three of you here," I said.

He smiled. "We just want to talk."

"Oh? What about?"

He motioned towards the workstation. "A… flaw, in our plan. We want to discuss a potential agreement."

I stared at him. The balance had been easier to maintain up until now, because evil had a tendency to be a lot more prevalent than good. Sure, there were a lot of people in the world who would hold open a door for somebody, do volunteer work, or donate to charities. Those were good things, but when you compared them to brutal murder, rape, genocide, war, it took a lot to even it all out.

Eight years, and only now were the angels moving to gain the upper hand.

Abraham was stalling. Buying time to get a Fist here? Did they know we discovered where their toys were being produced? Would they try to shut it down and move it before I could get there, or would they do their best to end this right here and now?

Time was never on our side. We had less of it now.

Eight years, and now I would have to kill them.

Like I had said to Rose, I didn't want to do it. I didn't like doing it. It made me feel dirty, because following God or not following God, killing was wrong.

It was also necessary.

I threw the power out, catching Rose's dagger with it, tearing it from her grip and sending it into Abraham's chest. He glanced down at it, and then looked at me accusingly as the poison started to spread.

His companion reached for the holy water at his hip, the salve that would stop the demonic poison from killing him. The other drew his sword.

Gervais was himself again, and he leaped forward, grabbing the dagger from Abraham's chest, catching the second angel's stroke in a strong hand, and reversing the knife back and up into his throat. All in one motion, he kicked the holy water from the first angel's hand, sending it spilling out onto the floor.

"No cheating," he said. He stabbed the remaining angel in the stomach, and then freed the blade by kicking the seraph out the window. He was still screaming, even after his body thumped against the cement below.

I looked at Rose. She was frozen in place, tears running from her eyes. I couldn't blame her for her reaction. I had cried the first time, too.

"We need to go," Gervais said, pointing out into the night. "Your friend is coming. He brought reinforcements."

"We can't outrun an angel," I said.

"No. We can hide."

"There's no time." I looked back at Rose. She hadn't moved. "You need to get her out of here."

"Ugh." He curled his lip and shook his head. "Why did you bring her along, again?"

"Just do it."

I could see them now, a dozen angels. It was a massive force considering how few of them there were on Earth. Two of the armored Fists dangled from their arms. I didn't see Adam. Was he out there?

Gervais ran over to Rose, bending down and lifting her. She went limp in his arms at first, and then started screaming and fighting against his grip.

"Put me down. Damn it. I'm okay."

I didn't have time to see what happened next. I took three quick steps and jumped out the window.

Breaking my fall with the power had been a lot of trial and error, a lot of broken bones. At first I had used a helmet to make sure I didn't smash my skull on a particularly bad drop. In time, I graduated to greater and greater heights, learning to measure the amount of energy to use to come down in perfect, and perfectly cool, three-point landings. My personal best was sixty-one stories.

Ten was easy.

I hit the ground and rolled to my feet, shifting the energy into my limbs, hitting the gas and running as fast as I could. It was nowhere near fast enough to outrun a seraph in flight, but I wanted to lead them away.

I looked up and back. They were closer now, much closer. The parking lot was in front of me, and beyond it a fence. On the other side was the drab brown wilderness I had been disparaging earlier.

I was halfway across the lot when the first angel landed in front of me. She was short and stocky, with a cherubic face and long brown hair. Her sword was already in hand.

I didn't slow. I swept my arm out in front of me, and she flew from my path, her wings unfurling and shifting to keep herself from falling.

The fence was getting closer. So were the angels with the Fists, the heavy machines making them just a little bit slower than the others. The rest of the angels had split away, and I saw them going for the building. For Rose and Gervais. I was tempted to turn, to make a move on them. Gervais would handle it. He was an evil son of a bitch, but he was a survivor. The armors were my problem.

I reached the fence and vaulted it with a flow of energy, easily clearing the barbed wire and landing in the trees on the other side. The angels wouldn't be able to drop the Fists there, the space was just too small, their momentum too great. I thought I heard one grunt as they were forced to go up and over.

I stopped running.

It was eerily quiet in the thin copse of trees. I closed my eyes, feeling the light breeze against my face, feeling the density of the earth beneath my feet, the unhurried beating of my heart. I gathered the power, holding it in my soul.

The calm before the storm.

I felt the earth shake when the Fists were dropped onto it. I heard the breeze blow past my ears from their displacement of the air. My heart began to beat harder, and I pulled the stone from my pocket and brought the spatha to my hand. The trees weren't much, but against two of the Fists, with four arms laden with bolts, I needed all the obstacles I could find.

A cracked branch on my left. Another on my right. I could see the faint blue glow of their activated scripture out of the corner of my eyes. I dropped to my knees without thinking, letting my intuition guide me. I felt the bolts go past, crossing one another in perfect harmony, missing my body by fractions of an inch. I caught them with my power and twisted, turning the energy with me, spinning like a tornado and casting them back towards large, dark shadows. My aim was a little off. The trunks of two trees splintered from the force of the missiles that hit them.

One of the trees didn't survive.

The first crack was followed by a second, and it started to fall behind me. I jumped up, vanished the sword, turned, and ran towards it in a mad dash, watching the branches sweeping down, the trunk moving ever closer to the ground. I could hear the motion behind me, the two Fists breaking from cover together, their motions mirrored perfectly. I dove ahead, my stomach hitting the ground, my momentum carrying me under the falling tree and through to the other side. I was lashed with leaves and branches, one of which dislocated my shoulder as I went by. Then it made a final, loud, echoing sound when it completed its crash, the thickness enough to block the angelic knights for a few seconds.

I got to my feet and grabbed my arm, pulling it back into place. The pain was intense, and I was grateful for how quickly I was able to heal. I kept running, moving out into the grassy hills, away from the woods. I had been wrong about the cover of the trees. It gave them a better opportunity to catch me in a crossfire. If I could see the bolts, I could stop them. If I could see the Fists, I could avoid them.

For how long?

CHAPTER THIRTY-THREE

I KEPT RUNNING, PUSHING HARDER, sending myself hurtling along the landscape. I glanced back every few seconds, checking on the Fists and making sure they weren't gaining.

They weren't. They weren't losing ground either. They kept pace behind me in complete synchronization, their feet moving and falling at the exact same time. I wondered if they would take a shot at me - when they would take a shot at me. I was surprised they hadn't already.

Except, I couldn't keep this up forever. Sooner or later, I was going to have to turn and fight.

I reached a small hill and barreled up it, deciding then that I would hit them from the other side, where I could launch something of an ambush. I hit the decline and dropped onto my ass, letting the speed slide me down the hill. I stopped myself about halfway, drew the obsidian blade, and waited.

The moment their heads crested the rise, I pushed out with my power, sending a cloud of dirt out behind me, and shooting at them like a rocket. I held the blade out wide, swinging it hard at the Fist on the right, my aim for the space between the helm and the body.

The blade crashed into an angled bit of metal that had been welded to the original design, scripture connecting and covering the new addition, which made the junction of head and torso even smaller then before. The lettering flared as the sword smacked it, catching the blow and throwing me off balance.

I must have spun thirty times before I even hit the ground, and another thirty as I rolled back down the slope. I hadn't even come to a stop before I was back on my feet, the Fists turning themselves, their arms out. Two more bolts came my way, and I swept the power out, pulling them down into the ground ahead of me. The neck had been a weakness I exploited once. They had updated the design to make sure I couldn't use it again.

I set myself in a crouch, holding the sword out in front of me. They drew closer, their blades extending from beneath their wrists.

They were bearing down on me from the slope.

A glow behind them caught my eye.

It was airborne, distant, barely noticeable over the Fist's shoulder at least a mile away. It would have been easy for someone to mistake for a star, or an airplane, or any number of things, except it was in my line of sight.

It was Divine.

Adam.

It had to be. He was here. He was watching. Was he commanding them? Did he know I had seen him?

They slowed as they reached me, leading with their blades. I was skilled enough to bat the first round aside, to parry and turn and parry and duck and parry and twist. I pushed back against them with my power, using their mass to throw myself back. I took the split second to look out to the sky again, finding the blue glow framed by a wisp of clouds.

It was obvious to me that I couldn't fight the Fists on my own and win. That left me with only one other option, a long shot hope. I gathered my power and pushed it into the ground with enough force to catapult myself high into the air, a hundred feet or more. The Fists tracked the movement, their bodies shifting, their arms coming to bear and their entire payload of bolts sparking and releasing towards me.

Did they think I couldn't catch them all?

I couldn't. One grazed my thigh, while another sank deep into my gut. I felt the pain at the same time I did catch the rest, wrapping them up in my power and redirecting them, pushing so hard that for a few seconds I couldn't breathe at all.

I didn't see if they had hit their target. I reached the top of the leap and started to fall, all of my energy spent on throwing the missiles. I must have done something right, because as I fell I saw the Fists turn away from me and sprint away from the scene.

I hit the ground hard, the force pushing the bolt in my gut deeper into me. I spit up blood at the same time I pushed the power to the site, using it to wrench the missile the rest of the way through my back and then heal the damage. I rolled over and jumped up. I had to see why the Fists had run.

I reached the top of the hill. They were half of a mile away, headed for the blue glow that was now resting on the ground. I could make the figure of the angel out now. It *was* Adam.

I gathered my power, feeling lightheaded at the exertion of it, the disruption in my soul renewed. If Adam was here, commanding these Fists, he couldn't be in Shenzhen, or in Heaven warning the rest of the Inquisitors about what we had discovered. There was no way I was going to be able to kill him with the Fists there, but I needed to at least slow him down.

The answer was beneath my feet. It was going to take all of my strength to make it happen, and I wasn't sure if I even could. There was no other choice.

I started running towards them, as fast as I could. I needed to get there before Adam or the Fists could pull the bolts from his body, before he could heal and get airborne again. I needed to reach them while they were distracted, and their guard was down.

I covered the ground quickly, my legs churning, my arms out at my sides. I got within a hundred feet, close enough so I could see

Adam's pained expression from his position between the Fists kneeling on either side of him. Close enough so I could see the blood-soaked toga, and the three bolts still embedded in his body.

Close enough that he could see me, too.

His metal hand shifted on the ground, and the two Fists turned their attention towards me.

Too late.

I slid to a stop, throwing the power down into the earth. The dry, loose earth. Then I pulled.

The ground started shaking around us, as the composition was changed in a near instant. Adam didn't even have time to say anything before the sudden sinkhole swallowed him and the Fists, dropping them into a deep pit.

I pushed the top layer of earth, using it to fill in the new hole.

Using it to bury the seraph alive.

CHAPTER THIRTY-FOUR

I RETURNED TO THE PARKING lot on rubbery legs, fighting to keep moving, to get back to Rose and Gervais. My heart was pounding, my head ached. I was even sweating. I hadn't forced that much from the energy before, and the resulting discomfort was threatening to drop me with every step.

The lot was still mostly empty. Everything was quiet. I found Sarah's Ford in her assigned spot.

Rose was sitting on the hood, knife in hand, her hair disheveled, her clothes bloody. Gervais was leaning up against the side of the car, looking like he'd missed the entire thing. His eyes opened a little wider when he saw me.

Rose slid off the car, walking towards me, a smile forming on her haggard face. She threw her arms out wide as I neared, and I took her up on the offer.

"Are you okay?" I asked. She held me tight, pushing herself into me.

"I'm fine, all things considered," she said into my neck. "I was worried about you."

I pulled away and turned her back towards the car. We were on the clock. "Are you injured?"

She twisted to show me a light nick on her shoulder. "That one was close. Otherwise, none of the blood is mine." She was sad when she said it, and I knew why. The blood of angels. "Did you destroy the Fists?"

"Not exactly."

We reached the car and Gervais. He straightened up. "You're alive," he said.

"So are you."

"He almost wasn't. I saved him."

His face twisted when she said it.

"You saved him?" I didn't hold back my laugh. If I had a chance to upset him, I was going to take it.

"I was fine," Gervais said. "I knew the seraph was there."

"Right. Whatever you say. Did any of them escape?"

He glowered and shook his head. "No."

I didn't want to say 'good', even though it was good. Adam wouldn't remember our fight, but I was sure he would put two and two together once he got out of his predicament. Why else would he be buried right outside of Los Alamos?

"There were two Fists, and Adam was here. I think he has a connection to them, that he's commanding them. Maybe through his mechanical arm. I couldn't kill them. I buried them out there." I pointed back to the hills. "He can't suffocate, and the soil there is loose. I bought us some time, nothing more. We need to get to Shenzhen, to get to Matthias before he digs his way out." I looked at Gervais. "We need reinforcements. Someone strong enough to use a rift."

"And you think I know this person? My domain is in Europe."

"You're seven hundred years old. You're telling me Valerix is the only demon you knew here?"

"Let me think on it."

"Fine. In the meantime, you need to drive us out of here. Let's head back towards Santa Fe." I took hold of the power, the act making me nauseous. I pushed it out towards Rose, using it to break apart the blood and scrape it from her clothes. It floated to the ground as ash. "Just in case any of the perimeter guards are Awake. I don't really feel like getting shot at again right now."

She smiled. There were goosebumps on her arms. "That felt weird. Good weird."

Gervais went around to the driver's side, morphing back into Sarah Mitchell. "You two want to screw around in the back seat? I can pretend not to be disgusted."

I walked over to the back door of the car and opened it. Rose slid across the seat, and I joined her in the rear. Gervais got behind the wheel and got us moving.

"Tell me what happened," I said, leaning my head back and closing my eyes. The whole world felt like it was spinning out of control in the darkness.

"We ran for the elevator, but we didn't make it. The first group came in through the windows. They didn't pay me that much attention at first. They went right for Gervais. He killed three of them before I could even think to fight. Then I remembered what you told me. I remembered Anita. I thought about all of the people who would suffer."

"How noble," Gervais said over his shoulder.

"Shut up," I said.

"He's still pissy about me saving him. Like I said, he killed three of them, but there was a fourth - a boy. He looked like he was maybe fifteen, sixteen. He came out of the office behind him, his sword already raised to stab him in the back. I grabbed him and cut his throat." Her face paled. Her eyes teared.

"He wasn't fifteen," Gervais said. "I knew that one. Siculus. He was older than me. He was a Spartan. One of the three hundred. He died at Thermopylae."

"Bullshit," I said.

"Why do you say that?" he asked.

"The Greeks didn't go to Heaven, they were polytheists."

The demon laughed. "You aren't going back far enough. God

was very patient with His creations. He gave them quite a while to settle into the idea of His existence, seeing as how it is so very magnificent." His voice dripped sarcasm.

"Were you trying to make me feel better, or worse?" Rose asked. "Whether I killed a fifteen year old boy, or a two thousand plus year old angel. I still killed an angel to save your disgusting ass. You killed my sister, and I saved your life? How messed up is that? Nothing is ever going to make me feel less dirty for that one."

"I suppose there is always a silver lining," he replied. "Needing a mortal to save my life is the meaning of embarrassing. How weak and pathetic I have become."

"Can you both stop?" I said. I wanted to be more sympathetic to Rose. I just wasn't in the mood, and their arguing wasn't doing anything for my headache. "Rose, do you know what happened to the angels that were carrying the Fists?" I had forgotten about them until now. If they had escaped, we were going to be in trouble.

"They caught us on our way to the car. That's how I got this." She pointed at the cut again. "It would have been deeper if I hadn't managed to get my knife up in time."

"They must have been initiates, the way they fought," Gervais said. "Clumsy."

"I hope that isn't true," Rose said. "I barely beat one of them in the same time he killed the rest. I know you wanted to train me, and to find others like me to train. I'm not feeling very positive about that idea right now."

I looked at her, trying to calm the doubts in my soul. I didn't just want to. I needed to. It was the only way I would ever be able to rest. If it took a hundred years, a thousand, ten thousand. I could be patient as long as I knew the end would come one day.

In any case, she'd gone into this whole thing with a minimum of experience, and no real protection from the Divine. I wasn't going to tell her, but the fact that she was still alive was an achievement by itself. Her odds of survival would only go up once I could get her with Elyse. The Nicht Creidem knew every trick in the book for defending themselves against the Divine, and she would pass that knowledge on.

"You'll get better with more experience," I said. "I believe in you."

She smiled and wiped the tears from her face. "Thanks."

"Please," Gervais said.

He slowed the car as we went back out through the access point, and then we were away. He got us back out onto the highway and pointed us towards Santa Fe. We rode in silence for a while, taking comfort in the minutes of peace. I closed my eyes and worked to steady my breathing, to calm the storm of power in my soul.

My eyes were still closed when I felt a pressure on my leg. I opened them to find Rose's head there, the rest of her curled up on the seat next to me. Her eyes were closed, and a moment later a soft snore started rising from her.

"Touching, really," Gervais said. I saw his eyes watching us in the rear view.

"Do you have to be like... that... *all* of the time?" I asked.

He looked away. Was he actually embarrassed?

"You wouldn't understand, diuscrucis. You aren't capable."

"Try me."

"I miss my sister."

"You're kidding?"

"No. Think what you want. I loved her, in the way that I am capable. Especially when we were mortal. I protected her. I cared for her. Now she is gone. To where, I don't know, but her soul is lost. Never again will I sense it. Never again will I speak to her. I find I am capable of sadness and I feel it at these thoughts."

The honesty made me uncomfortable. "I miss her, too, but I know for a fact that her soul isn't lost. It's up there, a part of the universe, a shared part of all creation." She was with Charis, with Clara, with the essence of the Beast, and with all the angels and demons we had killed. With every soul that had finished its journey. It was pure energy, the energy that allowed all universes to be in the first place. It was part of the balance. "Nothing else has ever made you sad?"

"No. Angry, yes. Violent, yes. Not sad." He took a deep breath and sighed it out. "I will kill you one day, if someone else doesn't do it first. Now that you know this flaw, I have more incentive."

I didn't respond. I closed my eyes again, and started absently stroking Rose's hair. In that moment, I wanted the human connection.

"One other thing, Landon," Gervais said.

"What?"

"I have thought of a demon that can help you, if you can talk him into it. I'm going to bypass Santa Fe."

"Where are we going?"

"Mexico."

CHAPTER THIRTY-FIVE

IT WAS A FIVE HOUR drive from Santa Fe to the border. I slept for three of them, waking up feeling a little more composed and a lot more hungry. Rose was awake by then, too, though she had left her head on my lap, and shifted so she was laying on her back. I opened my eyes to see her looking up at me, watching me.

"Hey, handsome," she said.

For once, Gervais didn't make a comment.

"Me? No. How are you feeling?"

"A little better. I'd love a shower and a change of clothes."

It was true that the blood, sweat, and dirt hadn't done much for her smell. We had some extra clothes for her in the trunk. We'd need to do something about the shower.

"Gervais, any hotels coming up on the route?" I asked.

He pointed at the dashboard. "I don't know how to work this thing. The user interface is sloppy, the heuristics are terrible."

Rose sat up, leaning between the seats. "You whine too much," she said, tapping the screen until she got into the nav system. "I'll give you a pass because you're an old man, not used to this newfangled technology."

He glared at her. I smiled. She certainly seemed refreshed.

"Ten miles. Can we stop there?"

"Thirty minutes, max," I said.

"More than enough."

Ten miles brought us into Las Cruces, and we pulled off I-25 and into the parking lot of a Fairfield Inn. Rose grabbed the extra clothes we'd bought from the trunk and we went inside together. Ten minutes later I was sitting on the king bed in our room, listening to her singing in the shower.

She was quick enough that she only got through one song, popping out of the bathroom wrapped in a towel. I handed her the stack of clothes, and turned my back when she dropped the towel.

"You're cute," she said. "You weren't so chivalrous when I was doing the pushups."

"Truth be told, I barely noticed you then."

"Oh." She seemed surprised. I imagine she wasn't used to men not noticing her. "What changed?"

"I've spent more time with you. I've been so distant from people for so long. I feel like I'm getting too close, too fast. I've known you for what? Two days? I hardly know anything about you."

"So you're saying you aren't looking because you have more respect for me?"

"Kind of. I have more awareness of you. Of your humanity. And of my own. I admire your strength, your courage. I think you're beautiful."

She put her hand on my shoulder. I glanced back. She had her clothes on, so I turned around.

"I don't get what the problem is," she said. "You know I'm not shy. I don't care if you look."

"I care. Even so, it's not the physical part of it. It's the emotional. I don't trust what I feel. Not in this. It's too easy for me to latch onto the first person I spend time with. Because I'm really attracted to you? Or because I've been alone for so long? Or because I'm just glad to feel more human? I can't answer any of that right now, and that's before I factor in all of the complications that go with being near immortal."

If she were someone else, someone less self-assured, I might not have felt as comfortable saying those things as I did.

"You're probably also afraid you'll get attached, and I'll die."

That was her response. She said it straight, just part of the conversation.

"There's that, too."

She leaned down and kissed my cheek. "It's okay, Landon. I understand. I'll try not to be so obviously sexy around you. Just know that I'm here, and right now I'm interested. Varium et mutabile semper femina. That's Virgil. Dante probably heard that one straight from the horse's mouth. If and when you want to talk about it, tell me."

A shifty, fickle object is woman, always.

I laughed and stood up. "Time to go."

We went back down to the car. Gervais was standing there, drinking coffee.

"You like coffee?" I asked.

"More than blood," he replied. "I never had to resort to such grotesquery as an archfiend." He tipped the cup up and downed the rest, and then threw the empty paper onto the sidewalk. "I do prefer it in a nice porcelain."

We swapped drivers. Rose took the wheel, I rode shotgun, and Gervais regained the back, spreading himself out on the seat.

"So, you were right that we don't know each other very well," Rose said a few minutes later. "We have some time."

"I don't know. You might want to be careful about what you say in front of him."

"You think I care about her family, or her childhood, or her favorite color? Or yours for that matter?" Gervais said.

We'd already talked a lot about her sister, her time at school, and a little bit about her parents during our first day together, when we'd gone shopping for the clothes to attract Gervais, and the food that was probably going to spoil before she got to eat any of it.

"Have you ever been to Mexico?" I asked.

"No, believe it or not. My father was born in Mexico City, but he came to the States as an illegal back in the '70s. He started out mowing lawns, washing cars, working hard until he got his citizenship. He never wanted to go back. He said to Anita and me, 'Forget that culture. This is our home, this is our culture. Be proud of where you are. Trees have strong roots, and when there is a drought they wither and die.'" She took on a deeper accented voice to mimic her father.

"Your father sounds like he has a good approach to life," I said.

"I think so. He's a strong man, and he made sure to raise us to be strong. He never wanted us to fall into bullshit female stereotypes. 'Anything a man can do, you can do. You know why that makes you better? Because you can do something a man can never do.'" She laughed. "I know he was never that happy with Anita and me when it came to some things, but he raised us to make our own decisions, to stand on our own. He always respected us as much as he respected our mother, and I love him more for that. What was your father like?"

I shook my head. "I don't know. He ditched my mom and me when I was a baby. From that, my guess is that he was an asshole."

Gervais laughed at that statement. "It sounds like he was smarter than you give him credit for."

I ignored his remark.

We spent the next hour telling stories. Gervais was mostly quiet, save for his occasional jabs and barbs, though he did share one tale about a time he and Josette had collected money for the poor, and then used it to buy themselves candy instead. Their parents had discovered the deceit, and punished them for their trickery. I had heard Josette tell the story. She had made her parents sound stern and well-intentioned. To hear the demon tell it, they were self-serving idiots who sacrificed their own well-being and comfort in search of some kind of emotional fulfillment from an unresponsive and useless God, and took His ambivalence towards them out on their children. He blamed them, and he blamed God. It was what made him who he was today.

It was four in the morning when we reached El Paso. The city was quiet this early, and we cruised through without having to slow for too many lights. I was thankful we had made pretty decent time down from Los Alamos. I was also nervous. I didn't know how long it would take Adam to get free.

The border crossing was open twenty-four/seven, and it was relatively quiet. We waited in line for ten minutes before reaching the Mexican side, and we were fortunate enough to get the green light and avoid a search by customs. A little bit of misdirection and sleight of hand by Gervais to manage our passports, and we made it through as uneventfully as I could have hoped for.

"So, we're in Mexico," I said. "Now how do we find this demon of yours?"

CHAPTER THIRTY-SIX

"His name is Espanto," Gervais said. "He's a fiend. A fiend with more power than he deserves. Whatever bad things happen in this city, they happen because he wants them to."

"Espanto?" Rose said. "Terror?"

"Yes. I sent Izak to speak to him once, when he still had his tongue. Izak wasn't afraid of anything, but he was wary of him."

"So, you don't actually know Espanto?" I said. The idea of Izak being cautious around any demon made me a little uneasy.

"I know of him. I know where to find him. I know he has a rift, and that he can use it. The rest is up to you."

We drove through the streets of Juarez. It was more brown here, more sparse, more poor. There was a lot of traffic for the early hour, the border crossing providing plenty of reason for people to be passing through. Gervais followed the navigation to a place called 'Ghost Salvage'.

It was a junkyard.

The gates were closed when we pulled up to it, a ten foot tall, faded green fence blocking our view of the inside of the property. We rolled to a stop and Gervais got out of the car, beckoning me to follow him. A moment later, a face appeared at the top of the fence.

A vampire.

"We're closed," he said in spanish, peering down.

"Don't be your usual annoyingly polite self," Gervais whispered. "Espanto respects toughness and power above anything else."

"Even if I kill half his servants?"

"You can kill every servant here. He'll enjoy that. He has plenty more. This entire city is his. Not just the Divine. The murderers, the drug lords, the pimps and prostitutes, even the crooked corporate suits."

"Why isn't he an archfiend?" I asked.

"He's not as, shall we say, ambitious, as some of us. He's content with his single city."

"I said, we're closed," the vampire repeated. "Get lost."

Gervais raised his eyebrows at me.

"Fine." I used my power to pick up a small piece of cement, and threw it at him. It struck the vamp between the eyes, knocking him from his perch.

"This should be fun," Gervais said, reaching down and finding his dagger. Rose hopped out of the car, already armed.

"What's going on?"

I reached out and took hold of the wooden gate, pulling it and breaking it into splinters that exploded to either side of us. I could see the junk behind it now: stacks of cars both crushed and whole, mounds of scrap metal and engine and wires. It was arranged in a chaotic pattern, organized to prevent a quick rush into the center of the yard.

I started moving in.

They started shooting at us.

"Guns?" I said, as the pops echoed in the night, the bullets whizzing past, or digging into the dirt around us. I looked back and saw Rose duck behind the car, covering her head to keep from being hit while bullets pinged against it and shattered the windshield. "You could have warned me."

"I didn't know," he said, dashing away, towards a pile of junkers to the right. I could see the light of muzzle flashes coming from there. More gunfire was pouring in from the left.

Only for a second. I threw out the energy, pushing the stack of cars over, crushing the vampire beneath it.

The shots stopped from the right as well, Gervais having reached the demon and put him down. He rose from the position, firing back at another stack.

A bullet hit me in the leg. Another in the chest. I cursed and pushed them out, healing at the same time I got the spatha to my hand. I leaped forward, landing on the stack of cars and tumbling over. They had been arranged so that the open space was a nest in the center of a square of junk, and four vampires all turned as I came down, trying to get their weapons trained on me. Enough bullets would slow me down long enough to lose my head.

I ducked low, sweeping the sword across, making deep gashes into two of their legs with the blessed side. The afflicted vampires stopped aiming and began to scream, their wounds hissing and steaming. The other two dropped the guns and jumped at me, claws and teeth bared.

I punched one in the face, rocking him back into the cars, turned and grabbed the other by the neck, throwing him into the wall. The first bounced back up, only to impale himself on the sword. The second managed to get his claws on me, scraping through my shirt and drawing a line of blood.

Everything paused for a second, while he waited to see the black lines of poison spread from the wound. When it vanished instead, he put up his hands.

Toughness and power. I cut off his head.

I leaped to the top of the stack, catching another bullet in my thigh for the effort. I had passed the first row of cars, and from up here I could see there were three more before we would reach an aluminum barn in the center. I looked back for Gervais, finding him and Rose crouched under cover, returning fire. I didn't know how well Lucifer had protected him from normal projectiles, but he didn't seem too keen on being blasted.

I jumped from one stack to the next, coming down on the shooters and ending their lives, before hopping back up and heading for another. I was nearly done with the second row when the doors to the barn opened, and a man and woman walked out.

The woman shifted, her body morphing and growing into the massive form of a Great Were. The man found me, and then launched a heavy blast of hellfire my way. I jumped backwards, coming down behind the cars even as they were turned to molten slag. I made my way back to Rose and Gervais.

Espanto was starting to take things a little more seriously.

"He's got a Great Were," I said.

"Oh, did I forget to mention that?" Gervais replied with a grin.

I heard it coming, the snarling and scraping moving at speed through the garbage. Great Weres were the most physically strong and agile demons on Earth, their strength borne of the gift of power bestowed on them from a higher order demon. They were vulnerable to scripture like any Hell spawn, but that was only useful if you could hit them hard enough to pierce their thick hides.

The Were barreled around the corner, planting claws off the cars to change direction and launch itself towards us. Rose and Gervais opened fire at her massive, fourteen foot frame, even as I pulled a car from our right and slammed it into the creature. She tumbled to the side, the shell of the car landing on top of her. She kicked it away and started to roll back to her feet.

I hadn't forgotten the other one, the fiend who had shot the hellfire at me. I spun, pushing the dry ground outward around us, lifting up dust and debris and sending it out like a sandstorm, using it to give us cover. Rose and Gervais opened fire through it, and I heard the Were yelp as she was peppered with bullets. They would only slow her down for a second or two.

"Get out of here," I said to Rose, pointing to the window of a car, aiming her towards the center of one of the nests. She got up and ran to it, climbing in, with Gervais right behind.

They had just cleared the space when the Great Were pounced into the middle of the maelstrom.

Her claws almost tore me in half. I fell backwards, pulling strength to my limbs just in time to catch the follow up blow and throw her back again. I saw a shape in the dirt and dust, and then the fiend appeared inside my circle, his hand coming up to burn me in hellfire.

I stopped the tornado and dove to the right, avoiding the flames, rolling to my feet, and rushing him. I heard the Were behind me, could feel her claws scraping at my leg as she tried to stop me. The wound burned from the poison, and I didn't stop to heal it. I dove ahead, hoping that the fiend didn't want to risk burning his accomplice at my back.

He didn't. He sidestepped and backpedaled, trying to avoid my attack. He was too slow. I caught his neck in my hand and drove him backwards to the ground, coming down on top of him.

"Wait," he said, his voice strained by my constriction of his airway. He wasn't talking to me. He was talking to the Were.

I looked back. She shifted again, returning to her human form. She stood completely still, her angry eyes watching me.

"You're him, aren't you?" the fiend said. "The diuscrucis."

I nodded. "I need to see Espanto."

"You're looking at him."

CHAPTER THIRTY-SEVEN

I LET GO OF HIS throat, and moved off him so he could get to his feet. He smiled as he pulled himself up, rubbing his neck with his hand.

"You're one tough hombre," he said. "You killed what? Twenty of my vampires? Alyx, how many ran away?"

"Two," the Great Were answered. "I'll get them later."

"You'll get them now. Make sure it hurts."

She smiled, the smile turning into a snout full of long, razor teeth. She turned and bounded off, back towards the center of the junkyard. I heard the screams when she found the deserters.

"You aren't here alone," Espanto said, pointing off towards where Rose and Gervais were hiding. "I hadn't heard anything about you keeping servants." He had a wide, bright grin. "Outside of the news that you were back to killing demons, I hadn't heard anything much about you at all the last couple of years. I take it you didn't come to off me?"

I turned back to him. I had been too busy trying not get killed to get a good look. He was short and stocky, with black hair, dark olive skin, and a square face. He was wearing a pink dress shirt rolled to his elbows, grey suit pants, and italian leather shoes. The demonic runes inked into his arms were smoldering like a dying fire.

"No. I didn't come to off you. And they aren't servants. They're my allies. Rose, Peter, you can come out."

They came out through the stack of cars. Gervais was back in his Peter form.

"You don't look Divine," Espanto said.

"They don't smell Divine either." Alyx padded back around the corner, her voice raspy and soft despite her monstrous appearance. She returned to human form a moment later.

"Not Divine," I said. "Human."

"Nicht Creidem, human?" Espanto asked.

"No, just human," Rose said.

"Hmm…" The fiend looked away from them, no longer interested. "Alyx, meet Landon. Landon, this is my wife, Alyx."

He didn't introduce Rose or Gervais. Toughness, and power. As far as he was concerned, humans didn't have any of either, and weren't worthy of his attention. Valerix might have called them 'sheep'. She had still acknowledged they existed.

"A pleasure," Alyx said. She was a tiny thing, athletic and toned. She was wearing a pair of skintight short shorts and a strapless black tunic. Her features spoke to her Vietnamese origins, and between that and her name I had a feeling she had been born a member of Ulnyx's pack. She looked to be eighteen or nineteen, which in were years meant she was closer to seventy or eighty.

For a demon to have a single partner was rare. For a were, especially a Great Were, to take a mate outside of their kind was rarer. For them to consider themselves committed as husband and wife was unheard of. Was that why Izak had been wary? There was something odd about Espanto. He didn't seem… evil… enough. Was it the result of finding some kind of love? Or was it something else?

Espanto reached up and put his arm around my back like we were old friends. "Why don't you come inside? You can tell me what you wanted to see me about. Although, I have an idea."

"You do?"

"I think so. We can discuss it inside."

He led us through the yard to the large barn. A were changeling came out of the door as he approached, holding a silver tray in his arms.

"Your shoes," he said in a meek voice.

Espanto started pulling his italian leathers from his feet. "If you don't mind. I like to keep a clean house."

Alyx was already barefoot. I guess she got a pass on the rule. I wasn't about to give up my boots, so I gave them a push, watching the dirt and dust spread away in a puff. I did the same for Rose and Gervais.

"Cute trick," Espanto said. "After you." He waved me in, not waiting for the rest of the group. I heard Rose mumble something in the background.

The inside of the barn had been converted to a living space, with walls that sectioned off different rooms, and a loft that appeared to overlook most of it. The entryway was purely defensive, an open space with a good line of sight from the doorways that fed from it, as well as from above. Besides the loft, I also noticed a catwalk running the perimeter of the rooftop. I could picture Alyx up there, stalking invaders.

"Strange days," Espanto said, leading me through the entryway, through a short corridor, and into the adjoining room. It was a large game room. Stand up video game machines, billiards, pinball. Under any other circumstances, I would have squee-d like a little girl and checked out the classic Pac-man box in the corner. "I had a feeling you would be involved in this. I didn't expect you to show up at my door."

"I wasn't planning on showing up at your door."

A vampire attendant came over to us, carrying a tray with three glasses of water.

"Drink?" he said. He took his and downed it. Picked up another and handed it back to Alyx.

I took mine and turned back to Rose and Peter. "You guys thirsty."

"No," Gervais said. I could tell he was amused by the whole thing.

"Yes, thank you," Rose said.

"I didn't offer it to them," Espanto said, taking it from my hand before I could give it to her.

"These are my companions. A problem with them is a problem with me."

The demon laughed. "I've got this intuition. It's helped me go from being a lowly fiend, fresh out of Hell, to controlling all of Juarez. I could have more if I wanted it. The archfiend, he's nothing to me. Weak. My army could destroy him in a blink. I don't though. You know why?"

"No."

"Intuition. A feeling that gaining too much, too soon, is bad for my health. It's bad for my long-term future. You're probably wondering what that has to do with you. I don't want to have a problem with you. My intuition tells me that you're here because you need something from me. And when you need something from someone, well then that person holds the cards, and you tend to not want to piss them off. Am I right?"

He was right. I nodded.

"So, you'll have to accept that I'm at least being gracious enough to allow your 'companions' into my home, and be satisfied with that." He handed me the water and stared at me.

Gervais had to be loving this. I drank the water and put the glass back on the tray. We kept walking.

There were other servants in the house, mainly vampires, both male and female. They were all naked, all completely shaven, their bodies bald. They wiped down the furniture, they swept the floors, they did everything they could to keep the place from collecting even a single spec of dust.

Espanto ignored them, even though they would stop what they were doing and drop to their knees as we passed. He kept us moving through the rooms in the barn, the path forcing us to spiral around towards the center. I was sure the demon had some better path through, a secret door here and there that he didn't want me to know about, just as I was sure he had a stock of 'sheep' somewhere in the barn that he used to feed all of these servants, as well as the crew he had lost outside.

"I've been hearing things for the last few weeks," Espanto said while we moved. "Entire nests of vampires getting wiped out. The angels having a new weapon. I tried to get in touch with Valerix about it, because our territories are adjacent. She was tight lipped about the whole thing, which hurt my feelings after everything the three of us have shared together." He glanced back at Alyx, who only smiled again. "I know her well enough to know that there was something she wasn't telling me, although she did give me one free bit of advice." He reached another door and pushed it open. "Protect yourself."

As I entered, I realized what he meant about having an idea. The outer part of the barn was a cover, a disguise for the demon's true home, a place to tend his herd and visit with the lessors who came for an audience. Here in the center was a cement floor, at the middle of which was what looked to me like the entrance to a fallout shelter, its cement frame rising up out of the ground, two large metal doors leading into the depths. All of it - the frame, the doors, and the floor - was covered in runes. The same runes that had decorated Valerix's mansion. Protection from angels.

Protection from the Fists.

CHAPTER THIRTY-EIGHT

"You know," I said.

"Valerix is dead, isn't she?" he asked.

He led us to the door. It began to open as we neared, the rattle of the chains and whining of the machine that worked it echoing in the room.

"She is. Killed by a Fist."

"Fist? Is that what they're calling those things?"

The doors opened enough for us to go through. Espanto led us into a long tunnel that dove deeper into the earth. The door closed behind us, leaving us in pitch black.

"Lights?" I asked.

"You can't see?" Espanto replied.

The demons would have no trouble seeing without light. I was faking my blindness for Rose's sake.

"Afraid not."

If they wanted to attack me, I gave them the perfect invitation. Instead, a row of dim light filled the room.

"Thank you," I said.

We cleared the corridor, spilling out into another living area. It was as sterile as the first, though the servants had already been ordered to leave us in privacy. We took positions on the available couches. This time, Rose stayed close to me.

"There was another attack yesterday. An archfiend in Russia."

"Darya?" I asked.

"Yes. She and all of her followers. They completely cleansed Moscow in less than an hour."

That was the hit to the balance I had felt. "Do you know how many Fists were there?"

Espanto walked over to a cabinet and pulled it open. Bottles of alcohol lined the shelves, along with a few unmarked containers that I knew held more macabre concoctions. "Drink?"

"No." I didn't make the mistake of asking Rose and Gervais again. It wasn't worth making the demon angry. Not yet, anyway.

He took out two glasses and poured a bit of bourbon for himself and Alyx. "I have demons monitoring every channel I know of for communications. We're still sorting through it, but my early estimate is six or seven. It could be more. I doubt it's less." He came back and handed Alyx the drink, settling down next to her.

Six or seven? I had enough trouble with one. I fought to keep my sudden panic from showing. The archangels had commanded Adam to find a way to defeat me, and to defeat the demons. Somehow, he had discovered Matthias Zheng. Somehow, he had succeeded.

"You're struggling to fight them, aren't you?" Espanto asked.

"Not as much as the demons are, but yes."

"As I guessed. Otherwise, you would be there, and not here. Perhaps you're regretting spending the last two years killing demons?"

"I must lack your intuition. I do what I have to do."

He laughed and took a sip. "Here is what I see, diuscrucis. I see the angels winning this war. I see the Rapture coming to pass. I see the demons that are left overrunning this world, enslaving man and devouring one another. I also see you dead."

He said it as a matter of fact. As far as he was concerned, the fight was already over.

"So what are my options?" he continued. "I'm safe in here, beneath the runes and the earth. I've already removed the tongues of my servants, to ensure they can't betray me to the Heavenly host as I imagine Valerix's minions did. I have enough stock to survive many, many years of ignorance. To spend it with my beloved in peace."

"Hiding? That doesn't sound very ambitious."

"Buying time. To see how the whole thing plays out. Which demon will emerge the strongest? We do not die, and patience is an easy practice to master when you have what you want the most." He patted his wife's leg.

"Your goal is to be second fiddle?" I asked.

"My goal is to be comfortable." He finished his drink and placed his glass very carefully on a nearby table, checking it first to make sure it wouldn't leave a spot. "I'm comfortable here. The angels can't touch me. Tell me why you came, diuscrucis. Tell me what you need from me, a lowly fiend. Let us be clear that regardless of what it is, my price will be exponentially high."

He was confident and smug. I wanted nothing more than to grind him into the floor, and mess up his painstakingly flawless environment with his blood and ash. A demon who wasn't actively interested in gaining power was the most dangerous of all.

"I need transport through a rift. I need reinforcements. I know where the Fists are being made. I know where to find their creator."

He laughed again. "You aim to stop them? I thought maybe you needed weapons, or perhaps information. That is something I would be willing to trade. Why would you think I would ever help you keep your precious balance?"

I glanced over at Gervais. His eyes danced away. Did he know Espanto would react this way? Or had he given me the only option he knew of? It would have been so much easier if I could trust him.

"You want the angels to win?" I asked.

"Someone is going to, sooner or later. Why not now? In the end, it's all the same to me. No, you have nothing I want, nothing you can provide me that is valuable enough for me to help you with this. I've decided."

He stood up, so I stood up. I didn't tell him that much about the situation. I didn't want to give him any more leverage over me. He didn't understand how important his assistance was. That he was even willing to dismiss me so readily... he was confident in his power. A fiend and a Great Were against me and my humans. He wasn't even counting them.

"I'll walk you out," he said. "I'm sorry you came all the way here for nothing."

I looked back at Rose and then over to Gervais. They knew the gravity. I could see them both tense.

"Why would you think I would waste my time coming here, and then walk away because you decided?" I asked. I knew one way I could get his help.

The runes on his arms flared in response. "Don't make me dirty my home."

Alyx gained her feet, baring her human teeth, ready to make the change. "You've been dismissed. Best be on your way."

"I don't think you understand what I'm asking you for," I said. They were so focused on me, so worried about my ability to fight them, they didn't even notice when Rose and Gervais got to their feet.

"I do," Espanto said. "And I said no."

He was getting angry. He was about to get even angrier.

Rose grabbed Alyx from behind and put her knife to her throat. Gervais took the fiend and did the same. The Great Were was immensely powerful in monster form, and she was still stronger than normal in human form. The difference was that her throat would be much easier to slit.

"What the hell do you think you're doing?" Espanto said. He

squirmed against Gervais' grip, finding the demon was stronger than he expected.

He morphed from his Peter form. "Hello, Espanto."

The fiend stopped struggling and turned his head, just enough to see his captor. "Gervais?"

"I bet your intuition didn't see that one coming. You should pay more attention to your enemies, regardless of their supposed origin."

Alyx growled, and found the knife pressed tighter against her neck for it.

"Don't," Rose said. "I'll take your head off before you can change."

"You're going to power the rift for me," I said. "I need to get to China, and I need to get there now."

Rose and Gervais kept a tight grip on the two demons, while they led us deeper down into the underground facility. More than once they had to order aside servants as they appeared in the long cement corridors and saw their masters held hostage. I could tell by Espanto's strained voice how embarrassed he was. How much the situation pained him.

I didn't doubt he would kill every one of those servants once he was free, rather than live knowing what they had seen.

The rift was in a small room behind what looked like an ops center, filled with workstations and monitors, and manned by a number of still unclothed and bald demons. They were monitoring communication channels - phone services, internet packets, satellite feeds. They were also monitoring the demon's interests, tracking the drug dealers and whores, the Turned and the vamps. It looked like a sophisticated operation. The work of someone who knew that knowledge was power, and did his best to command as much of it as he could.

It was how he had known about Valerix, and about Russia, and probably a lot more than he had revealed. Given more time, I would have liked to find out how much.

"Let him go," I said to Gervais, once we were at the rift.

He relaxed his grip and pushed the fiend forward. Immediately, the runes on Espanto's arms began to flare, his eyes turning into empty black orbs.

"Don't even think about it," Rose said, pulling the knife tighter against Alyx's throat. The fiend paused.

"Damn you to hell, diuscrucis," he said. He went to the ring of stones that formed the outline of the rift, and began filling in the missing runes.

"That's what you get for falling in love," Gervais said. "A foolish emotion."

"Shut up," I said.

It only took the fiend a few minutes to wire up the rift. He knelt at one of the stones and began feeding his power into it. Fiends that were strong enough to activate rifts were incredibly rare. It was a privilege normally reserved for the most powerful demons.

It came to life, flaring into a ring of flames that illuminated the small room.

"There. It's done. Let her go."

Rose looked at me. I shook my head. "Sorry, I can't do that. Alyx is coming with us, to make sure you made the connection to the right place. If you did, she lives. If you didn't-"

"It goes to China. The closest rift is in Kowloon." His voice was strained, hinting at desperation.

I'd never seen a demon so upset. He stood at the edge of the circle, his face sweating, his hands clenched in fists. I was sure making a mortal enemy of Espanto wasn't the best idea, and I might have killed him and been done with it if I hadn't needed Alyx. A mortal couldn't travel a rift without being in contact with a demon. They would be ripped apart by the power, and Gervais' nature made me unsure if he was qualified to act as the conduit.

"Ladies first," I said, motioning to the Great Were.

They moved to the edge of the rift.

I put my hand on Rose's shoulder. "You're going to feel a little dizzy when you come out. Don't lose your grip."

She set her jaw and nodded. Then they stepped through.

"If you hurt her-" Espanto said.

"I'm not going to hurt her. I told you I needed transport and reinforcements. I'd say a Great Were is a quality reinforcement. It's not personal, Espanto. You know I can't let the angels win."

He stared at me, his eyes betraying his rage.

"Too-da-loo," Gervais said.

He stepped into the rift.

I followed after.

CHAPTER THIRTY-NINE

ONE FOOT WAS IN MEXICO, the other was in Kowloon. That was how transport rifts worked, creating a connection between our world and Hell and back again that made the distance negligible.

Rose was on the other side with Alyx. She was pale and sweating, but she managed to keep the knife pressed against the demon's throat.

"You can let her go," I said.

Alyx's hand snapped up and caught Rose's forearm, while she used her other arm to elbow her in the gut. I could see Rose's muscles flex as she tried to pull the knife into the demon's throat, but she was stronger than I had guessed. She twisted around and got Rose to drop the blade, positioning herself behind and holding Rose's arm tight against her back. A single finger elongated into a claw, pressed against her throat.

The Great Were looked over at the rift, and then at me. I was static. Disarmed. Gervais chuckled next to me.

"You really thought a human could overpower her?" he said.

I looked over at him, momentarily confused. Then Alyx took her hand away and shoved Rose into my arms.

"He means, I wanted to come," she said. She knelt down at the still burning rift, shifting her hand into a paw and pulling one of the flaming stones away. The smell of singed hair and flesh rose from it. The rift went out.

"Why?" I asked.

Rose pulled herself from my grip, a look of disgust on her face. She had told me she felt overmatched, and I kept trying to convince myself she wasn't. Without the tattoos and artifacts and upbringing of the Nicht Creidem, could any mortal hope to fight the Divine? Was I deluding myself because I didn't want to accept that my role as the so-called 'Great Equalizer' was an eternal one?

"He says he loves me," she said. She unbuttoned her shorts and pulled them down, just enough that I could see the fiend's brand resting on her pelvis. "This is love? He controls me." She pulled her pants back up. "He took me from my pack when I was a child. He did things to me." A low growl formed in the back of her throat, even as she spoke. "He branded me, trained me to be his bodyguard, his assassin. He took me as his mate. I couldn't break free of him, not with the brand. I learned it was easier to comply, to play along. Every day I hoped that something would happen to free me from this. Every assignment I hoped that I would be killed. I never imagined that anyone would save me." A tear ran from her eye. A tear from a Great Were? "I've heard that Ulnyx fought with you."

"He did. He was my friend."

"He was my true alpha. We would have been mated when I was older, if Espanto hadn't taken me."

"He took you?"

"He sent his demons into the pack. A distraction. I was only a pup then. He came looking for us. A female for himself, a pair of males for Valerix. My mother tried to protect me. He killed her, took me through his rift, and branded me. I've had no freedom since, until now."

"Espanto couldn't have promoted you?"

"No. He doesn't have that much power. We did a few favors for Valerix, a number of years ago. She imbued me with the power, raised me to Great as payment."

"I'm not sure what to do with you now. I was going to try to compel you to fight for me by threatening to lead the angels back to Espanto and tearing the runes from his little hidey-hole. Obviously, that isn't going to work. I don't want to force you."

She licked the tears from her cheek with a long tongue. "I don't need to be compelled. Espanto's information network is unparalleled. I know what happened in Mumbai. I know most of the pack was killed there, helping you and Ulnyx. I know he was alpha when he died." She looked at me, her eyes going soft and big. "I know you were alpha before him."

It had been on a technicality, because the Great Were's soul had been trapped in mine. "I don't have any right to that title anymore."

"The title is yours. There is no more pack. What was left of us was absorbed or destroyed. Either way, you got me out of there. You're the closest thing I have to family. I'll stand by you."

It was a surprising twist, and for once it actually went in my favor. I looked over at Gervais, who was trying to hide a self-satisfied smirk. Had he known about Alyx's past? Had he guessed the way this would work out? Was he helping me for real? Or was there some other plot simmering beneath this one?

Either way, she was in truth still a slave to the demon. Freeing her from the brand meant cutting it from the fiend's body. Until then, only distance from him would protect her.

"I don't know if or when I'll be able to confront Espanto," I said. "Right now, I need as many powerful demons as possible to stay alive."

"It isn't my place to question you, Master," Alyx replied. Then her dark eyes sparkled. "Besides, he'll be coming after you. He'll want me back. Then he'll die."

If he came after me, one of us would. "Please don't call me 'Master'."

"That is what mates call their alpha," she said. "That is what I will call you."

I felt a knot in the pit of my stomach. Mates? I wasn't sure what I was getting myself into, but the way she said it, I could tell there wasn't a lot of room for debate. I would deal with that later. We still weren't in Shenzhen, and we'd already burned almost seven hours.

"So, does anyone here have any idea where we are?"

CHAPTER FORTY

THE RIFT WAS IN THE bottom of a butcher's shop, tucked into a back corner and hidden behind a false wall. Once we pushed it aside, we were let out into the basement proper - a cold storage area where racks of meats hung from the ceiling.

Some of it was human.

"I'm going to be sick," Rose said. She still hadn't completely recovered from the rift travel, and the sight of the skinned bodies was more than enough to push her to the edge. The heavy smell of meat didn't make it any easier.

"Just concentrate on walking," I said. "One foot after the other."

The place was obviously home to any number of demons. None of them were in the basement at the moment.

"Weres," Alyx said. "Mongrels. I can smell them. What time is it?"

"Here? Close to seven."

"They'll be out readying for the hunt. The meat down here is for emergencies. We prefer fresh."

"How can you eat people?" Rose said.

"How can you eat cow?" Alyx replied. "Or pigs, or deer. Rabbits, dogs, chickens. The were are children of Lucifer. We eat human meat because we cannot survive without the blood of God's creation. Why do you eat meat?"

Rose turned red, her jaw clenching, her sickness forgotten. "Are you comparing people to cows?"

"Humans are like cows. A food source to the superior species."

"Superior? You can't even survive without us, and you think-"

I stepped between them. "Rose. This isn't the time or place. Alyx, can you lead us out of here?"

"Yes, Master." She smiled at me and walked ahead.

"I don't like her," Rose said, to Gervais' amusement.

"Because of who she is, or what she is?" I said. "Not all demons are hopelessly cursed to being evil. It isn't her fault or her choice to need human blood to survive."

"You're just saying that because she makes those big puppy eyes at you."

"I'm saying that because we need any allies we can get. To keep the balance, you can't take a side of good or evil. You need to accept both for what they are. Weres aren't evil because they eat human flesh. That's basic self-preservation. Weres are evil when they rape, or murder for sport, or work for others to help them do other rotten deeds. Yes, the prevalent attitude among them is to do those things. Most do, not all, and they can change. Ulnyx changed."

I was tempted to ask her if she was just feeling jealous. I was sure I would get hit if I did.

"Just give her a chance," I said.

We followed Alyx out of the basement, through a rusted metal door and into a crowded street. The buildings here were high and tight, the atmosphere subdued. Lit signs littered the sides of the buildings in bright colors, the pending darkness promising an amazing sight once night finished falling.

I pulled my phone from my pocket, and waited for it to get a signal. Once it did, I hit up the internet for an idea of where we were, and how far we had to go.

Too far.

"It'll take another two hours by car," I said. "An hour and a half by train, not including waiting times. There has to be a better way."

"What about flying?" Rose asked. "Maybe we can get a helicopter. Hospitals usually have one."

"Do you know how to fly it?" Gervais said.

"No. Landon?"

"I don't even like to drive," I said.

"Any other bright ideas?" Alyx asked. Hadn't it been bad enough that Rose and Gervais were always bickering, without throwing an apparently catty Great Were into the mix?

I looked up the nearest hospital. It was only a few blocks away.

"Let's head over to Kowloon Hospital. Even if we can't get a chopper, we can take an ambulance. The lights and sirens can't hurt."

We moved through the crowd at top speed, crossing over the few blocks in a hurry. The hospital was a huge, white stone building, modern and clean. It looked like any other hospital around, and could have easily been sitting in the middle of New York.

"How are we going to find the pilot?" Gervais said. "I doubt he's just hanging out in the cockpit waiting for us to ask him for a ride."

Rose shook her head. "I'm so stupid. He probably is hanging out in the cockpit. It's an emergency helicopter. He needs to be ready to go."

I looked up towards the roof. "Maybe we should drive. If there are any angels around, Alyx's aura is going to draw them right to us."

"We can leave her here," Rose said.

"We can't. We need the firepower." I kept staring up at the roof, trying to decide what to do.

"It's too risky," Gervais said. "They won't be able to attack unless we hit them first. What they will have is plenty of time to warn the others. We need the element of surprise, or they're going to spirit Zheng away before we can get close."

"Okay," I said. "Let's find an ambulance. Alyx, can you scout the perimeter?"

"Of course, Master." She smiled, her entire face growing and changing as she did. Within moments the petite woman was replaced with the hulking form of the Great Were. She stepped forward and put her muzzle against my cheek, and then turned and bounded off, vanishing from sight in a dozen long strides.

"I'm not ashamed to admit I'm a little jealous of that," Gervais said, casting a sidelong glance at Rose. He was trying to fuel the fire.

"I'm going to take the high road," I said, pointing to the rooftop. "I'll be right back." I gathered my energy and pushed it out into the ground, using the force to launch myself into the air.

Like jumping from high places, leaping to them was something I had practiced over and over again. The roof was near the limits of my reach, and I came down only a foot or so from the edge.

I looked back, scanning the front of the hospital, searching for a ride from above. Then I turned and started running for the opposite side.

An angel landed in front of me.

"Who are you?" she asked. She had dark hair, fair skin, golden eyes. "Not the demon I sensed."

I didn't slow down, barreling right into her and knocking her to the ground. Her wings spread beneath her, trying to find leverage to push me off. If all I had were mortal strength, she could have done it easily.

"I'm sorry," I said, even as I found the stone with my free hand and summoned the dark sword. I couldn't risk her getting away and telling the others.

I plunged the blade into her heart.

I'd never managed to kill an angel without feeling an overwhelming sense of failure after. This time was no different. My heart wrenched, my gut tightened, and I stumbled back to my feet, pocketing the stone and moving ahead while the poison spread and the seraph writhed and died. I looked skyward for more of them.

It was clear.

I took a deep breath and worked to force the sadness from my soul, to focus on the task at hand. Would it get easier over time? Would I want it to?

I was running for the opposite side of the roof when I heard a howl from the front. I switched directions and looked down, finding the Great Were on her haunches next to Rose and Gervais.

"Which way?" I called down.

Alyx took a few steps to the left, and paused.

"I need you to carry Rose."

Rose looked up at me, horrified. Alyx looked back at Rose. Even from the distance, I could tell she didn't want to. Even so, she didn't argue. She circled back and scooped her up in a massive paw, dumping her on her back. Then she took off, Gervais racing behind her.

I followed along the rooftop, keeping an eye out for more angels. Alyx tore around the corner, blasting past bystanders who would have no idea what they had seen. I wondered what their brains would tell them she was?

The motor pool was behind a large, barbed wire fence. Alyx leaped it without slowing, shifting upright as she did and wrapping a hairy arm around Rose to keep her from falling off. I jumped from my own perch, pushing the energy out and landing gracefully next to them. Gervais joined us a few seconds later.

"I'm fast. Not that fast," he said.

"How was the ride?" I asked Rose.

Her hair was windblown, her face blanched. "I prefer cars."

"Then you're in luck."

There was an ambulance a dozen feet away. It wasn't locked, and the keys were already in the ignition.

"I guess they thought a fifteen foot fence was good enough security," Rose said.

"Yeah, and who wants to steal an ambulance, anyway?" I said with a smile, taking shotgun. Gervais and Alyx found their way into the back.

Rose got us moving, angling us around and towards the gate. I reached out with my power, pulling it aside as we sped through, leaving the security guard stationed there with wide eyes and confused expression. By the time he recovered, he would have forgotten he saw us in the first place.

"Did you see the look on his face?" Rose's laughter was almost enough to sooth the sudden unease I was feeling.

Almost.

CHAPTER FORTY-ONE

WE HIT THE SIRENS ONCE we were a couple of blocks from the hospital, using them to get through lights and push the traffic out of our path. It definitely made things faster, but it wasn't doing much for the dread I was starting to feel.

Seven hours. Eight by the time we got there.

We were going to be too late.

"Are you okay?" Rose asked.

I thought about lying to her, deciding against it. "No. I don't think we're going to make it."

"Why do you say that?"

"It took too long to get here. I should have time walked. Come alone."

"Yeah, that sounds like it would have been a great idea. How do you know you wouldn't have walked right into a trap? Have you considered that maybe the angels planted the intel about Taylor? That they wanted you to find it? I mean, they knew pretty fast that we had accessed it."

I hadn't considered that.

"You said you think Adam is controlling them," she continued. "What if Adam is only one of many? What if there are others? You could have gone in alone against who knows how many Fists."

"We could still be going in against who knows how many Fists."

"Yeah, but you aren't doing it alone. I might not be strong enough to fight them directly, but I can be pretty distracting when I need to." She put her hand to one of her breasts and lifted it up suggestively.

I laughed at that. "I don't think the angels or the Fists will fall for your sex appeal."

She laughed with me. "That's better. I don't think so either. I can be distracting in other ways. You also have Gervais, and Alyx. I don't have to like her to see how badass she is in that monster form."

I looked towards the back of the Ambulance. Alyx was laying down on one of the gurneys, looking oddly content. Gervais was sitting on the floor, his head down as though he were praying.

"We might die," I said.

"If this whole balance thing is what you say it is, if we die, a lot of people are going to die. I think in that case I'll be one of the lucky ones."

The statement gave me a new level of respect for Rose. "You were worried before about feeling overmatched. When I saw how easily Alyx overpowered you, I was worried too. Afraid that I'm going to get you killed. Afraid that regular mortals can never be strong enough to fight back against the Divine."

"You said the Nicht Creidem are mortal."

"Mostly, yeah."

"They fight back against the Divine."

"They spend more time hiding from them. Guerrilla warfare. Anyway, they've had thousands of years to learn."

"And you're worried after two days?"

I stared at her. She shifted her eyes between me and the road. I could feel my face turning red with embarrassment.

"Seriously, Landon. You're too intense. I mean, I know this job has pretty strict performance requirements, but you need to show a little patience. You're immortal. If it takes you thousands of years to get us on the right track, then it takes thousands of years. If you break a few sexy little eggs like me along the way, then that's what you need to do."

"You're okay with that?" I asked. "Being a broken egg?"

"I'd rather stay in one piece. I know what you're trying to do. I've already seen some of the sacrifices you've had to make. I've already had to make a few myself." She motioned back towards Gervais. "Second guessing yourself isn't going to get you anywhere. Worrying about my lifespan isn't going to get you anywhere. Us humans have free will, right? I decided to seek you out. I decided to sign on the dotted line, metaphorically speaking. I believe in your cause. I know Anita would have, too. I'm willing to die for it. I'm willing to die for you."

"I can't ask-"

"You aren't asking anything. My decision. Calling you 'Master', that's Alyx's decision. Being an asshole... well, I don't think Gervais can help himself. Do what you need to do. Let your allies be your allies. I might die, and you better be sad if I do. You have to go on. You have to keep fighting. Your dream will never be real if you try to force it. Work for it. Have patience."

"I don't want to be doing this forever. I don't want to end up like the Beast. I don't want this universe to end up like his universe."

"Forever is a long time. You need to know what you want and figure out how to get it, not pin it all on hope and get yourself all worked up for it to happen right this minute. It wasn't easy to spend two years searching for Anita's killer. It's even harder sitting in the same car with him. If I can do that, you can do this."

"Wow. Good pep talk," I said. In that moment, I really wanted to make up for missing that first kiss. Her words and attitude were inspiring.

Even if we were driving to our doom.

CHAPTER FORTY-TWO

WE MADE GREAT TIME, REACHING the center of the city a little over an hour after we'd arrived through the rift. Between the strong words and the heavy foot, I found myself getting more impressed and enamored of Rose by the minute.

Beautiful? Check. Confident? Check. Smart? Check. Courageous? Two checks for that. Good with guns and knives? I'd never considered that as part of what made someone attractive before, but she nailed that one, too. All things considered, I was struggling to find something about her that wouldn't hit every mark on the attractiveness scale.

There *was* one thing.

She was mortal.

No matter what happened to us here and now, and no matter what happened to us in the future, if she lived she would age, and then she would die. If I fell for her, if I let myself fall for her, I was only setting myself up for heartbreak sooner or later. I'd just gone through it, and it had taken me two years to work through those emotions.

Of course, that was assuming she was even interested in me like that. Yes, she'd expressed a willingness to have sex, but her views on that were a lot more open than mine. She saw it as simple fun. I saw it as something a little more. Maybe too much more? Either way, there was a big chasm between friends with benefits and a committed relationship. I didn't believe in the first. She might not believe in the second, at least not with me.

Those were the thoughts that occupied me while we cruised through downtown Shenzhen, headed towards the industrial area near Deep Bay where the Taylor Heavy Industries factory was located. If we survived, if we stopped the Fists and the angels, Adam and Matthias Zheng, maybe then I would ask her what she thought. One thing I was glad to know is that she would be bluntly honest with me.

"Any sign of angels?" I said, turning back towards Alyx.

She raised her nose and took a few deep breaths. "Lingering scent, Master. They have been here, but not recently."

"Demons?"

"In a city this dense? For certain."

I expected as much. I also trusted they would stay far away from the hot aura that the Great Were was spilling out into our surroundings.

"How far to the factory?"

Rose glanced at my phone, resting on the dash. "Two miles."

"Let's ditch here, before the police wonder why a Kowloon Hospital ambulance is so far away from Kowloon."

Rose nodded and began searching for an open spot to leave our ride. She pulled to a stop a minute later, and we abandoned the vehicle.

"Alyx, stay alert. Tell me right away if anything Divine starts heading for us."

"Of course."

I was glad she dropped the 'Master' for once.

"Do you have a plan?" Rose asked.

I thought I did, until she had suggested that we might be walking into another trap. The angels weren't anywhere near as conniving and manipulative as the demons. That didn't mean they couldn't plan ahead.

"There's no way to know if Adam got out of the hole I left him in, or if it matters whether he did or not. We could be taking them completely by surprise, or they may have been planning for us to show up. That means we have a fifty-fifty shot at catching them off-guard. So, I think we should hedge our bets, and hit them from both directions."

"How would you suggest we do that?" Gervais said.

"Two teams. Gervais, you and Rose will do your best to sneak into the factory. If you need to kill people to take their form and get in, do it. Alyx and I will go straight for the front door. Hopefully we'll draw out whatever kind of defense they have, Fist or otherwise, and give you a chance to get in and find Zheng."

"What about the factory workers?" Rose asked.

"Try not to kill them. Don't let them stop you," I said. "I know you don't want to. This is bigger than they are." I looked at Gervais. "If you find Zheng, capture him. Do you understand?"

Gervais grinned. "Of course."

"I mean it. I'll kill you if you hurt him."

"I shall do my best, diuscrucis."

It wasn't much of a promise. I had to trust Rose would try to stop him if he decided not to listen to me.

"Remember, whatever shit we have on each other, whatever we think of one another, this is about stopping the angels from causing the Rapture. Everyone here has their own reasons for wanting to stop it, but the common thread is that we do want to stop it. We're one team right now, with one goal, agreed?"

Alyx moved up next to me and put her arm around my waist. "As you command."

"I'm with you," Rose said.

Gervais shrugged. "Eh. Why not?"

"I did this with Obi once. It worked out pretty well. Put your hand in." I put my right hand out. Rose put hers on top of mine.

Then Gervais. Then Alyx. She seemed confused by the action. "When I count to three, say 'break', and pull your hand away," I told her.

"As you say, Master."

I cringed at the word.

"Ready? One... two... three... BREAK!"

We pulled back our hands. Alyx smiled at the activity. So did Rose. Gervais looked nonplussed, and the people dividing around us in their subconscious desire to avoid the Great Were tilted their heads as if they heard our shout in a whisper on the air.

"Let's move out."

CHAPTER FORTY-THREE

My heart was pounding as I leaned against the side of a nearby building, and looked across a long, mostly empty parking lot and a few islands of trees to the front of the Taylor Heavy Industries factory. It was a long, wide, squat construct, made of dark stone with mirrored windows to hide whatever was happening inside. A stack near the center bellowed white smoke, while a number of trailers carrying shipping containers both came and went while I waited with Alyx for Gervais and Rose to make it around to the back.

"Master, why do you keep that human with you?"

I turned my head back to where Alyx was leaning against the wall, staying out of sight. "You mean Rose?"

"Yes. Is she your conquest?"

I almost laughed at the thought, except she was serious. "No. She's my friend."

"You are very powerful. Why do you want humans for friends?"

"You know I was born a human, don't you?"

She considered me for a minute. "When you were human, you were weak. Now, you're strong. How does one so strong find anything of interest in something so weak? Espanto was once human, too. He said the strong devour the weak. The strong use the weak. That is the way the universe was made. Ulnyx once said these things, too. I remember when all the pups in the pack would be gathered, and he would tell us of our duty, and our power."

"The strong need to protect the weak, because they can't protect themselves. Ulnyx figured that out in the end."

"I should protect humans?" She made a face, disgusted by the thought. "Protect my food?"

"It's a little more complicated than that. I know Espanto looked down on mortals, to the point that he barely saw them. People are capable of a lot more than he gave them credit for. Rose is a good example. She put a knife to your throat, after all."

"I could have killed her. I would have, if Espanto had Commanded."

"Exactly. She risked her life to help me. And because of that, you're free from Espanto."

She was silent for a moment.

"You don't want her for your conquest? I wouldn't be jealous. It is expected of the alpha, and Espanto had many such prizes. Even the archfiend Valerix shared our bed."

She caught me off-guard a second time. "What? No. Humans aren't a prize. They have feelings, desires, needs. Just like you do."

"Their feelings are inferior."

"That's Espanto talking. I'm telling you that isn't true. People deserve your respect."

She wasn't convinced. "I will try, Master. The idea is very strange to me." She lifted her head, her nostrils flaring.

"Angels?" I asked.

She leaned up to whisper in my ear, her warm breath tickling me. "The building is protected. I can't smell anything inside, or sense any Divine. I was smelling your sweat. You're nervous."

"This is very important to me." I glanced down at my phone, checking the time. They should be in position soon. "Are you ready to run?"

She smiled. "Yes, Master."

"You really don't have to call me 'Master'," I said again.

"You don't want me for a mate?" she asked.

I paused. The last thing I needed was to upset her when I needed her the most. "I didn't say that."

"Then why don't you want me to speak to you as a mate speaks to her alpha?"

Somehow, I doubted that Ulnyx's mate, Lylyx, had ever called him 'Master'. The way he had been smitten with her, I could picture the massive Great Were calling her 'Mistress'. Or maybe 'Boss'. I had to remind myself that Alyx's experience was that of a child in the pack. Her understanding of gender dynamics was bound to be a little skewed.

"Never mind," I said. I kept my eyes trained to the rear of the building. We'd picked up a prepaid phone on the way over, and Rose was going to send me a text when they were ready.

I closed my eyes and took a few deep breaths, focusing my energy, and trying to calm my nerves.

"Landon," Alyx said beside me.

I opened my eyes and turned towards her again. "Angels?" I asked for a second time.

She smiled. "No, Master. I… I wanted to thank you, for getting me away from Espanto. And I wanted to wish you good hunting."

At first, I wasn't sure what she meant. Then I noticed the look in her eyes, and the softness of her face. There were a lot of different sacrifices people made. When I leaned in and put my lips to hers, when I allowed her mouth to explore mine, it was to ensure her morale, and her ferocity. The closer to me she felt, the more intense she would be to protect me.

Not every sacrifice was difficult. Or painful.

She pulled away from me, her lips spreading in a wide smile. "I will not disappoint you."

"I know," I replied, returning her smile and trying to calm my heart again.

My phone vibrated against my leg.

"It's time."

She was shifting into her demon form before I said it. Once more, she took a moment to nuzzle my face, and then we both started running.

CHAPTER FORTY-FOUR

We were halfway across the parking lot when it started.

"The roof," Alyx growled next to me. I looked up, not seeing anything, trusting in her senses.

A moment later the bullets began digging into the pavement around us, the muzzles of rifles and the protected heads of a dozen Touched guards taking position to fire down on us.

They had been so quick to respond to our charge. Had my fears been realized? I scanned the sky for Adam, even as a bullet hit me in the leg and I tumbled to the ground, coming to rest behind a car

The bullets peppered it, shattering the glass and filling my ears with a sound like heavy rain. I pushed the bullet out and healed my leg, getting back to my feet at the same time Alyx reached me, changed back into her human form to fit behind the cover.

"Master?"

"I'm fine." Except, why were they using bullets? They couldn't kill us, only slow us down.

Something about that didn't sit right.

"We need to make a break for it, now," I said. "Don't wait for me." They wouldn't be able to fire down at us once we got to the entrance.

Alyx shifted again, bounding over the car in one pounce. I used my energy to push myself away, diving over the pounded metal towards the glass front of the factory.

I heard a scream, and saw the rocket launch from the rooftop. It exploded behind me, behind the car where we had been hiding only seconds before. The force pushed me forward even faster. I could see the explosion in the mirrored facade of the building. Red and blue flames. Holy flames.

They had missiles?

I hit the ground, rolling on my shoulder to my feet. Alyx was already near the entrance, waiting for me to catch up.

We were the diversion. Our part wasn't to go inside, not yet. It was to draw the defense out.

"Up," I shouted to her, pushing with the power, throwing myself towards the rooftop. I found the stone and brought the spatha to me.

The gunfire started again, a hail of slugs that whizzed past my ears and burned my scalp, that bit into my arms and torso and left me in burning pain, even as I landed in the midst of the shooters. My hamstring had been cut by one of the shots, and I hit the ground and stumbled, rolling away from the Touched towards the center of the building.

The gunfire didn't stop, it just changed directions. I threw my power out around me and curled into a ball, using it to stop most of the bullets, unable to get them all. I covered my head with my hands to protect it, and gritted through the assault.

A sharp growl told me Alyx had arrived. The Touched began to scream, the din of gunfire reduced with each wet smack and thud that reached my ears. I started to heal, the silver bullets dropping to the bloody ground around me.

Silence.

I felt her hot breath against my face, and then she was nuzzling me again. I got up and patted her head. "Thank you."

She responded with a soft whine.

The angels landed on the rooftop. They didn't need to wait for us to attack. By killing the Touched, we already had.

They were dressed in golden breastplates and helms above leather jerkins. They held blessed swords and shields. They looked out of place in the modern world. They looked even more out of place now that I had seen a blessed explosive decimate an entire demon army. They didn't speak, instead landing in a diamond formation and making a direct charge.

Alyx rose on her hinds beside me, spreading her arms and roaring at them. An angry Great Were was one of the most intimidating things I knew of, and it was no different for the seraphim. The charge slowed at her challenge, the less experienced soldiers losing some of their nerve at the sight and sound.

I brought the obsidian blade to bear and pushed myself forward, slamming into one of the angels, knocking him down and making a light cut along his cheek, which immediately began sprouting black lines of demonic poison. I wrenched his shield from his grip and used it to block an incoming attack, hopping to my feet and taking a defensive crouch.

When Ulnyx had fought, it was with pure brute power and rage, with a large measure of experience thrown in. The technique was all his own, all chaos and anger. Alyx had said Espanto trained her to be a bodyguard, and an assassin. She had the power of a Great Were. She had the form of a dancer.

It was an incredible thing to watch something that large move with such fluid efficiency. I had felt fortunate when I thought I had stolen her from Espanto, and could force her into the fight. Seeing her now, I wondered about the balance. It wasn't just about Heaven and Hell and Earth. The balance was in everything. It was everywhere, from this universe, to all universes.

Had it thrown me a bone?

She did a neat pirouette, catching one of the angels in her claw and using the momentum to throw him into the HVAC unit behind her, at the same time she swiveled down, deflected a sword stroke with her thick hide, and ran her claws through the breastplate like it was butter. She knocked a third seraph down and dove in, ripping her throat out with her massive jaws.

I was elated and crying at the same time, thankful to be winning the fight, horrified to be doing this to the angels. What would Josette have thought of me for this?

She would have told me to follow the path that God set out for me, even if it seemed contrary to His will. Even if I couldn't possibly understand how it was what He intended.

I deflected another sword, turned and sank the spatha into angel flesh. Another replaced him, her brown dreadlocks swinging wildly as she made a clumsy attack. I pushed it aside and cut off her head, feeling the wetness on my cheeks as she fell.

These weren't experienced soldiers, I realized. They were trying to slow us down. To keep us out of the building. There was no sign of any Fists, no sign of Adam. Did they even know where he was? The whole thing suddenly reeked of desperation.

There was a stairwell near the center of the rooftop. It was where the Touched must have exited from. The door was open. A round, silver, scripture covered ball was rolling towards us.

There were still angels on the rooftop. If the explosion tore them apart, they wouldn't be able to heal. Did they know the sacrifice they were about to make, or had it been made for them?

I threw my power out, launching myself towards Alyx. I was nowhere near strong or massive enough to move her, but I did get my arms around her neck. I threw out my energy again, at the same time the bomb exploded.

My wall of power blocked the shrapnel and heat. It caught the blast and we were battered backwards, thrown away from the explosion. The remaining angels were bathed in the fire, and the Holy Light, and as the force knocked us from the rooftop, I could see that while the fire was burning them, the Light was healing them.

That was my trick.

We tumbled in the air, my arms wrapped tight around Alyx's neck. She wrapped herself around me, huge muscled arms putting me in a protective shell. We hit the ground hard, or at least she did, landing on her back and absorbing the blow. The drop would have killed a human. She opened her arms and let me get to my feet, and then flipped herself over, sitting on her haunches next to me.

There were only a few angels left on the rooftop, and they must have been stunned, because they didn't follow.

"Inside," I said, pointing to the glass front of the building. She scooped me up again and leaped forward, turning her shoulder into the doors and smashing through the hardened glass as though it were paper. It shattered inward, leaving us in a large, open foyer with monitors on every wall. They were all playing the same clip about how Taylor Heavy Industries was making the world a better place through technology.

A better place for who?

There was a smaller door behind the reception area, and hallways that branched to either side. I could hear gunfire echoing from somewhere further in.

Alyx put me down and shifted back to human form. She motioned towards the door. "The human is this way."

We went through the door, through a space with some offices, a conference room, and a lunchroom, through the back and out onto the factory floor.

The room was huge. Conveyor belts sat still on massive machines that climbed up towards the roof, various gears and belts and robotic arms positioned at different intervals along the track. There were buckets of parts, monitoring stations, forklifts and packaging materials. A catwalk ran above it all, for easier visual checking.

I hadn't been in too many factories. I imagined that most of them probably looked similar to this. I couldn't tell what they were actually producing here, but I figured it probably wasn't Fists of God. If it was, they would have thousands of them by now.

The area was clear. There were no Touched guards hiding in the cracks and crevices along the assembly line, and the angels still hadn't followed us inside. I had been out of their sight long enough for them to forget about me, but they should have been able to guess something was up by the condition of the rooftop. Had they counted their dead and given up?

The gunfire had also stopped, so I wasn't sure where we should go. I pulled out my phone, ready to text Rose and get her position. No signal. If it hadn't been for Alyx, I might have spent hours trying to find them.

"This way, Master," she said. The size of the machinery had forced her back to human form to maneuver through smaller chasms.

"Do you sense any other Divine?" I asked.

"No. I smell others. They could be behind scripture."

"Thanks for breaking my fall." I could have stopped myself. I couldn't have caught her too.

She looked back at me, her eyes big and soft again. "Of course."

We navigated past the line, each passing second giving me more cause to worry. Were the angels regrouping? Was Adam on the way? Was Rose okay? I still didn't trust Gervais, and I hated having to send her off with him. His special talent was the only way for them to get in without drawing fire, though it had sounded like they hadn't gotten completely through the defense.

We reached the other end of the floor, almost half a mile away from where we'd started. Each step was making me more worried.

"Dead end," I said. The back of the building was a solid wall, with some small windows way up near the rooftop.

Alyx didn't answer. I turned back and saw her eyes were closed, her nose shifting and rocking. She stepped forward without looking, kneeling down at the wall and putting her hand to the floor. I followed with my eyes. There was nothing there, the joint between floor and wall was solid.

"Through here," she said.

"Where?"

"The whole wall. It is a glamour. A strong glamour. There is air coming out here. It's carrying their scent."

A glamour? I was highly resistant to Divine trickery. It would take a very, very powerful angel to place a glamour that could trip me up. I put my hand to the wall. It felt real enough. I slid it down to the floor where Alyx was pointing, closing my eyes and pushing my own power out. It helped me to find the seam.

I opened my eyes. Locating the beginning of the glamour allowed me to overcome the power, to see completely through it. Most of the wall was real, though it didn't have any windows and was clearly not the end of the building. In front of me was a massive elevator.

I found the button and hit it. The doors slid open. It was a freight elevator. A gigantic freight elevator, large enough to carry an entire semi if needed. It had a matching door on the other side, which I could only guess led to some route to the outside. I was sure this was how they were bringing the materials in. Maybe sending them back out, too. Scripture ran all along the ceiling, tiny lettering scratched into the metal, and glowing a soft blue that illuminated the space.

"I guess we go down," I said, stepping over the threshold.

Alyx followed behind me, crying out when she crossed over.

I whipped around to see what was happening. Her entire body was beginning to steam, the smell of frankincense growing more heavy with each second. She stood paralyzed in fear and pain.

I picked her up and carried her out. The steaming stopped at once, and I watched the burns on her skin begin to heal.

"You'll have to stay up here."

She shook her head. "You need me."

"I do. Up here. If anything tries to get in... don't let them."

She wasn't happy about it. Neither was I. "As you command, Master," she said at last. "Nothing will get past me."

I leaned in and kissed her on the cheek, and then went back into the elevator. I hit the button and waved to Alyx as the doors closed and I began to drop.

CHAPTER FORTY-FIVE

It took almost five minutes for the massive lift to settle at its base. I spent the entire time pacing the length, worrying about Alyx above and Rose below, worrying about Adam making an appearance, worrying about Gervais doing something stupid. I wanted allies, I wanted help. I wasn't sure I wanted the emotional roller coaster that was coming along with it.

The doors opened quietly, all things considered. They revealed a small loading dock, with a platform to carry stuff out onto the trailers, and wide twin doors behind it. There was nobody here, and the dock was empty. The smell of gasoline and oil lingered, and I was amazed that Alyx could pick out Rose's scent through it.

I wasn't going to go in softly. I vaulted forward and slammed the doors open with my power, bursting through ready to rip the place apart.

Everything was quiet. In front of me was a new assembly line, one made up of more machines, bigger and more complex then the first set. It reminded me of videos I had seen of automotive plants, though it seemed a bit less automated. There were stations spread around the floor, where it looked like some of the work could be done by hand, or where someone helped guide the system through its maneuvers.

The station closest to me was a tall rack, a crossbeam with a pair of hooks mounted on it, inside a gyroscopic type setup. Attached to the three swiveling arms were small appendages that looked like pens, with the smallest little hole in the center. I didn't need to be a scientist to guess what they were. Lasers. Etching lasers, able to burn the tiniest scripture into the metal suits that would be hanging from the hooks. There were no Fists in production at the moment. Looking around again, there was nobody here.

Where the hell had Rose and Gervais gone? Where had the gunfire come from? Hadn't anyone been down here?

I moved more slowly through the room, checking around the machinery, past computers that had gone dark, into every crevice and space I could find, looking for anything that might give me a clue. I kept expecting to stumble over a body. Rose's, a Touched. Despite myself, I kept hoping to find evidence of a dead angel, a hint of ash and dust to prove that something had happened down here. I just didn't understand how it could all be so clean.

I was losing hope in a hurry, my heart sinking to my gut like a stone. Rose and Gervais were gone. Matthias was gone. Had the demon double-crossed me? Had he somehow overcome the strength of the binding we had made? I didn't think it could be possible, and yet there was nothing else to explain it.

I turned back towards the doors, towards the elevator.

I heard a small beep.

It was the slightest sound, coming from one of the machines. I walked over to it, searching with my eyes. I wasn't sure exactly where the noise had come from. It was hard to track such a slight intonation.

The beep came again.

My eyes darted to a short belt that traveled through some kind of square box. I ran over to it, leaning in on the belt and peering into the box.

Rose's phone was resting in the center, the LED on the top a solid red. I pulled it out with my power, bringing it to my hand and turning the screen on.

It beeped again.

Low battery?

I stared at it. Why would the battery be low? What could drain it that fast? It wasn't an expensive phone, and we didn't have time to charge it all the way. Even so, we barely used it, and I doubted Rose was playing Candy Crush in the middle of our assault.

I navigated into the menu, and went to the photos. There was one. A video. I checked the battery. Five percent. I hit play and tracked to the end.

Rose had turned it around so it was recording her face. She was sweaty and scared, a bit of blood on her scalp. "...Bad timing. She's coming for me. I think they got Gervais already. Not Adam, another angel. Her aura is so bright, its blinding. Shit, she's coming."

The video stopped there. She must have turned off the phone and tossed it to keep it from being discovered. At least now I knew what happened to them. We came for Matthias, and they took her and possibly Gervais instead. I took a few deep breaths, trying to calm myself. The angels wouldn't kill them if they surrendered. They might try to use them as leverage. They might just hold them until they won and then let them go. More likely, they would force them to Confess, to find out what they knew. There was nothing there that they could use to help them, but I had seen with Josette how traumatizing the process could be.

I was going to go back to the elevator, when I realized that there was no way Rose and Gervais had taken that route. It was too slow and too loud to go unnoticed. There had to be another route.

I pushed my power out towards the walls, knowing what to look for now. I found the glamoured door easily, and I shoved it open. A spiral staircase led upwards, each metal rung of the ladder inscribed with scripture similar to the stuff in the elevator. More protection against demons. Gervais had gotten past it, which meant

Lucifer had cooked up a demon that could even fool the Heavenly power. If not for the imminent threat from the Fists, that thought might have been even more chilling.

I hopped the steps four at a time, getting to the surface in less than a minute. It opened up on what I imagined was the other side of the elevator, where the trucks would roll out. It was the rear of the building, where Rose and Gervais had probably come in. How had they gotten past the glamour?

I went to the elevator and forced the doors apart, first on the near side, and then on the far. Alyx was waiting on the other side. She turned and waved at me, her eyes bright.

"We need to get out of here," I said. "Meet me outside."

A heavy thump behind me shook the ground.

Another one followed it.

CHAPTER FORTY-SIX

ALYX DIDN'T WAIT TO MEET me outside. She shifted into her monster form, taking two steps back and charging forward, leaping the fifty foot chasm between us. The distance was easy. The scripture made it painful.

She landed right behind me, her skin sizzling and hissing, blood running from the wounds. She fell to her stomach, whining in pain, waiting to heal.

The bay doors twisted inward as the Fists charged through it, blades out, bolts reloaded. "Bad timing," Rose had said in the video.

I couldn't agree more.

The bay was empty, leaving nothing to distract or displace the armors with. They charged towards me in perfect sync, not wasting their bolts again, not leaving them open to be returned. I found the stone in my pocket and called on the spatha, glancing behind me at Alyx. She was struggling to get to her feet, the wounds healing slowly, but healing.

I threw the blade at the Fist on the left, letting it deflect it with its own, throwing out my power and catching it, pulling it back in behind the thing. It wasn't expecting the attack, and the blessed edge dug into its shoulder. It slowed and turned towards the blade, even as I pushed it back out and whipped it in, an invisible swordsman keeping one of them occupied. It took a lot of concentration for me to keep it going and get back to Alyx, wrapping my arm around her neck even as the second Fist bore down on us.

"Alyx, you need to get up. We need to get out of here." In her Great Were form she was bigger and faster than a horse.

Her eyes found me, and she growled and forced herself up, letting me hang onto her back while she gained her footing. The second Fist was a dozen feet away.

"I'll push it back, hit it hard and it should fall."

"Yes, Master," she said, bunching and springing towards it.

I pulled my energy back, the spatha with it, catching the sword in my hand and then throwing the power back out. It slammed into the Fist, slowing its forward momentum, getting its weight off balance. Alyx pounced at it, both fore and hind legs bunching and slamming it hard in the chest. Her claws skidded off with the sparkling of blue light, but the force remained. It started to fall backwards beneath the weight, and as it did she pushed off it, getting even more forward momentum.

The ground shook when the Fist hit the floor. The second one angled our way and took a chance with the bolts. I cast the power out and caught them, redirecting them over and down, into the fallen Fist. The missiles pierced its arms and legs, nailing it into the floor.

Then we were out of the bay, out into the evening sky, charging ahead.

"Stop," I said. "Stop!"

Alyx hit the brakes, her feet digging into the ground. I held on tight, trying not to get thrown by the maneuver.

Adam was standing in front of us.

"Landon," he said with a smile. There was no hint that he had ever been buried under tons of earth.

I turned my head back, looking for the Fists.

"They won't come. Not yet," he said. His metal hand was quiet. "I was hoping we could negotiate."

"Negotiate on what?" I asked. The pause gave me a moment to consider how I must look, perched on top of the Were, dark sword in hand. Heroic, or stupid?

"I have your human companions. Rose, and Peter, they said their names were."

"And?"

"We can stop this now. I know you've felt what the Fists can do. That was two of them. We have a dozen now, and there will be more once we can get the resources. You don't need to fight. Repent, and we'll let them go. No, even better. Repent, ask them to repent, and you'll all be afforded a place in Heaven. Even this one." He motioned to Alyx.

"This again?" I asked. Alyx growled in agreement.

"Come on, Landon. You know you can't fight them. Only two, and you ran away. It was smart to think they would protect me, it bought you time. Not enough time. You know how much I respect you, admire you. I'm trying to save you. You can't beat two, what are you going to do against twelve?"

"I'm going to do what I've always done," I said. "Keep trying. Keep fighting. I'm not afraid to die. I don't want to die a coward. I made a promise."

"I know. They want you dead, my friend. They want you gone. You know I'm only doing as My Lord commands."

"I know you're doing what you think you should. You can keep Rose and Peter. We'll settle this soon enough."

He shook his head. "I'm sorry, Landon. We'll settle this now." His wings spread wide, and he rocketed into the air, getting way out of my range.

"Alyx, go," I said, twisting around. The Fists appeared in the broken doorway of the factory. He'd stalled me long enough for one to get the other loose.

She growled her assent and launched forward again, covering the ground with incredible speed. I heard the thumping of the Fists behind us, breaking into a full run that allowed them to keep the pace. Like before, Alyx would tire eventually. The Fists wouldn't.

"Head back into the city," I said. "We need to lose them."

She turned and found the road, leaping a small berm and landing smoothly on the pavement, her claws leaving marks each time they hit the ground. The Fists followed behind, and I watched the sky, watched the aura of the First Inquisitor from two miles away. He was commanding them, that much I was sure of. Yet it was still only the two, and he said they had twelve. Did they need more angels to control the rest? Or were they assigned to other tasks? It wasn't like they needed more than two.

We hit the city proper, Alyx charging into traffic, leaping over and around cars that slowed and swerved without even knowing what they were slowing and swerving for. The Fists continued behind, though they were hampered by the human density, forced to trim their pace to avoid hurting anyone. Even if the people wanted to get out of the way, to avoid the Divine among them, they couldn't always do it. It was the obstacle we needed.

"That way," I said, aiming Alyx down a narrow alley.

There were all kinds of fruit stands and shoppers here, and we recreated movie cliche history, barreling through them and knocking everything aside, coming out the other end and racing across the next.

We nearly speeded headlong into one of the Fists.

"North," I yelled, holding on as Alyx planted her feet to turn.

I threw my power out between us and the Fist, catching the bolts it launched, at the same time she surged forward again. I was so used to being disguised, I had forgotten about Alyx's hot demonic aura. Her power was a blinding red beacon they could hone right in on. We needed to cover it up somehow.

We raced down the street. I could hear the Fists running behind us, falling back as we pushed through the mortal traffic. I winced when Alyx's foot came down on the roof of a car, causing her to slip and regain herself, sending the vehicle off into another, the driver surely wounded. Even so, I didn't ask her to slow. Not until we got further away.

"We need to go in there," I said, pointing at a tall, residential apartment building. She gave me a confused grunt, but made the adjustments to get us going that way. I vaulted from her back when we neared the revolving doors, and she shifted and came to a standing stop next to me.

"What are we doing?" she asked.

"He can follow your aura. We need to hide it."

"How?"

The aura was like a Divine radio signal. I'd learned to mess with it, to disguise it a long time ago. If we got close enough, I was hoping I could cover it over like a blanket, or deflect it like a piece of tin foil. If we could stay undiscovered long enough, Adam would forget about me, forget about us.

I grabbed her hand and pulled her into the building. The Fists were coming hard, but it would be a challenge for them to get into the small space without hurting anyone. They weren't made to fight in close quarters. That didn't mean Adam wouldn't send others in to try to draw us out.

We walked through the lobby, past the other people who were milling about on their way to here or there. We headed right to the elevator, crowding into the first one that opened heading upwards.

"Where are we going?" she asked again.

"Home," I replied.

"I don't understand."

"Trust me."

She smiled. "Yes, M-"

I put a finger to her lips. I didn't want her calling me that at all. I wasn't going to let her in public.

We got out on the seventeenth floor.

"Find us an empty one," I said. "Fast."

Alyx started running down the hallway, while I kept my eyes on the windows at either end of the corridor, waiting for angels to come bursting in. Would Adam send them, or would he wait me out? We both knew I couldn't hide in here forever.

"This one," Alyx said, facing us towards a door.

I reached out and unlocked it, shoving it open, pulling her in, and slamming it closed, almost at the same time the glass outside shattered. At least I had my answer.

I threw her down on a leather couch and brought myself down on top of her, putting my arms around her and holding her as tight as I could. I closed my eyes and focused on my energy, sending it out around me, running it around my limbs and connecting the spaces in between, acting like the tin foil I'd conceived. Would this work? I thought it would. I wasn't sure.

I felt Alyx's hands tighten around me, her breath against my neck, and then the wet softness of her lips against my flesh. She kissed my neck, pushing herself into me suggestively.

"Alyx," I whispered.

"Mmm… yes, Master?"

"This isn't what I had in mind." I kept my eyes closed, listening for the approach of the angels. I counted the seconds down. Thirty seconds to forget, thirty seconds more for good measure.

"You don't want your mate?" she asked.

Again her naiveté was forcing my hand. "I do. Just… not right now."

She kissed my cheek and pressed her face against mine. "They're right outside the door," she whispered.

I held my breath, waiting for them to open it. If they saw me, this game would be over.

"I never had this much fun with Espanto," she said, her breath hot against me. "He never let me go anywhere unless it was to kill something. I love you."

Did I hear that right? "What?"

"I love you."

I squeezed my eyes tighter. This wasn't happening. "Where are the angels?" The thirty seconds had come and gone. I wanted to be sure they had left.

She didn't answer right away.

"Alyx?"

"Do you love me?" she asked.

"Where are the angels?"

Silence.

"Alyx," I said, doing my best imitation of a snarl. "Tell me where they are, now."

She nuzzled her face against mine. "Gone, Master."

I gave myself permission to breathe, and let her go.

CHAPTER FORTY-SEVEN

"Alyx, I know that things are different for weres, and you don't have a lot of experience of the world outside of your pack and Espanto. I don't know you anywhere near well enough to love you."

We were still sitting on the couch. I don't know why I was even having the conversation. For some reason, I felt like I owed it to her after she helped me get away from the Fists.

"What is wrong with the way of the pack?" she asked.

"There's nothing wrong with it, if you're a werewolf. I'm not a werewolf."

"You're the diuscrucis. You're strong and powerful. You were also the alpha. You freed me from Espanto. You trusted me with your life. I love you."

She said it firmly, convinced that it was true. Maybe it was for her. She was a demon, and power was their most desired quality. It didn't help that she felt like she was supposed to be, deserved to be, mated to her pack's alpha. Ulnyx was gone. Lylyx was gone. The pack was scattered and in ruins. Why not?

"Okay, say that you do. I loved someone before. I know what it feels like. I don't want to hurt your feelings. I don't feel that for you. We only met a few hours ago." I really didn't want to hurt her feelings. I needed her power.

She was quiet. She put her head down, thinking. Then she looked at me. "Do you think you will ever love me?"

"I don't know. It takes time to find out if you can love someone or not."

"Would you not love me because I'm a demon?"

Izak was a demon. He had once been as evil as it came. Love had changed him. "No."

"Then why do you think you wouldn't love me?"

I wasn't sure what to say. Truth be told, I already had a bit of a soft spot for her. Maybe it was the way she nuzzled my neck, or the fact that she could bowl over a Fist of God. There was something cute about her innocent exuberance and demeanor, and I felt guilty that I could probably get used to, and grow endeared to, the way she called me 'Master'. At the same time, she was so inexperienced with the outside world. In some ways she wasn't much more than a child. It was hard to see past that part.

Then there was Rose.

Did I have to get all confused and emo about every girl I met?

"I'm not saying I never will or won't. I'm saying I don't know. I need to spend more time with you."

She smiled and leaned over, putting her head on my shoulder. "Okay."

I took another deep breath and reached for my phone.

"What are you doing?" Alyx asked.

"Phoning a friend. We need to find out where they took Rose and Gervais."

She tilted her head, confused. "I thought you said the angels could keep them?"

"I know what Confession does to angels. I can't imagine what it will do to a mortal. Also, wherever they took them… I bet that's where they took Matthias, too."

I found Alichino in the contact list and made the call.

"What is it?" the demon asked.

"The angels have Rose. I need to know where they took her."

"Landon? I haven't heard from you in two years, and what, you don't even say hello? Seriously. It's like you were raised by wolves."

That comment got a positive response from Alyx, who pushed her head harder against my shoulder.

"Alichino, shut up. She was taken by an angel, she said its aura was blinding. Also, I think they're moving the armors from the factory to another location."

I heard mumbling on the other end of the phone, and then some thumping and static.

"Signore," Dante said.

"Dante. Did you hear what I told Allie?"

"Yes. You said another location?"

"Yeah."

"It makes sense. The scripture on the metal is useless on its own. It requires an angel to give it Divine power and activate it. I have been traveling back and forth in order to help Alichino work out the requirements, based on our observations of the scripture. We haven't got it calculated yet, but it is quite a lot. More than a single angel can provide."

I knew what he was getting at. "A sanctuary."

"Yes. To power the scripture on the Fist, they would need to bring it to a sanctuary and bathe it in the light of Heaven."

"Okay, but they aren't flying them out. They had a loading bay, a whole setup to drive them."

"They likely can't carry them until they are activated. Ordinary metal is quite heavy, even for a seraph."

"So wherever they're going, it needs to be nearby. Where's the closest angel sanctuary?"

"I'm not aware of one in Shenzhen," Dante said. "I don't know all of their locations. They don't like to advertise, for obvious reasons."

"They would need a road," Alichino said, his voice muffled by his distance to the phone. "One that could bear the weight. I'll get on that."

"Ah, yes. The demon is correct. The Fists are very heavy. They must have added or reinforced a road. Please, signore, allow us a little time. We will discover the location."

Time was the last thing we had. There wasn't much choice.

"Okay. Wait! The angel."

"What about it?" Dante asked.

"Rose said its aura was blinding. I've been face to face with some powerful angels before. I never felt anything like that."

There was silence on the other end of the line. It wasn't a good sign.

"Dante?"

I heard him take a heaving breath. "I am hoping that it is not what I think it may be, signore."

"Just spit it out."

"It is possible that there may be an archangel involved."

I froze on the couch, feeling like my jaw was resting on the carpet. "Oh. Shit. I thought that was against the rules?"

"It normally is. If Lucifer knew about this, Hell would have already come to Earth. They must be moving about in secrecy."

"What if Heavenly light wasn't enough?" I said, the thought springing to the front of my mind.

"Excuse me, signore?"

"What if Heavenly light wasn't enough? The Fists, the bombs, the Holy flame, even the crazy powerful scripture we ran into in the factory? This kind of evolution doesn't just happen. What if the archangel is giving some of his own power over to make all this stuff work?"

There was another pause.

"Then you best put a stop to it," Dante said.

I hung up without saying goodbye, feeling my body shaking

from the implications. It was getting worse with every minute that swung by.

"Is it time to run?" Alyx asked.

"Not yet." I hit another name on my phone. The odds were fifty-fifty that she would answer.

It rang three times before she picked up. "Landon?" She sounded surprised. Considering I'd never called her before, it made sense.

"Elyse. Hey. Where are you?" I tried to be a little more polite than I had with Alichino.

"Cape Town. What's up?"

"How fast can you get to Shenzhen, China?"

"Not fast. It's probably about a twenty hour flight."

I tried to hide my disappointment. I was desperate for a little more backup. "You don't happen to have any quicker routes, do you?"

She laughed. "I take it you're in trouble?"

"We're all in trouble. It's a long story, but the bottom line is that the angels are kicking demon, and my, ass."

"I only have three rift stones. And retrieving one of them was the whole reason I came here."

"Do they do what I think they do?"

"Yes."

"There's a rift in Kowloon, about an hour drive from here. This is important enough to burn a stone on."

She didn't hesitate. She was a former Nicht Creidem. She knew the score. "I'll call you when I get to Shenzhen."

"Thanks, Elle. Oh, and watch out for weres when you come through."

"Got it. Thanks for the warning."

"Write this all down, so you don't forget." I could prevent people from forgetting me when I was near them. Phone calls? Not so much. Elyse was used to the small complication, and she retained the memory of when we had first coordinated the system.

"I'm already doing it. See you soon."

She hung up on me.

"Who is she?" Alyx asked. There as a slight hint of jealousy in her voice.

"A friend. She's going to help us."

"So what do we do now?"

"There's nothing to do but wait."

She smiled mischievously. "I can think of something else to do."

I wondered how many men would turn down two offers in one day. Or how many men would even turn down one offer in one day. At least I wouldn't have to worry about that with Elyse.

"Do you remember what I said about not knowing you very well?"

"Yes, Master." She blinked her big eyes, her mouth open and inviting. I could smell a change in her, that reminded me of Gervais and his pheromones. It probably worked great on other weres.

"Yeah. So… let's try to wait until I know you better and the mortal world isn't threatening to fall apart in the next twenty-four hours."

"As you command, Master." She backed away from me a couple of feet and made a face that left me feeling guilty for turning her down. It was intentional, manipulative. Despite her inexperience with people, she was still a demon.

I leaned back on the couch and closed my eyes, trying to take a minute to relax and recharge. I managed a couple of deep breaths before my gut wrenched again, the tickling pain causing me to groan.

"Landon?" Alyx said. She slid over, putting her arms around me. "What is it?"

The balance. Again. Adam wasn't about to let me slow him down.

He was moving forward with the angels' plan.

CHAPTER FORTY-EIGHT

Whatever he was doing, it was big enough to keep me unsettled the entire time we were waiting for Elyse. I leaned against the arm of the couch, feeling more desperate and more angry with each twist of my soul, with each shift of the needle. It would take the death of a lot of demons to throw the balance altogether. Weeks at the current pace.

Who knew if the current pace would last?

My phone rang.

"Elyse. Where are you?"

"I'm here. Shenzhen. Where are you?"

"Somewhere downtown. A big apartment building. I'm not sure what the address is. Just look for the bright hot aura of a Great Were."

"You're kidding."

"Not this time. I'm getting too desperate to kid."

"Okay. I'll be there in fifteen."

She ditched me again.

Alyx was laying across the couch, her eyes closed. She was snoring lightly, her mouth hanging open. She looked peaceful, content. I was sure she didn't understand the gravity of the situation. I wasn't pretty sure she wouldn't care, even if she did.

I watched her stomach rise and fall with her breath, watched her nose twitch, watched her hands and feet shake a little. What did weres dream about?

I didn't realize I was staring for so long, until her eyes snapped open. She didn't say anything to me, or pay me any mind. Instead, she hopped up onto her hands and feet, her eyes on the door. She was ready to pounce.

Someone knocked a few seconds later.

"Human," Alyx said. "A strange smell. Different."

"It's okay. It's Elyse. You can stand down."

She finally looked at me, her face violent and serious. It softened, and she smiled. "I saw you watching me." She fell backwards, putting her back against the arm of the sofa and pulling her knees up to her chest.

Of course she did. I could only guess what she thought about it. I reached out with my power and pulled the door open.

It was easy for me to forget sometimes how young Elyse actually was. She had the wisdom of years drilled into her by her father from the time she was born, and that kind of upbringing had brought her to carry herself with a confidence that was more akin to a two hundred year old angel than a twenty four year old mortal.

She was some part German, some part Japanese. Pale skin, almond eyes, short and lithe in a leather jacket and tight blue jeans. She had a dozen necklaces around her neck, rings on every finger, earrings, a nose ring, and I knew that underneath the clothing her entire body was tattooed and scarred in scripture and rune, an artistic mutilation to give her maximum protection against the Divine, protection that I hoped she would be able to pass on to Rose once she had time.

She wore a black do-rag over her scalp, hiding the mess of a scar her father had added to her forehead, and the bald head that refused to grow hair since the day he had done it.

She smiled when she saw me. "Landon. You still have my sword, right?"

I pulled the stone from my pocket and tossed it to her. "Of course. It wasn't worth having to deal with your wrath to risk losing it."

She caught the rock and walked over to me, reaching up so I could give her a massive hug. "It's been too long," she said.

After the Beast, after I'd finished mourning, I had sought Elyse out. She had made a lot of sacrifices to help me, and the loss of her father and the shunning by her family had left her pretty much alone. In a lot of ways, we were in a similar place at the time, and while I never talked to her about Charis and Clara, and all the crap that had spilled out to Rose, we had talked about a lot of other things. Mainly, about Heaven and Hell, good and evil, my place in the universe, and hers. It had taken a few weeks, but I won her over in the end.

Now, she was more like a sister to me. Closer than Obi in some ways, and not in others. Putting my arms around her, holding her close, feeling her warmth against me... only then did I realize how isolated I had become. Maybe I would live forever, but she wouldn't. Obi wouldn't.

"I'm sorry I've been so out of touch," I said, breaking the embrace. "I guess it's taken the threat of the Rapture to get me out of my funk."

"Apology accepted." She turned to Alyx. "Who's your friend?"

"Alyx, meet Elyse. Elyse, Alyx."

"Cool to meet you," Elyse said, holding out her hand.

Alyx sat on the couch, staring at it. Then she looked at me.

"Remember what I said about Rose? Same deal."

She looked uncomfortable, getting up and reaching out to take Elyse's hand. We would need to work on that.

"Nice to meet you," she said, quiet and meek. A quick shake, and she retreated to her spot. Elyse glanced over at me, confused.

"It's a long story," I said. "I have a different one for you first. You want something to drink? This isn't my place, but I'm sure they have water."

"No. Just let me sit for a few minutes. The demon I dragged through the rift clocked me pretty good when we got to the other side. My head is still spinning a little bit."

"I'm sure you gave better than you got."

"Of course."

She sat down on the couch, opposite Alyx. I could tell the Were was doing her best to not look like she was put out by the presence of a human.

I spent the next twenty minutes going over everything that had happened, from the moment Rose had shot me, which drew a nice laugh, to the conversation I had with Dante and Alichino. After that, I pulled out Rose's phone and used the last one percent of the battery to show her the video.

"That's your new friend?" she asked. "She's cute."

"She's sweaty and has blood on her face."

"Nothing that a shower wouldn't fix. I like her eyes."

"If we get her back alive I'll be sure to introduce you. She wants to fight, but she's out there naked right now."

"There are worse things-"

"Elle, can you be serious for a minute? She needs some trinkets, some tats, that kind of thing. I was going to talk to you about all this when it was over. I know you understand why I called you now instead."

She nodded. "This is what we talked about, isn't it? New recruits? If we survive this, and she's willing, I can start getting her ready. She doesn't have the Nicht Creidem bloodline, though. I don't know if she'll do what it takes to make this stuff work."

It took a small measure of Divine power for the runes and scripture to activate. The Nicht Creidem had been passing what they had amongst themselves via inbreeding for thousands of years. If Rose wanted it, she would have to drink angel and demon blood.

"We'll worry about that if we get to it."

"Right. I know you said this was important, but I wasn't exactly expecting to have to attack an angel sanctuary with an *archangel* inside it."

"Good, because attacking it would be stupid. We need to sneak in."

CHAPTER FORTY-NINE

MY PHONE RANG AGAIN TEN minutes later.

"Signore," Dante said. "I don't quite remember what we talked about, but I wrote a note to find an angelic sanctuary with new road construction to it, and to call you when I did."

"Do you have it?" I asked.

"Here, let me give the phone to Alichino."

The phone passed hands.

"Landon. It's been a long time. How are you?"

"I'll be better once you give me the location of the sanctuary."

He cackled and hissed. "Yeah. You always need something. No 'hello'. No pleasantries. It's like you were raised by wolves or something." I didn't know if he was just messing with me. They had the note, so he had to know we had talked already. He cackled a little more. "Yeah, so I went digging through permit applications and construction receipts. It was a pain in the ass because its all in Chinese, but you know, I'm good like that. Anyway, the place is called Ming Shan monastery. It's a really secluded place, a patch of private land sitting in the corner of a Chinese national park. Somehow, they got a permit to build a heavy road through the public trees and grass to connect it to the rest of the world. All of a sudden. After three thousand years."

That had to be the place. "Do you have any kind of intel about the site? Satellite images? Photos? Anything?"

"Nope. I asked Google. I asked Bing. I even asked freaking Jeeves. The place barely exists. Three thousand years."

"What about private satellites?"

"I tried the Pentagon, Chinese National Security, and the NSA. The NSA had some interesting stuff, but no satellite imagery." He cackled into the phone again.

I figured as much. "I don't suppose the monastery is owned by Taylor Enterprises?"

"Bingo, buddy. The permit application was signed by one Adam Taylor, C-E-O."

Adam Taylor? I'd never heard of him, but the shared first name with a certain cyborg seraph didn't skip my attention. "Text me the GPS coordinates."

"Doing it now. Here, I'm going to put Dante back on. Nice talking to you, D."

"Whoa, hang on. You have anything new on the head?"

"Oh, yeah. I totally forgot in all the excitement of reading thousands of lines of Chinese. Dante helped me with some more of the scripture on the inside, and it didn't make a lot of sense until we wrote down 'archangel' after I guess you talked to us last. The scripture is nothing that's been used in this realm before. It has some similarities though. The nearest we can figure, its some kind of force field or something."

"You mean like a wall, so demons can't get through even if they pierce the outer scripture?"

"Yeah, kind of. Except, it only works from the inside out."

That was strange. Very strange. I heard the phone shift users again.

"Signore. I hope we have been some help to you."

"You've been a lot of help. Thanks, Dante."

"Landon, before you go, I... I know things have been a bit strained between us. I want to apologize to you. So many things have happened, and it is my fault. Since the day I listened to Mr. Ross and brought you back to this world... none of it has gone the way I planned."

I wasn't sure why he was apologizing now. Was he sure I was going to fail? "Okay."

"I feel responsible for this, for you. Especially now that I am struggling to find my own balance, and recover what I lost. I just wanted you to know that I am sorry. If you need anything else, please consider me your humble servant."

I was quiet for a few breaths. It was hard for me to see the poet as a humble servant. Still, his apology was sincere. "Don't worry about it," I said at last.

I hung up before he could say anything else.

A few seconds later, the latitude and longitude of Ming Shan monastery popped up on my phone. I plugged it in and watched the dot settle on the map.

"I guess we're going in blind," I said, turning to Elyse.

"I guess we are."

Alyx got up off the couch and moved to my side.

"What is your command, Master?"

CHAPTER FIFTY

THE BIGGEST PROBLEM WITH ANGEL sanctuaries wasn't that they were filled with angels, because in all likelihood, it wasn't. Normally, they were manned by Touched monks and a small contingent of more elder seraphs, whose job was to guard the Heavenly Light, its primary purpose being used as what amounted to an elevator between Earth and Heaven. While more experienced angels didn't need it, the younger ones used the Light to help guide them between the worlds, meaning reinforcements were only seconds away. The Light had other properties too. It could heal the seraph, it could be used to force Confession, or apparently it could be used to power robots.

Worse, the altar that focused the Heavenly Light was behind heavily protected doors that could be sealed from the inside. I had stopped a demon attack on a sanctuary once. Now I needed to organize my own.

Not really an attack. What we needed was more like a Mission Impossible style break-in, an inception that would allow us to get in, find Rose and Gervais, find Matthias Zheng, avoid the archangel, and get the hell out. Once that was done, I would still need to do something about Adam and the Fists before they managed to tip the balance, and I was pinning a lot of hope on the idea that Zheng would tell me their weakness, either intentionally, or through less... polite... means.

We stole a cab to make the first leg of the journey, from downtown Shenzhen to the side of the single road that split the Plover Cove national park in two. It was a twenty mile hike from that position to the monastery, and we could have gotten much closer - even driven right up to the gates - if we weren't trying to keep Alyx out of the angels' attention until we needed to call on her. That, and driving to the gates was a little less sneaky than what I had in mind.

She wasn't happy when I told her she wouldn't be going in with Elyse and me. She protested the decision with a fierce and almost violent anger. Not because she was eager to kill angels, but because she felt an insanely powerful and irrational need to protect me. Knowing I was walking into danger and not being able to do anything about it caused her to curse, whine, tear up the apartment we had borrowed, and otherwise throw a fit worthy of a two year old. Elyse had watched the whole thing with an odd mix of amusement and fascination. I had gotten angry, and thrown Alyx to the ground, standing over her and barking orders.

I found that she wasn't the delicate flower she looked like, or that I had feared her to be, in her human form. She didn't skulk or pout or otherwise shrink up. She beamed at my dominance, and I realized I had only dug that hole even deeper.

"You know what to do," I said to her. We were in the middle of the forest surrounding the sanctuary, about half of a mile from the road we had discovered, a road that Alyx said still smelled of gasoline, rubber, and exhaust.

"Yes, Master. I will wait for your signal."

"Elyse?"

"I'm ready," she said. I had let her keep the spatha. It was hers anyway. She had given me a pair of nasty looking daggers in return. Normally it took time for a cursed edge to spread the wound through an angel, giving them a chance to heal themselves with holy water. According to Elyse, this particular cursed weapon would kill in seconds. I wasn't sure why she wanted to trade.

"Nervous?" I asked.

She smiled. "Very. This is what we're here for." She leaned in and gave me a short hug. "We can do this."

"Master? Might I wish you good hunting?"

There was no point in complicating things. I stepped towards Alyx, letting her wrap her arms around me, and lowering my head so she could kiss me.

"Don't let them catch you," I said. "No matter what happens. That's a command."

"Of course."

We left Alyx standing there, making our way through the trees and brush, covering the ground at a solid run. It was a long distance for Elyse, but she was so well-conditioned that she never slowed.

Ten miles.

We covered it in an hour.

We slowed when we got within a mile of the place. The growth was dense here, dense enough that we couldn't move without pushing through some leaves, or stepping on twigs, or otherwise making what would be a racket to anyone paying attention. We slowed down even more, careful where we placed our feet, being as gentle as we could. The foliage and darkness would let us get close without being seen. It might not let us get close without being heard.

We still hadn't gotten the actual sanctuary in sight when Elyse put up her hand to stop me. She motioned to our left, holding up one finger, and then four. She'd caught an aura, most likely a Touched sentry. She pointed to herself, and then back out.

I shook my head, motioning in the direction of the monastery. I didn't want to risk taking anyone out and having them be missed.

We kept creeping forward. Twice, I got a sharp pain in my soul, feeling another quick shift of the balance, the needle tilting ever closer to Heaven. When it happened, I paused and leaned down against the ground, or found purchase on a tree, and did everything I could to stay quiet.

The good news was that if Adam was out killing demons, he wasn't defending the sanctuary. It was as much as I could have hoped for.

We didn't so much find the monastery, as the monastery found us. One second, there were thick bushes and trees, branches heavy with leaves, and the next there was an old stone wall, coated in a thick moss that ran along the uneven stones that had been piled to make it. It was twelve feet tall, and I could see the scratches of faded scripture on the small bits that weren't hidden beneath the growth.

"This looks like the place," I whispered, putting my head against Elyse.

"I can sense a few weak auras on the other side. If there are angels in here, they're being muted."

"How else would an archangel hang out here on Earth without the demons knowing?"

"I'd feel better if we had some idea of the numbers."

"Numbers only matter if you get into a fight. Let's not get into a fight."

She smiled at that, turning to the wall and starting to scale it. She stayed tight up against it, muscles flexing, getting her head up to the top. I waited below while she scouted the landscape.

She dropped back down a minute later.

"Touched. Four of them. Swords across their backs. There's also a watch post near a tall iron gate, a tower with another Touched in it, keeping lookout. The gate is new, it looks like it was installed when they added the road. The road goes through a second inner gate, to the inside of the sanctuary. It's going to be tough to get there without being seen. Have you ever been to the Forbidden

Palace in Beijing?"

"Not yet. I've seen pictures."

"The monastery looks kind of like that, but a lot smaller. Traditional Chinese architecture is long and low, with an emphasis on symmetry, courtyards, and not a lot of vertical walls. I'm sure you've at least seen a samurai flick or two?"

"Yes."

"There you go."

"Okay, so how do we get in?"

"First, let's circle around back. That will get us out of view of the gate. Then I'll jump the wall and take out one of the sentries."

"I think they'll notice if we drop a guard."

Elyse pulled a glove from a pocket of her jeans. It was made of some kind of leather and covered in runes. "This will let me glamour myself to look like the guard. They won't know he's missing right away. I'll cover you while you get over the wall and into the main building, and keep the way out open for you."

"I wanted you to go inside with me. It would be a lot easier to stay unseen if I could sense them coming."

"I don't know how else to get you through unnoticed. If you want to try brute force, I'm still with you."

"No. We'll do it your way. Do you have anything on you that I might be able to use?"

She held up her hands to examine her rings. "This crap against your power? There's a reason I'm carrying so many, and it isn't because of my fashion sense."

I smiled at that. "Right. Let's go."

We circled around the outer wall, staying tight against it and keeping constant watch for any of the outer sentries to return, or any of the inner guards to decide to make a round on top of the stone barrier. The complex was larger than I had pictured it would be, much larger than the sanctuary I had been to in the Catskills. We chose stealth over speed, taking our time getting to the back, reaching it at the same time a light rain began to fall.

Elyse didn't say anything before she scaled the wall again, resting near the top, holding her weight with the tips of her toes and the strength of her arms. She glanced back at me once, rocked down, and then vaulted over.

I didn't hear her land on the other side. I pushed my power into my limbs and followed her track up the wall. I stuck my head up just in time to see her go up behind the guard, put one hand over his mouth, and use the other to cut his throat with a small cursed knife. She scooped him up over her shoulder and ran him back to the wall.

I reached out and used my power to pull, lifting the body up and over, dropping down and catching it on the other side. I lowered him silently to the ground, feeling a short wave of regret when his bloody throat came into view. It was never simple. It was never easy.

I moved back onto the wall, peering over. Elyse was standing near the center of the open patch of ground between the outer barrier and the inner sanctuary. A small haze shifted around her in the visage of the guard. The glamour. I was able to see through it. The Touched wouldn't be.

She scanned left and right, keeping her arm out and down, her palm facing outwards. I looked to the left and saw a second guard, making his way to the corner of the grounds and then spinning around and heading back. The moment he vanished from sight, she closed her hand into a fist.

I sprung from the wall, up and over, landing smoothly at a run, heading straight for her. She turned her fist and stuck her thumb out, pointing it at a heavy wooden door between a pair of scripture covered columns and putting up a finger. I kept running, not even looking at her, crossing the open space in a matter of seconds. I bent my legs slightly as I approached the other side, pushing off the ground and using the force to send me arcing into the air at a tight angle towards the slanted tile rooftop ahead.

I pushed back against it as I neared, fighting to control the energy and keep the balance centered. Too much effort in any one direction would threaten to dislodge a tile, and make all of our sneaking around for nothing.

I landed almost gently, my boots making a slight *clink* along the clay when I landed. I was still for a few seconds, waiting to hear new movement. When none came, I climbed to the apex of the rooftop. There was another guard on the other side, a second outer courtyard with another building ten feet away. The guard was at attention, but he wasn't looking up. I leaped the distance over his head, coming down without a sound on the other side.

I was in.

CHAPTER FIFTY-ONE

THE INNER SANCTUARY WAS QUIET, the three layers of guards on the outside expected to keep anyone from getting as far as I had. I crouched at the top of the building and surveyed the grounds. I was standing on part of a long, rectangular building that boxed in the rest of the space, the rooftop running out of sight towards the front. Beyond it was a second building that was wider and shorter, and a few more that were positioned to create the symmetry that Elyse had mentioned.

The Heavenly Light was in the center.

I didn't need to see it to know it. The building there was three stories high and had a sharp gold roof that spilled downward as though it had been made from the falling light of Heaven itself. It was painted white, with blocks of prayer layered into it in gold paint.

There was a balcony that ran around the third floor of the pagoda, where columns rose at intervals to help support the roof.

An angel was standing on it, looking east.

She was beautiful. Magnificent. Her hair was red and gold and brown, falling in waves down her back. Her face was soft and angled, her neck long and pale. She was wearing a gown of gossamer white and gold that shimmered in the light and framed her from behind, revealing the most perfect body I had ever laid eyes on, and at the same time somehow keeping the most private parts always hinted at but never displayed. She was love and peace, strength and courage, beauty and art form all at once. The sight of her brought a sudden jolt to my soul, lifting it to immediate elation, and dropping it as fast. I felt the cold calm of her, her Heavenly power just as Rose had described.

Blinding.

She was unaware that I was crouched a hundred feet away and staring, trying to regain control of my emotions after setting eyes on something so amazing. I had to remind myself over and over that right now, she was the enemy.

I rolled off the rooftop and down into the sanctuary, landing back on the ground without a sound. I needed to find Rose and Gervais, and hopefully Matthias. I needed to do it without her seeing me.

There was no easy way to search for them. There was no trick I could use to discover where they were being held. Instead, I moved from shadow to shadow, building to building, pushing open screen doors on wooden tracks and looking in, scanning rooms and moving on, constantly aware that I could be discovered at any moment.

I found the kitchen, where I was lucky enough to avoid the eyes of the Touched monks who were preparing the next days' meals.

I found the barracks, where more monks slept on simple cots in small rooms separated only by rice paper partitions.

I found the barn and the livestock, the communal baths, and even an old-fashioned loom.

I didn't find Rose and Gervais.

My search led me around the center building, to the front side where a black painted trailer was parked, an odd contrast to the old stone and wood of the ancient seraphim waypoint. The THI logo adorned each side of the trailer, and the back doors were hanging open. The inside was empty.

A rut ran out from behind the trailer, the ground impacted by the many feet that moved the armors away from the truck and inside the base of the pagoda. I followed it to a large door, the outside of which was decorated with a carved depiction of the face of Jesus, head down, forehead bloodied by the crown of thorns resting on it. It was easy to tell that the columns at the base had been recently replaced, both by the lighter tone of the fresher wood, and by the volume and size of the scripture that covered them. The lettering glowed so faintly it was barely noticeable. It was active, the power in use. If I had to guess, it was to keep the archangel hidden.

I watched it intently as I crossed the threshold, waiting to see if any more of the scripture began to glow, or if the intensity changed with my passage. It didn't appear to be a tripwire, at least not one that could pick me up. I put my hand on Jesus' face and pushed gently on the door, watching it shift inward without a sound, leaving just enough room to slip through.

I entered the sanctuary, finding myself in a square room lit by a few LED lamps that had been placed along the floor and powered by a small generator that was sitting in the corner. Like the rest of the compound, the space inside was a square ring that ran the perimeter of the building, leaving the center open all the way up to the roof, surrounded by a series of metal columns emblazoned with scripture. In the middle of the open space, bathed in soft white light, was a simple stone altar, weathered and worn. Water pooled at its top and ran over the sides in a gentle trickle, landing in an array of white and gold flowers growing around the base.

The inner sanctuary. I was expecting it to be hidden away behind massive doors, the way it had been in New York. I was expecting it to be more protected. Was this place so unknown to the demons that it wasn't needed? Or was I just not able to trigger any of the defenses?

Someone was humming to my left.

I turned my head, tracing the wall.

First, I found the new Fists, connected to a steel and stone contraption that allowed them to hang lifeless from a pair of hooks, similar to what I had seen in the factory. There were twelve of them, their metal faces and bodies suggesting animation and displaying none, like marionettes waiting for their puppeteer.

Next, there was a desk, facing towards the wall. A laptop screen glowed on top of it, displaying what looked like a video game. I followed the screen to the keyboard, the keyboard to fingers, the fingers up to the face of the person at the controls.

Matthias Zheng.

He was humming as he played, so focused on the game that he hadn't seen or heard me. Was this really the guy that was helping the angels to bring the Rapture? Or was I looking at another fake?

I started walking towards him as though I was supposed to be there. Trying to sneak up might make him scream, and screaming would attract the attention of the archangel above.

I was almost sitting in his lap before he noticed me. He froze at first, his entire body locking up with tension, before he shoved his chair back and away from me.

"Whoa! What the he...heck? You shouldn't sneak up on people like that." He looked me over. "Who are you?"

"You're Matthias Zheng, right?"

He shrugged. He wasn't afraid of me. "Yeah."

"Come with me. We need to talk."

CHAPTER FIFTY-TWO

HE DIDN'T ARGUE OR ASK any questions. He got out of his chair and waited for me to lead the way. I brought him outside to the empty trailer.

"Hop up."

He looked at me, still unsure of my intentions, and then shrugged and pulled himself into the trailer. I followed behind, easing the doors most of the way closed behind us.

"Go up to the front and sit."

Matthias kept walking, following my instructions. He flopped down at the front of the trailer, landing on crossed legs.

"My name is Landon," I said. "Did Adam tell you about me?"

"Adam?"

"The angel."

"Angel? What are you talking about?"

Not quite the answers I was expecting. "Yes. Big wings, metal arm?"

He laughed, putting his hand to his head and rubbing his temple. "Angels don't exist."

I stood there, feeling more than a little confused. I decided to try a different approach. "You've been building robots."

He nodded, taking his hand away and smiling. "Yeah. Isn't that what you wanted to talk to me about? My Forward Operational

Grunts? Are you an auditor?"

Forward Operational Grunts. Fists of God. Project Fog. Auditor? The words circulated through my mind. "Yes. They sent me to check on your progress. We're eager to get your units into the field."

He shook his head. "Only eight are operational so far. I'm having trouble getting my requisitions filled for power supplies."

"Power supplies?"

"Yes. I keep asking Gretchen to send in new forms, and to call Nathan to see if he can expedite the acquisitions. According to her, there have been some setbacks at the factory due to the complexity of the engineering process. I mean, I get it, the fuel cells are still experimental. It's frustrating though, because you guys... well, our bosses, they keep pushing me to get the rest of the units up and running, and I can't."

I stared at him, trying to make sense of the way he was talking. "Matthias, do you mind if I ask you a question? It's going to sound really strange."

"Sure, I don't mind."

"Where are we right now?"

He laughed. "What do-"

"I told you it was going to sound strange."

"We're in one of the transport trailers, outside the lab."

The lab? "Can you describe the lab to me?"

"Kind of drab, and the laptop you guys gave me is so last year. I'm making progress on the models though, taking the feedback you've been giving me to improve the specs." He paused and smiled at me again. "I was working on it, I swear. The game was just a break, to let off some energy and refresh."

I reached behind my back and drew the cursed knife, holding it out to him. "Do you know what this is?"

"I've seen guns before. This isn't one of the ones I designed though." He took it and put the point to his eye, his hands somehow managing to grip it without touching the sharp edge. "You should get one of mine. I wrote an algorithm to correct the boring to get another two, three hundred feet of accurate range."

I held out my hand, and he dropped the weapon back into it.

"Have you ever seen anything... out of the ordinary?" I asked.

"Like what?"

"Angels. Demons."

He started laughing again. "Are you screwing with me? I told you, that stuff doesn't exist."

I put the dagger away and sat down across from Matthias. I had been baffled by his immunity to the Divine. I had thought maybe he was like me. The truth was even stranger than that.

Not only was he immune to Divine power, he was completely unable to See them. He was one of the Sleeping, helping Heaven to tilt the balance and not even knowing it. Somehow, his mind was trapped in the subconscious denial that all mortals succumbed to, and not even daily interaction with the Divine had broken him out.

He was the most blissfully ignorant mortal I had ever heard of.

"I was just testing you," I said. "I've been getting reports that some of the other engineers are suffering from fatigue and lack of sleep, and its leading them to develop symptoms, such as hallucinations."

"Oh. That sucks. No, I haven't had that problem. I get plenty of sleep. Gretchen set me up with a nice room right on campus."

"Excellent. We need to make sure our top people are being taken care of."

"Yeah, I am. I'm happy. I mean, I don't get out much lately, but - deadlines, you know."

"Yes, and believe me when I say we're grateful to you. I just have a few more questions I need to ask you about your work, so I can put it in my report."

"Okay. Shoot."

"The communication system to coordinate the fogs. Can you

describe it to me?"

His eyes lit up. "Sure." He looked around the trailer. "It would be better with a whiteboard."

"I have a good visual memory."

"Okay. Well yeah, one of the problems we were having with the units was keeping them synchronized and performing without having to load massive memory banks and CPU cores, which I'm sure you know would have led to much higher power requirements, which leads to added weight for heat sinks, that sort of thing. So me and Gretchen, she's my assistant, we devised a static comm system. Basically, it gets fitted onto a UAV or other HAO, and it can send and receive signals, and pass information between all of the fogs that are in range. In simple terms, it's like cloud-based warfare."

In more ways than he realized. I didn't know what Gretchen's real name was, but I could guess who she was, and I could start to piece together the clues to this mystery.

Somehow, the angels had discovered the work Matthias was doing with the organic wiring. Somehow, they had learned that for some reason he had a strange inability to grasp the concept of the Divine. They had used their contacts at Los Alamos to reach out to the company he was working for, and recruit him to their cause. Then they had shipped him off to the lab, put him on Project Fog, and told him whatever they wanted to about what he was doing. He couldn't see through the veil to the truth, and so he had followed blindly in the name of his country, and not only perfected the robotics, but also developed the systems needed to control them, at least as far as his mortal brain could take it.

Gretchen, the archangel, had picked up the slack, using his knowledge of technology and enhancing it with her knowledge of Heavenly scripture. Between the two of them, they had created a perfect system.

He had also confirmed what I had suspected. Adam's hand was

acting as the server, syncing the data between the Fists and helping keep them coordinated.

"Let's say our enemies wanted to disable the fog," I said. "Where are we on that front?"

"It wouldn't be easy," he said. "The value of organic wiring isn't just the cost savings. The fog is completely immune to EMP. So is the comm system. The armor can take high-caliber fire, and we just recently added some new bolstering to protect some of the vulnerable joints." He paused, looking up to the ceiling in thought. "No. Short of a high-powered explosion, the fogs themselves are pretty much indestructible, just like you ordered. I mean, if you could manage to hit the UAV and bring it down, I think that would be the weakest link. Shut down the server and the units lose their brains. Last time I checked, there wasn't a military on Earth that had the tech to see a drone at fifty thousand feet, let alone knock it down."

"Impressive," I said, my mind reeling. It wasn't enough to knock Adam out of the sky. If I wanted to stop him, stop the Fists, I needed to cut off his arm. That was easier said than done when he could fly, and I couldn't.

"Oh yeah, its totally cool. What do you think about the warheads we designed? And the close combat capabilities? Oh, and my success in miniaturizing the circuitry. That was a real challenge. I didn't sleep for weeks trying to work that one out."

"We've been very impressed with all of your efforts."

He was beaming at the praise. "I'm going to call my mom after this. She'll be so happy to know how well I'm doing."

"There are a dozen of the fog units in the lab. Are all of them only waiting on a power supply to be operational?"

"Mmm Hmm. Once you guys get us the fuel cells, we can switch all of them on."

"What about comm systems?"

"We only have the one right now. It was a prototype, you know.

But we should be done with the load testing in the next week or two, once we get all the units online, and then we can start building more."

"Exciting times."

He laughed. "Yeah, it's been a lot of fun. If you're done with your questions, I should probably get back to work."

I stared at him, trying to decide what to do. It was clear I couldn't risk leaving him here, which meant I had two options. Take him with me, or kill him.

No, I couldn't kill him. What if he went to Heaven, and decided to continue playing along? What if he didn't even realize he had died? There was something about him, something that made him unique to all of mankind, and I needed to understand what it was, and what the fallout of that would be.

"I had heard there were two new engineers being brought in today," I said. "Have you seen them?"

"No. I've been in the lab all day. I hadn't heard anything about new blood."

"If they had arrived, do you know where they would be?"

"Yeah, probably bunked near me."

"Can you take me over to them? I'm not familiar with the layout yet. I spent the last couple of weeks in New Mexico."

He was hesitant. "I don't know…"

"You can get back to work as soon as you get me there."

"Okay, why not." He got to his feet. "Why did you want to do this in the trailer anyway?"

"They haven't given me an office yet, and I wanted our conversation to be private. I'll be speaking to Gretchen a little later, to get her feedback, too."

"Sounds good. Follow me."

CHAPTER FIFTY-THREE

WE DIDN'T MAKE IT OUT of the trailer.

I was just about to push open the rear door when the familiar thump of something heavy hitting the ground next to us caused me to freeze in place. It was followed by three... no... four... no five more thumps.

Six Fists. A dozen angels. Adam.

Then I heard the voice.

"What are you doing? You can't do this to me. Angels don't use torture."

There was a small crack in the trailer doors. I wasn't going to risk being seen.

"I really have to get back to work," Matthias said. "Gretchen gets pissed when I disappear on her."

I couldn't afford being discovered right now, and if they found Matthias gone they were sure to go looking for him. I rounded on him, grabbing his arm and pushing him against the wall. "Nobody knows I'm here, got it? You'll jeopardize the whole audit."

He nodded and smiled. "No problem. I won't say a word."

"If you see me watching, act like I'm not there."

"Okay. Okay."

I let him go and moved back into the shadows. He pushed open the trailer door and hopped down.

"Matthias?"

It was Adam's voice.

"Hey, Captain Rogers."

"What were you doing in the trailer?"

Matthias laughed. "Oh, just taking a little break. I needed someplace quiet to think. You took the fogs out for a field run? I didn't even hear you."

"Yes. Just some short maneuvers around the base."

"Cool."

"I've got something for you."

"Hey, what are you doing? Get your damn hands off me. You son of a bitch. I'm going to-"

It was a third voice for sure, muffled at the end, as though something had been shoved into the speaker's mouth.

I moved up the edge of the trailer, dropping to my stomach and peering through the opening. I was almost at eye level with Adam and Matthias, standing less than ten feet away. I could see one of the Fists standing to his right, clutching a demon by the shoulders, one of its large hands over the fiend's mouth. He was wiggling and squirming beneath the machine's grip. It was a waste of time.

"You got me another unit," Matthias said, his eyes lighting up.

I noticed he was looking at the demon.

"Yes, and I should have the rest by tomorrow. I wanted to bring this one by and make sure the outputs were compatible."

"Let's bring it inside so we can test it. Gretchen is going to be so excited."

Matthias led Adam into the sanctuary. The Fist holding the demon followed behind, while the others moved into an organized line and went still.

Another unit? Compatible outputs? I slid back to my feet. Could it mean what I thought it meant?

There was only one way to find out.

I eased out of the trailer, dropping to the ground and rolling back below it, hiding behind the wheels. I watched the Fists for a few seconds, making sure they wouldn't react, and then circled around towards the side of the sanctuary, keeping an eye out for the angels that had delivered them.

My path was clear.

I looked up, finding the balcony where the archangel had been standing. She was gone. I pushed out with my power, throwing myself upwards and landing softly.

The upper floor of the sanctuary had been claimed by the archangel. Beyond the balcony was another ten feet or so of bamboo flooring that vanished at the central sky well, which tumbled down to the altar. Resting on the floor was a red woven mat, threadbare on the sides where the knees would rest, as well as a quill and a bottle of ink. Pages and pages of parchment sat alongside it, some of them blank, many of them written on, and many more written on, crumpled, and tossed aside. Hanging from the walls was even more scripture. It was black ink, and it didn't glow. Prayers.

I inched my way over to one of the balled up pages and picked it up. It was scripture. Like a composer writing a song, she was trying to create new bindings of power, to go beyond what she and Matthias had already accomplished with the Fists, or the holy hand grenade that had leveled the warehouse in San Francisco.

"Matthias, you're supposed to tell me when you're stepping outside." It was the first time I heard her voice. It echoed in my mind, resonating through my soul. It was more than beautiful. It was disarming.

"You weren't here," Matthias said. "Anyway, aren't you supposed to be *my* assistant?"

She laughed. It was a melody that burned me. "Yes, and you need someone to keep an eye on you. How many times have you wandered off when you were supposed to be working?"

"I get bored."

"You don't have time to be bored now."

I walked over to the edge of the well and looked down. The archangel was standing near the altar, looking back towards Matthias. There was the sound of castors on the stone floor, and then one of the lifeless Fists rolled into view. Adam placed it to the left of the altar, leaving it hanging from its rack.

"They made some modifications to the power supply," the archangel said. "You may need to adjust the thresholds so we don't overload the circuits."

"Okay."

I waited a few heartbeats, until Matthias came into view. He went around to the rear of the armor and plugged a pair of wires into its back. He was cradling a laptop in his arms.

"Whenever you're ready," he said.

"Adam," the archangel said.

There was some rustling, and the angel appeared, holding the demon in his arms. They had done something to him to knock him out. Adam carried him to the altar and placed him on it, ripping off his shirt and exposing a scarred chest.

I sucked in a deep breath, my heart hanging as everything started to become clear. Alichino had said the scripture on the inside was to keep something contained, and now I knew what. Unlike the angels, the Fists were able to attack without provocation. It wasn't some special grant from God that made it happen, it was because they were demons. At least, they were powered by the souls of demons. It was the communication system that controlled them, the cloud-based brain that separated the angels from the machines. It was a loophole. A damn hack.

Something hit me in the head.

CHAPTER FIFTY-FOUR

It came up from the second floor, down and across from me, smacking into my ear and flying off to the left. It clinked on the ground behind me, not loud enough to be heard below.

The strike took me by surprise, and I fought against my instincts in order to stay still and not reveal myself unless there was a true danger. If Adam or the archangel had seen me, they would have used more than a pebble to attack.

I shifted my eyes in the general direction of the small stone's origin, down to a wall that obscured part of the lower floor. Peeking out from behind it was Gervais.

He was giving me the finger and smiling.

I should have expected as much. The angels had probably locked them in a room or something and forgotten about them, thinking they were just your run of the mill human beings, and of course the fiend had gotten them out. It wasn't only the demons who were capable of miscalculation.

He lowered his finger, and then pointed down below and shook his head. He brought his fist into his hand, suggesting an attack.

I shook my head in return. An archangel, the First Inquisitor, and six Fists of God against the three of us. It was straight up suicide. The only thing we had in our favor was the element of surprise.

He pointed up to me, flapped his hands like wings, and drew a line across his throat. Then he pointed at himself and then made glasses on his face, symbolizing Matthias.

I looked down below. The archangel was leaning over the demon on the altar. She had a small inkwell in her hand, and she was dipping her finger in it and then drawing scripture on the fiend's chest. He was still out cold, with no idea what was about to happen to him.

I pointed at Gervais, back at myself, and then held up three fingers. Where the hell was Rose?

He motioned to the other side of the well, directly beneath me. I tilted my head, and saw the hand rising up out of the shadows, giving me a thumbs up.

By the time I looked back, the demon was already on his way down.

I had half a second to make the choice. It didn't seem like a long time, but a lot of thoughts could flash through the mind in that small space. Should I follow him down, or leave him to die? I didn't care at all for his future, but I did care about what he knew, and I did care if Rose got screwed because of his stupidity. Then again, if I died here and now on some overly impulsive, ill-conceived attack, it was the whole world that would wind up paying for it. If I let it happen, there would still be the Fists. There would still be the archangel. There would still be Adam. Was it going to get easier to stop it later? It wasn't much of a chance, but what if it was the best chance I ever got?

I pushed, sending myself sliding off the edge of the balcony, falling headlong towards the archangel. I pulled, bringing the jagged dagger to my hand. I saw Gervais hit the ground beside Matthias, wrenching the laptop from his hand and putting his knife to the engineer's throat. The action startled the archangel, causing her to stand up and turn towards him.

I pushed again, outward, using the upward force to turn myself over and land on the altar with a light splash, my legs spread to either side of the demon, my body crouched low. I grabbed the archangel by the hair, pulling her head back and putting the dagger to her throat.

Time stopped. I could feel my breath as though it was a stream of energy flowing into my mouth and down my throat. I could hear my heart beat, a solid thump that echoed and vibrated in the stillness of the moment. I was bathed in the light of Heaven, dropping into this world from that one, or maybe rising up. It was cool and peaceful and seductive. It made promises to my soul, of rest and hope and joy. I could sense every strand of hair I was holding, soft and firm in my hand. I could see the long, pale neck of the archangel, and the grimy, speckled matte of the weapon I was threatening to kill her with.

It was a struggle not to let go. It was a struggle not to fall into a heap and bawl like a child, or beg for forgiveness. This was the promise I had made. The responsibility I had accepted.

"Stop," I said, pushing the knife into her throat, tight enough that a deep enough breath would cut in, deliver the poison, and end her existence.

"Mr. Landon?" Matthias said. "What's happening?" He was standing completely still, Gervais' weapon against his throat. He wasn't scared or upset, just confused.

"Landon-" Adam was six feet away, the runes on his arm glowing.

"Don't," I said. "I know how it works. Keep it still."

His arm went to his side.

"Diuscrucis," the archangel whispered. "Please. You don't know what you're doing. Let me go, and we can talk about it."

There was power in her voice. I could feel it slamming against me, the pressure of her Calming words. I pushed back with my own power, balancing it out, preventing the words from swaying me.

"Not another word," I said. I glanced up to the second floor, checking for Rose, wondering why she hadn't dropped after us. She was there in the shadows, out of sight. Was she staying out of this one? I couldn't blame her if she was.

"Landon. You can't get out of this. There are five more of the Fists waiting outside. Even if you kill Matthias. Even if you kill Margaret."

"How can you do this?" I said. "How can you think this is right?"

"The Lord allows-"

"Bullshit! Your arm. The Fists. You're using demons. There's no way God is supporting you. There's no way this is anything but a cheat." My eyes found his, burning into them. "Of all of the seraphim, I can't believe that you're going along with this."

His face tightened as his anger grew. "You of all people think that you can judge me, judge my actions? You're a slave to your duty. I'm a conduit to mine. I do what I must to protect what I believe in. It doesn't matter if I respect you. It doesn't matter if we were friends. Ultimately, you're an enemy of Heaven, an enemy of God."

"And that means that you can bend and twist the rules however you see fit? What do you believe He would think about breaking His laws to win? Or do you think because she is here, that makes it okay?" I held the archangel a little tighter. "What are you doing here, anyway? Do you know what would happen if the demons knew you were on Earth?"

"They will never know. I travel only from the factory to the sanctuary, to aid in the production of the Heavenly Weapons, the tools of our victory. Of all the archangels in Heaven, I alone have accumulated the knowledge and skill to create the new scripture. I alone have harnessed the blessing of the Lord to turn evil to good, to use chaos to create order. If that is not God's will, then why do I exist?"

"Why are you guys fighting about the fogs?" Matthias said. "I thought the budget was approved?"

"Even the seraphim have free will," I replied, ignoring Matthias. "You have pursued the path of scripture, have come into your own power. He will not stop you. That doesn't mean He will always support you."

I felt her throat move and clench beneath my blade. "Don't pretend to have the slightest feel of His desires, diuscrucis. You are worse than any demon. You don't champion mankind, you prevent them from rising and being with their Creator."

I held steady, returning my attention to Adam. "Adam, think about this. She's leading you down a path you don't want to travel. You may get your wish. You may kill me today. At what cost? At what price? The victory of angels on the backs of demons."

"A victory is a victory. I learned that from you, and your battles. 'Find a way to destroy the diuscrucis.' That is what they said to me, Landon. That is my command. You know well enough not to attack first. You don't have the demons' blind hatred to slip you up. There was no other way. There is no other way. If I fall, I fall in His service."

My heart was pounding, my hands were sweaty. I could feel the coldness of my grip on the dagger, the clammy moisture tight against the hilt. Maybe he was right. Maybe there was no other way for the angels to come after me. It wouldn't be the first time God required sacrifice to meet his will.

"Kill me, diuscrucis," Margaret said. "Kill me, if you can. Kill me if your heart is so filled with evil and hate that you can bring the end to one who has served in the name of good for centuries. I am secure in my place in His universe. Are you?"

Her words carried power. I felt it wash against me, a rough sea against a rocky shore. I tightened my grip on the dagger, beginning to feel dizzy. I had told Rose that what made us strong was our unpredictability, our strength of emotions. Even though the seraphim had once been mortal, they were qualities that were easy to forget in service to Heaven. They were qualities that were easy for any Divine to forget, as the Beast had.

She had miscalculated me. She had underestimated who and what I was.

"Yes," I said, running the blade across her flesh.

CHAPTER FIFTY-FIVE

SHE DIDN'T SCREAM. THE POISON spread through her like a bolt of lightning, turning her entire face and chest dark, turning her hair white, the feathers dropping from her folded wings and floating to the ground as dried out husks. She didn't even have time to bleed.

Her ash dropped to the base of the altar in front of me, mixing with the water there and quickly turning it an inky black. I dove towards Adam even as he backed away, raising his hand, the scripture glowing as the commands were sent.

I was less than a foot from him when the Fist slammed into me, driving me sideways and into, and then through, the flimsy paper walls of the sanctuary. I tumbled on the wet ground, rolling and getting to my feet. I looked back towards the altar, feeling my anger double as I watched Gervais' dagger sink into Matthias Zheng's chest.

"No!" I shouted, pushing out, throwing him away from the engineer. Of all of us there, Matthias was the only one that was completely innocent. He was the only one who didn't know what he was doing.

I was too late. He fell to the ground, clutching at his stomach, the dagger still protruding from it.

It was all I got to see, because the Fist hit me again, its blade sinking deep into my gut. It used it to lift me from the ground, holding me above its head and drawing back its other arm, ready to decapitate me.

I could see Adam behind it, wings out and headed into the sky. His face was grim, his eyes cloudy with tears. In that face, I could see that Margaret was more than his superior.

Sharp echoes rippled across the night, blinding flashes launching from the balcony to my left. The Fist's elbow shattered as dozens of bullets pounded into it, ripping the delicate joint apart and forcing it to drop me. I slid off the end of the blade, choking on my blood, forcing my energy into the wound to heal it. The Fist turned towards the balcony, launching its bolts at the shooter, and I saw Rose drop, land on the ground and roll to her feet. She had a rifle cradled in her arms, and she turned it and continued to fire, the bullets doing nothing to the thicker chest armor, but keeping its attention fixed on her and giving me time to get to my feet.

The ground began to shake.

The rest of the Fists were active. I didn't need to see them to know it.

I felt a breeze behind me, turned and caught the arm of an angel before he could bring his blade around and into my skull. I twisted, breaking the arm, and then brought the dagger around, shoving it up into his chest and watching him fall to ash in my grip. Another landed in front of me, and a bullet caught her in the head, knocking her backwards.

I pushed, throwing myself back and away, avoiding the reach of the one-armed Fist. It didn't fire its bolts at me, turning back towards Rose instead. She dropped the gun and ran, disappearing around the corner of the sanctuary, opposite the other Fists.

I landed on a rooftop, scanning the sky for Adam. The only way to stop them was to break the link. The only way to break the link was to destroy his arm.

Two more angels landed on either side of me, launching their attacks in unison. I blocked the angel on the left with the dagger, leaning back to avoid the sword of the one on the right. At the same time, I saw the flashes from the Fists, and heard the screaming of the bolts.

I couldn't manage all of it at once. I dropped from my feet, sliding down the side of the rooftop, even as I caught the bolts and threw them into the angels, impaling them and sending them off the roof in the other direction. I slipped from the decline and landed on the ground, right next to Elyse.

"I thought we were going for stealth. What the hell are you doing?" She had dropped the glamour, and she held the spatha in hand. There was blood on it.

"Making mischief," I said, gritting my teeth and pushing, sending myself hurtling towards the one-armed fist. It tried to block me, but it wasn't as strong with a missing appendage. I barreled into it, continuing the push, using the force to send it backwards, feet dragging along the ground until it finally fell back and into the others. I rolled forward off of it, forcing the Fists to turn around to track me. The one thing I had over them was speed, and I needed it.

I pushed off again, going high into the air towards the top balcony of the sanctuary. I saw Elyse squaring off against an angel, one of the bracelets on her arm flaring red as it caught a sword strike, and the spatha coming up and around and digging deep into the seraph's arm. The wound didn't matter, the poison did. It abandoned the fight to heal.

"Where are you?" I screamed into the night, searching for Adam in the darkness.

"Here." He appeared behind me, slamming me in the gut with the metal arm, the force of it throwing me off the balcony. I fought to regain control, to stop my descent, and failing. I went through the roof of the opposite building, and then through the wall, coming out on the other side.

I watched him launch high into the air, the arm glowing and

moving, fingers tapping. A Fist blasted through the wall of the building I'd just gone through, blades flashing in the night. I rolled away from its attack, kicking it hard enough in the side to push it off balance. I tried to slide the dagger into its elbow joint and missed, the scripture flaring and knocking my arm aside, leaving it numb. I backed away as it turned, looking for a path out.

"Master!" I heard her soft, raspy growl, and then she was on top of me, pushing me to the earth and bounding away at the same time the bolts flew through the air where we had just been. Alyx landed on her stomach and slid along the ground, bunching up and pouncing on the nearest Fist, her own monstrous weight throwing it to the ground. She leaped away from it before it could recover, getting away from its blades. Bolts launched behind her, and I reached out and caught them, pulling them into the ground.

I scanned the sky again, searching for Adam, gaining a moment of relief thanks to Alyx's distraction. The ground shook around me, the Fists still coming. I was starting to feel tired, the power becoming unstable in my soul. I couldn't do this forever.

I found another rooftop and pushed, sending myself towards it, trying to get a better vantage point. I found Alyx and Elyse together, the Nicht Criedem and the Great Were, engaging the Touched and the angels that entered the fray while trying to stay away from the Fists. I found Rose near the sanctuary, cornered by a pair of seraphim, her hands in the air. I found Gervais leaning over the body of Matthias Zheng, his face near his pelvis, covered in blood. He was being ignored in the chaos around him. I knew what he was doing, and I didn't like it.

I found the blessed dagger at my calf and drew it, ready to dive in on the demon and put an end to him once and for all, ready to forget about his claims that there were others attempting to summon Abaddon. He wanted what Matthias Zheng knew. He wanted to know how to make the machines. He could figure out how to power them later, and I knew if I gave him the chance he

would.
　That was when I spotted Adam.

CHAPTER FIFTY-SIX

He was a speck in the corner of my eye. I wouldn't have noticed him at all, if it weren't for the feeling of him in my senses. He was high in the air, over the sanctuary, sitting in the Heavenly Light that was now piercing the night sky. It was an alarm, a call to arms, a request for reinforcements.

This had to end now, or it was all going to end.

I couldn't reach him. I couldn't touch him. He was a mile away or more, drifting through the clouds. Of all the tools the angels had, it was one of their best defenses against me.

I couldn't fly.

I heard a yelp, looked down and saw that Alyx had been hit by a bolt, watched as she lost her monster form. Elyse leaned over her, doing something with one of her artifacts, even as a Fist approached them. I found Rose again, held by the angels, her arms locked behind her back.

My gaze returned to Adam. He knew he was going to win. He knew he could stay up there, guide the Fists, and tip the balance. He was resolute before I had killed his love. He wouldn't take any chances now.

I had one chance. One crazy chance. It was unpredictable, and aggressive to the point of being stupid. It was something Rose probably would have loved.

I focused my power, gathering it in my soul, pushing it tighter and tighter, making it dense and heavy inside me. Then I pushed it out ahead of me, and at the same time pulled it behind. I started to feel lightheaded, even as the way became clear, Adam appearing as though we were only a foot apart.

It was my special sauce, my ultimate use of power. I would be lucky to stay conscious when I got to the other side. I didn't have a choice.

I stepped forward, through the fold of time and space, out into the sky way above the sanctuary. I appeared in front of Adam, literally out of thin air, reaching out and wrapping my arms around his neck before I had a chance to fall. My head swam, the world spinning around me, my eyes refusing to focus.

"What the-" I heard Adam say, even as I gripped him tight and rested my head on his shoulder.

"Going down," I said. I was drained, wasted. Rose had given me another idea and I used it now, turning my clothes to lead and weighing myself down.

It was more than he could handle, and we began to fall.

His arms pummeled my sides as he tried to get free, but I held on tight, ripping him from the sky. We went straight down, bathed by the Heavenly Light, twisting and rotating in the air, but still descending. I fought to stay alert, to be ready for when we hit. I would need to heal faster than he could heal. I would need to destroy him before he could destroy me.

The sanctuary approached in a hurry, growing larger and larger beneath us. We were going too fast for him to recover now, and so I pushed the energy out, returning my clothes to normal, giving myself the mobility I would need to attack.

"I'm sorry," I said, right before we reached the well and continued down. We landed on top of the altar, the stone splitting with a massive crack that reached across the night, sending ripples of thunder out to the horizon.

My limbs shattered. My back, my legs, my arms. The pain was unbelievable. It took all of my strength to focus, all of my energy to stay lucid and begin to heal. The world faded in and out of view as I stumbled to my feet, finding them still broken, and falling to the ground. I pushed myself up again, gathering myself at last.

Adam was still on the ground, his arm bent and twisted and mangled by the force of its impact against the altar. He lay there with his clothes torn, his mouth open, his eyes red with rage.

Red eyes? I stared down at him. His wings were bent beneath him, no longer white and gold. They were brown and black, with flecks of red.

He had fallen.

"Why," he said, looking up at me, anger and pain and sadness all colliding. "I did what was asked. I did what was demanded."

"You know why," I said. I still had the cursed dagger in my hand, and I knelt down next to him. "Look what you did to this place."

The sanctuary was defiled. The altar was cracked, the water black with the archangel's remains.

"What I did? What... *I* ... did?" His face twisted into a gruesome snarl. "You caused this, Landon. You did this."

I was calm in the face of his storm. "No. You should have found another way. You had eternity."

"There was no other way. I had no choice."

"We always have a choice."

He sat and stared at me, his chest heaving.

"It's over," I said. "The arm is destroyed. The Fists are broken."

He looked over at the crushed arm, as if he had forgotten he even had it. He looked back at me, and then his foot lashed up, catching me in the chin.

"This isn't over," he said, leaping on top of me. I was weak. Too weak to fight back. Too weak to stop him from killing me.

There was a crash from the front of the room, as the door flew open. Alyx landed a dozen feet away, snarling at the angel.

"It isn't over," he repeated, spreading his wings. He rose into the air, back up through the well, the Heavenly Light lost to it, and to him. The tears continued to stream from his eyes as he vanished into the night.

CHAPTER FIFTY-SEVEN

"Landon," Alyx said, losing the Great Were form and rushing to my side. She knelt over me, leaning down and kissing my forehead.

"Help me up?" I said. Adam might have left, but my own anger was still smoldering.

Alyx got her arms under me and lifted me to my feet. Rose and Elyse made their way inside together. Rose had a cut on her cheek and her clothes were torn and muddy. She had an angel's sword in her hand. Elyse looked hot and tired, but otherwise unharmed.

"Landon?" Rose said.

"Where is he?" I asked. I scanned the room.

"Gone," a new voice said.

I turned towards it. The fiend that had been on the altar. He had woken at some point, and was hiding in the shadows. Now he came out to us.

"I saw him leave. That way." He pointed through the hole I had made in the wall. I found Matthias' body a few feet away from it. It was laying in a pool of blood, the stomach torn open with none of the care that had been taken with Gervais' other victims.

"I can't take the chance that you're lying to me," I said. I didn't know if Gervais could take the form of demons, or only humans. "Rose?"

She didn't hesitate to grab the demon's shoulder and run him through. His eyes went wide, and he fell over.

I waited for him to change.

He didn't.

"Damn it," I said, lacking the energy to put much force behind it. I stumbled towards Matthias, with Alyx continuing to hold me up. "He can't have gone far. Alyx?"

"I'm sorry, Master. I can't track a scent I'm not familiar with."

Or one that he could change constantly.

"He took his form," Rose said.

"He doesn't care about his form. He cares about what he has in his head. The archangel was powering the Fists with the souls of demons, and she was using scripture to do it. He can't replicate that, but he can rebuild the control system, and he's smart enough to work out how to use it to his advantage."

"Hell already has one of the Fists," Rose said. "The one you crushed in L.A."

I had forgotten about that. "You're right. Hopefully, it's too damaged to be much use to him."

"I don't know. We both sensed the archangel when we went into the factory. I told him we should turn back. He insisted we take our chances, to try to find Zheng. He was almost crazed about it. He wasn't even upset when we were captured. It was almost like he knew what would happen, and that he wanted it to happen. He could have broken us out any time, and I think we would have escaped, but he insisted that we wait."

"He knew I would come for you."

"Not only that you would. He seemed to know when, or at least make a solid guess. I don't think he planned everything from the Underground, but… seven hundred years? That's a lot of experience. I think he's unbelievably good at improvising. Remember when he said there was always a game, and he would find another way?"

"You think this is his other way?"

"Don't you?"

I wasn't sure. It might have been a full plan, or a stepping stone, but there was no denying the demon's intelligence, or his ability to calculate and improvise. He had pushed me into attacking the archangel, knowing it was a risk, and weighing it against the reward. It worked out in the end, and I had stopped the Fists. He had used the chaos to get what he wanted, too.

"It doesn't matter right now," I said. "We had to stop Margaret and Adam. What happened to him after only proved that even Heaven wasn't completely aligned to their way of thinking. Gervais will turn up again sooner or later. We had a deal made in blood. I held up my end by defeating the Fists. It will be agonizing for him to resist fulfilling his side."

"So what do we do now?" Elyse asked.

"We have to figure out how to take apart the Fists. We can't risk that Gervais will rebuild the communication system and work out how to bring the active ones back online. We also have to go back to the factory and get rid of the machinery that miniaturized the scripture. Angels with guns…" I shook my head. "That's one escalation we can't afford to allow."

"Espanto had a compactor in the junkyard that could crush anything down to a slab of scrap," Alyx said. "And I mean anything. There must be something like that somewhere around here."

"Good idea," I said. "Can you help Elyse get the Fists loaded back onto the trailer?"

"Of course, Master." She started to extract herself from me, forcing me to stand on my own. I was good for a few seconds, and then started to stumble.

"I've got him," Rose said, ducking in and pulling me back upright.

"I don't really like to time walk," I said, trying to get my head to stop spinning. I turned myself so we were facing one another. "You did pretty well for a mortal."

She laughed at that. "You did pretty well for a... whatever you are. The aggressive approach worked out for you."

"This time."

"Emotional and unpredictable, right?"

"Yeah."

She leaned up and kissed me. I could taste the sweat and dirt and blood on her lips, mixing with my own. It was nice as kisses go, but it was missing something. From her? From me? I'd done the checklist, and she had hit every mark. Maybe I was just tired.

"Like ships in the night," she said, staying close and looking up at me. She'd felt it, too. "We'll always have the Happy Bay Inn."

I tried to laugh, but it wasn't worth the dizziness that followed. "Help me over to Matthias?"

"Sure."

It was hard to look at him after what Gervais had done to his body, but I felt like I needed to give his passing a moment of my time.

"He was clueless about the Divine. Completely unaware of the hidden world that existed around him, even though he was knee deep in it. It's a rare thing to be that innocent. A gift. It's my fault he's dead."

"You did what you had to do," Rose said. "And the next time we cross paths with that asshole, don't try to stop me from making sure he gets what he deserves."

Matthias certainly hadn't gotten what he deserved.

I hoped it was worth it.

CHAPTER FIFTY-EIGHT

"Good," Elyse said, stepping back and using her twin daggers to block Rose's furious assault. I sat on a couch with Alyx, in the corner of the space we'd cleared for the sparring.

"No. It's not right," Rose said, coming to an abrupt stop. "My elbow is too low, my feet are too wide. You're being too easy on me."

Elyse put the daggers down. I tossed her a couple of towels that were resting on the arm of the couch. "You have to start somewhere. The training you did brought you a long way in a short time, but you know the Divine are faster than you can ever be. Which means you need to be smarter, more prepared."

"An unpredictable egg," I said.

Rose laughed and wiped the sweat from her brow. "Right. So when do we take some of this training out into the real world?"

It had been three weeks since we'd come back to New York, after doing everything we could to dispose of the Fists of God, and make sure whatever remained of them would never see the light of day again. I'd sent Alyx out looking for Gervais three or four times that night, trying to catch a scent, or listening for someone moving through the woods alone. I'd asked Elyse to scour the newly empty and unholy sanctuary in search of him.

They had both come up empty.

I wasn't sure how he could have gotten away so easily. Elyse's guess was that he had kept a rift stone secreted away, ready to use the moment he needed a quick escape. It made sense. As much sense as anything about the demon did.

Somehow, he had reneged on our deal, and had never surrendered the names of the demons that were working to bring Abaddon back into the world. I couldn't imagine how that was even possible, when all Divine were subject to the same rules, one of the very few things both sides had ever agreed on. And yet he had managed it, and in doing so had forced Obi, Dante and Alichino scrambling to discover the origin of the demon's warning, and to try to come up with the identities of those involved.

So far they were coming up empty, too.

"Not for a while," I replied. "The balance is leaning towards Heaven right now, and you just said yourself that you still need a little more work."

"I did say that, didn't I?" Rose said.

I glanced over at Elyse, catching her return look. We had yet to approach Rose about the tattoos and the artifacts, and what she would have to do if she wanted to make use of them. She was still struggling to come to grips with what she had done, having visited me in the middle of the night a few times to talk about it. Just because she wanted to help, and was willing to use violence to do it, didn't mean it didn't take its toll. It was something we all had to go through at some point.

Alyx lifted her arms up over her head and yawned, stretching her body languidly back like a cat. Her head was resting in my lap, and she looked up at me with big, dark eyes that simmered with the contentment that had filled her since I'd gotten her away from Espanto.

Well, maybe not all of us had to go through it.

Even so, and maybe despite the fiend's best intentions, Alyx wasn't just a killing machine. Her heart was warm and open enough to at least make an effort to be sensitive and understanding, and she was fiercely loyal in a way that Obi, Rose, Elyse, or even Dante could never be. It was more than a decision for her. It was a basic instinct, a raw desire to protect and care for her alpha, who just happened to be me. I wasn't too fond of bossing her around, or her insistence on calling me 'Master', but she had found whatever soft spot remained in my soul and latched herself tight onto it.

I was willing to deal with the complications.

"I love you," Alyx said.

She said it a lot, and I knew that she meant it. I smiled back at her and ran my hand across her forehead. I couldn't say the words back. I wasn't there. Yet? I didn't know, and I didn't have to right now. There was no reason to rush into anything, and she had accepted my perspective after the third or fourth time I had given it.

"What do you say we call it a day?" Elyse said. "I'm going to hit the shower and then grab a bite from that Italian place down the block."

"Do you mind if I join you?" Rose asked.

"In the shower, or the restaurant?"

Rose laughed, but she didn't clarify. I knew she and Elyse had hit it off over the last couple of weeks. What they did outside of my presence was none of my business.

"Someone is at your door," Alyx said, her nose flaring and wrinkling, a motion that got cuter every time I saw it.

"Who?" I asked. "Obi? Dante?"

"I don't know. I haven't smelled them before. This one reeks of paper and aftershave."

She sat up instinctively as I got to my feet and headed to the door. We were four apartments down from mine, in a space we had emptied to make room for the sparring.

"Divine?" I asked, reaching out for the knob.

"No," Alyx replied.

"Gervais?" Rose said, reaching down and picking up her weapon again.

He still knew where I lived. Right now, I wanted him to.

I finished opening the door and stepped out into the hall. There was a man standing in front of my apartment, in a brown shirt and shorts. UPS.

"Hey, you have a package for Landon Hamilton?" I asked.

He turned and looked at me. He was young and lean, with a mop of brown hair showing under a company baseball cap. "Yeah. Is he home?"

"He's me."

We started walking towards each other. He held out a slender package, too small to be anything but a letter, or maybe an optical disc of some kind. I took it from him, and signed for it.

"Have a nice day," he said. "Ladies." He tipped his cap to the others as he passed them, and looked back at me with a jealous smile.

"Hang on a second," I said, getting Alyx's attention. She stepped out in front of him, grabbing him and throwing him against the wall, and then locking his arms behind his back. Rose and Elyse came over to see what I had received.

"Hey! What the hell are you doing? Let me go!"

"In a minute," I said. "Maybe."

I tore the strip off the package and slipped it open. There was a piece of parchment inside, light and pale, with scrapes and scratches throughout. Dark stains ran along it in tight, formal cursive.

My Good Friend Landon,

My apologies for bowing out of the party early. I was concerned you might not be very amiable to my decision to do what I wanted, instead of what you wanted. Regardless, I did make a pact with you, and while I have made every effort to ignore my promise, I find that I am barely able to think straight over the last few days. As such, in order to assuage my own pain and continue to try to ruin your existence, I have sent this missive on a journey that will both fulfill my end, and keep you in the dark for a number of weeks.

I only do this because I care.
In any case, here are the names that I promised you.

1. Who cares
2. Who cares
3. Randolph Hearst
4. Who cares
5. Who cares

Not that it matters.

Yours in brotherhood,
Gervais.

P.S. I may have exaggerated the number of demons who knew about the summoning ritual.
P.P.S You may want to sit down.

"Not that it matters?" Rose said, reading the letter over my shoulder.

I didn't have the chance to answer her.

My stomach clenched, my body froze, my blood turning to ice. There was a sudden maelstrom in my soul, a shaking in the balance that caused me to start shivering at the force. I stumbled forward, reaching out to catch myself, only Elyse and Rose's quick reaction preventing me from falling. My eyes closed involuntarily, a dark spot finding purchase in my existence.

Diuscrucis.
A voice in my mind.
A voice that echoed in emptiness, and filled me with hopeless dread.
A voice that cursed me.
Abaddon.

Thank You!

It is readers like you, who take a chance on self-published works that is what makes the very existence of such works possible. Thank you so very much for spending your hard-earned money, time, and energy on this work. It is my sincerest hope that you have enjoyed reading!

Independent authors could not continue to thrive without your support. If you have enjoyed this, or any other independently published work, please consider taking a moment to leave a review at the source of your purchase. Reviews have an immense impact on the overall commercial success of a given work, and your voice can help shape the future of the people whose efforts you have enjoyed.

Thank you again!

About the Author

M.R. Forbes is the creator of a growing catalog of speculative fiction titles, including the epic fantasy Tears of Blood series, the contemporary fantasy Divine series, and the world of Ghosts & Magic. He lives in the pacific northwest with his wife, a cat who thinks she's a dog, and a dog who thinks she's a cat. He eats too many donuts, and he's always happy to hear from readers.

Mailing List: http://bit.ly/XRbZ5n

Website: http://www.mrforbes.com/site/writing

Goodreads: http://www.goodreads.com/author/show/6912725.M_R_Forbes

Facebook: http://www.facebook.com/mrforbes.author

Twitter: http://www.twitter.com/mrforbes

Printed in Great Britain
by Amazon